"I need no Norman wench telling me how to arrange my hall."

His voice was low and threatening, but Kathryn felt no fear, only a shuddering awareness of his body.

"Mayhap it takes a Norman to carry out the task." Her words came out in barely a whisper as she sensed the same kind of melting heat that she'd experienced with him earlier.

She felt the pressure of his hands upon her shoulder, pulling her toward him. Edric lowered his head. Kathryn gazed up at him as he gently brushed his lips across hers. Her eyes drifted closed and he drew her even closer, and Kathryn returned his kiss with all the ardor of their earlier encounter. She shifted her body against him but he broke away, growling, pressing his forehead against hers.

"I must be insane," he muttered.

Taking note of the fire in his gaze, Kathryn thought he might truly be mad.

But the madness was not only his . . .

Other **AVON ROMANCES**

Be Mine Tonight *by Kathryn Smith*
From London With Love *by Jenna Petersen*
How to Seduce a Bride *by Edith Layton*
No Man's Bride *by Shana Galen*
Once Upon a Wedding Night *by Sophie Jordan*
Sinful Pleasures *by Mary Reed McCall*
Sins of Midnight *by Kimberly Logan*

Coming Soon

Deliciously Wicked *by Robyn DeHart*
Taken By Storm *by Donna Fletcher*

And Don't Miss These
ROMANTIC TREASURES
from Avon Books

The Duke in Disguise *by Gayle Callen*
His Mistress By Morning *by Elizabeth Boyle*
Tempting the Wolf *by Lois Greiman*

MARGO MAGUIRE

The Perfect Seduction

AVON BOOKS
An Imprint of HarperCollinsPublishers

AVON BOOKS
An Imprint of HarperCollins*Publishers*
10 East 53rd Street
New York, New York 10022-5299

Copyright © 2006 by Margo Wider
ISBN-13: 978-0-06-083732-7
ISBN-10: 0-06-083732-2
www.avonromance.com

First Avon Books paperback printing: September 2006

Printed in the U.S.A.

10 9 8 7 6 5 4 3 2 1

This book is dedicated to everyone who has cared for a terminally ill loved one, doing whatever it takes to keep him or her comfortable and at home until the end.

It was written in memory of my mom, and dedicated to my sister and three brothers.

Chapter 1

Castle Kettwyck
Late summer, 1072

"**T**aken?" 'Twas the dignified Lady Beatrice, sitting across from Kathryn de St. Marie, who'd spoken. "If the barbarian Scots took me, they would have to kill me before I would ever show my face in civilization again."

A shiver ran down Kathryn's spine. Surely Kettwyck's new walls were sufficient to keep any raiding Scotsmen out. And there were many strong and powerful Norman knights present for the festivities here at her father's holding.

Still, they were very near the border, far from the safety of the Abbey de St. Marie where she and her sister, Isabel, had spent the last ten years. Were they vulnerable here at Kettwyck? The fortress was not yet complete, and Kathryn had seen workmen adding mortar and stone to the walls that very day. She dearly hoped this welcoming banquet was not premature.

"What they do to captives is unspeakable," added Lady Alice, Kathryn's mother.

"*My* daughter would certainly know enough to throw herself from the nearest cliff before returning to society. She could never come bac—"

The old biddy's words faded into the night when Sir Geoffroi Le Chievre came up behind Kathryn and touched her shoulder. Slivers of heat raced down her arm at the touch of the young man who'd attracted her attention earlier in the day. They'd flirted some, and she'd been intrigued. But she had not expected him to come to her here. "Come and join in the dance."

Kathryn stood, but her mother's words followed her as she accompanied Geoffroi away from the cluster of old women in her father's great hall. "Once you become a Scotsman's whore, you might as well be dead."

"Don't listen to those old flap dragons," Geoffroi said, leading her to the courtyard where the musicians played and the young people had gathered to dance. "I mean no offense to your mother or the other ladies, but Kettwyck's walls are stout and strong. No Scotsman will ever breach them."

"Of course you're right," Kathryn said, smiling up at the young knight. She put away all thoughts of Scotsmen and her father's castle walls and gave her attention to Sir Geoffroi Le Chievre.

To his credit, he'd barely taken note of her sister, Isabel, the comely one. Isabel had pleaded with their father to allow them to choose their own husbands. Lord Henri had agreed, to a point. He'd drawn up a list of favored candidates and gathered them here for the festivities marking the two sisters' arrival at Kettwyck and their reunion with their parents. Over the next few days, each sister would choose a husband.

Kathryn was certain that even without a generous dowry, Isabel would have no trouble settling on a bridegroom. The lords and knights here were mad for her attention, while Kathryn quietly yearned for the honest affections of one man, a bridegroom who would honor and revere her for what she was, not for the wealth she would bring him.

'Twas a foolish wish, she knew. The daughters

of powerful Norman barons married to achieve strategic goals, not to satisfy silly yearnings. Besides, she held not the same appeal as beautiful Isabel. Kathryn's eyes were merely brown, and her hair was the color of a mouse's pelt, so different from her sister, whose eyes were stunningly golden and her hair a striking, glossy black.

Kathryn had grown up in Isabel's shadow, but the two sisters could not have been closer. She did not begrudge the attention Isabel garnered with her beauty and her many talents. Both young women had been exceptionally well educated at the abbey, and Kathryn had a head for languages. The abbess had said her skills would serve a husband well, but Kathryn had never spoken of the fire that burned unquenched within her.

She'd been too embarrassed to ask the holy woman about the deep yearnings she felt for the caring touch of a husband. She'd imagined her bridegroom's kiss and his gentle caress too many times to count. Such thoughts were surely sinful, for she'd heard of no other maid who admitted to such desires—not even Isabel.

Kathryn admired Geoffroi as he danced so well, wishing she could match the grace and elegance of his movements. Yet not once did the intricate steps of the chain dance require that he take her in his arms, or even touch her hand. At this rate, Kathryn would never know if Geoffroi was the one she should choose as her bridegroom. She needed to know if his touch . . . if his kiss . . . could flame the fires that burned within her. She seemed destined never to know, for Geoffroi was a proper knight who would observe custom and keep her under the watchful eye of the matrons.

Taking matters into her own hands, she beckoned him away from the crowded courtyard.

"Lady Kathryn?"

She made no reply, but took his hand and moved quickly into the bailey adjacent to the keep. With so many people about, no one took note of their departure. Laughing, Kathryn led Geoffroi to the yard behind the stable and stopped in a dark corner. A mere sliver of the moon lit their faces, but Isabel could see puzzlement in Geoffroi's expression.

She knew her actions were much too bold for a well-bred lady, but she had to discover whether Geoffroi's touch, his kiss, could satisfy the hunger within her. She wanted to know if he'd sought her out because she pleased him, or because he realized Isabel had already made her choice, giving him cause to settle on her.

Was this the man who would cherish her, who would give her the children she craved?

"Kiss me, Geoffroi." Her voice sounded too

breathless, too anxious for one who had never been guilty of cowardice. Yet Geoffroi's motivation had taken on a great deal of importance. Kathryn had to know if *she* was what he wanted . . . or if it was just her dowry that attracted him.

"Kathryn, I don't think—"

Her breath whooshed out in a rush of frustration, along with all her hopes. If he needed time to think, then she had her answer.

Quickly, before her disappointment became evident, she whirled away from the handsome knight. She took one step, but he grabbed hold of her arm and turned her, pressing her back against the rough wood of the stable. He put one hand at her waist and the other upon the wall near her head. "You've never been kissed, have you?" he asked, his face moving close to hers. Kathryn could feel his breath on her lips, smell a hint of wine.

Mayhap she'd drawn the wrong conclusion. 'Twas all so confusing, dealing with men and their strange ways, trying to understand the signals they sent and the ones they did *not* send. She trembled as he bent closer, touching his mouth to hers.

Kathryn let her eyes drift closed. Her heart pounded and her knees went weak as he pulled back and then kissed her again, this time deeply. He opened his mouth slightly and slid his tongue against the barrier of her lips. Kathryn sighed and let him inside, returning his touch. 'Twas a pleasant feeling, but odd. Geoffroi seemed to be aroused, but when the excitement of her first kiss passed, she felt little more than curiosity. 'Twas not the magical experience she'd hoped for.

He broke contact. "Kathryn—"

Shouts in the courtyard interrupted whatever he was about to say, and the ground shook with the thunder of horses' hooves.

Geoffroi grabbed Kathryn's hand and ran toward the disturbance at the keep. Terrifying, barbaric warriors rode through the gate, swarming like bees 'round the keep, slaughtering those who impeded their path.

"Where are the guards? Where are all of my father's knights?" Kathryn continued to rush toward the keep—toward Isabel and her parents. Could these be the raiders the ladies had spoken of? *Scots?*

"Kathryn, stay back!" Geoffroi shouted. He caught her by the arms and shook her once. "Don't be a fool! Hide yourself!"

A dozen more Scottish barbarians thundered through the gates and turned to bear down on them.

Kathryn backed away to flee, but there seemed to be no place to hide, not with so many men on horseback pursuing her. She lost sight of Geoffroi, but she had no chance to search him out, for two of the horsemen split off from the rest and came after her.

Running for her life, Kathryn ignored the strain on her lungs and the painful stitch in her side. If she stopped, they would catch her and kill her. Or worse . . . carry her away. Had not her mother and the other ladies made it clear 'twould be better to die than be taken by Scots? Was she to pray for a swift death?

The acrid smell of smoke reached Kathryn's nose and she risked a quick glance back to see what was burning. 'Twas the stable, but worse yet—the two riders were still after her.

She stumbled and almost fell, but recovered in time to make a sharp turn 'round the corner of a storage building. Dashing inside it, she slammed the door shut behind her and prayed the foreign warriors would ride past.

Her prayers went unanswered. The men dismounted and followed her into the building, kicking open the door and laughing as they flanked her, speaking in their strange, guttural tongue. If only she had studied Gaelic instead of wasting her time with Latin and English, she might be able to bargain for her freedom.

Backing up to the wall as the two men stalked

her, Kathryn desperately tried to think of a way out, but in the flickering light from the burning stable, she could see she was cornered. There was no way out, no back door.

Desperate, she lifted a wooden crate that lay nearby, hefted it into her arms, then threw it at one of the men. Hoping 'twas enough distraction for her to make her escape, she made a frantic run for the door, but was not fast enough. They caught her before she made it outside, grabbing her and knocking her to the ground. Her hair slipped from its neat chignon and they tore the sleeve of her beautiful gown from her shoulder.

Kathryn scrambled away, but one of the men took hold of her ankle and pulled her back through the dirt, even as she kicked at him. The second man laughed and called out some words of farewell before mounting his horse and riding into the melee in the courtyard.

Kathryn screamed even though 'twas not possible for her voice to be heard above the shouts and cries of the other victims running wildly across the grounds. Her captor shoved a rag into her mouth and held both her hands in a viselike grip above her head.

He tore off the necklace she wore, and ripped the jeweled girdle from her waist. When he shoved her skirts up to her knees, Kathryn bit back a sob and kicked frantically. Her captor suddenly changed his tack and bound her wrists together with a rope. She was helpless as he shoved her onto her face and tied her ankles. Grunting with effort, he lifted her and tossed her onto his horse, forcing the air from her lungs and making bright spots of light appear behind her eyes. Still struggling to get free, Kathryn tried to spit out the rag, but her mouth would not work. She was suffocating! She was going to die here, ignominiously, with her carcass lying across a Scotsman's filthy steed.

She rose onto her elbows and tried to throw herself from the horse, but her captor shouted at her and struck her.

No! she cried soundlessly. *I don't want to die this way!*

He hit her again and Kathryn felt her brain shudder inside her skull just before she lost consciousness.

Chapter 2

The border lands north of Braxton Fell

"**W**hy are you so angry?" Bryce asked his elder brother as they rode north toward their Scottish enemy. "You've never before objected to making war on Léod Ferguson."

"I don't like taking orders from the Norman bastard," replied Edric, the Saxon lord of Braxton Fell.

"King William, you mean?"

Since the answer was obvious, Edric saw no reason to reply to his brother. In the past year, he'd received an increasing number of directives from their Norman conqueror, most of them unreasonable. The duties Edric was required to pay as the price for keeping his estates increased with every year that passed. More men, more goods, bushels of wool . . . and little in return. 'Twas Edric's responsibility to protect England's northern borders and he was certain there would be repercussions if he shirked his duty. Edric had directed his steward to send letters of protest, for Braxton Fell suffered a dire lack of resources of late.

Even so, there had been no change in the Norman king's demands.

Word of a Scottish raiding party riding across Edric's lands required that he take action. He hoped it was the Fergusons who trespassed, for it was past time they paid for their last damaging raid upon Braxton lands. As Edric and his men pursued the Scottish raiders, he had no doubt they would be carrying their spoils with them, and herding some pathetic Norman's cattle as they traveled.

'Twould be an additional boon to confiscate those valuable goods for himself, although he would have to conceal that fact from his Norman wife, Cecily. She need not know he was sending *Norman* goods in place of the tributes demanded by her king. In truth, Edric had no choice. When Ferguson and his men had harried Braxton Fell two years before, they'd burned the fields and killed whatever livestock they could not scatter or carry away. These days, there were no extra goods at Braxton Fell.

Upon Edric's marriage to Cecily, her dowry had provided some relief, so no one at Braxton Fell had starved in the past year.

Yet this autumn, Cecily's father, Baron Gui de Crispin, had refused all requests for assistance.

"I thought you might be angry because you do not wish to travel so far from Cecily." Sarcasm oozed like mud from Bryce's mouth.

Edric kept his silence, refusing to allow his brother's taunt to affect him. Everyone at Braxton Fell knew Cecily had no love for Saxons, especially her Saxon husband. Yet he'd had no choice but to wed her for her dowry, and to assure his alliance with the Norman kingdom.

The past year had been a daily challenge, trying to keep the peace in his household. Cecily might have the beauty of a Norse goddess, but she despised him and took every opportunity to berate him. She'd made no attempt to learn the language and customs of her husband and his people, and had treated her servants—all but her old Norman nursemaid, Berta—with disdain.

Fortunately, she'd become pregnant within weeks of their nuptials. He'd had no reason to visit her bedchamber once she was with child, but she managed to make his life hell with her tantrums and petty jealousies. At the slightest hint of an infidelity, the woman went off on a tirade, demanding that he abide by his marital vows. Edric had agreed, but his patience was wearing thin.

"Do you suppose Cecily's mood will improve after she is delivered of your child?" Bryce asked.

"I wouldn't hold my breath," Edric muttered.

"What's that?"

"We can only hope," he said, loud enough to be heard. But Edric had gone past the point of reconciliation with Cecily. She had the temperament of a shrew. No, that was too kind. He had never known a woman so harsh and unbending. She had not allowed him to touch her after the first month of their marriage, nor had Edric wanted to.

But worst of all, and unforgivably, she did not want the child.

Cecily had tried to rid herself of the pregnancy early on. Fortunately, she had not been successful. Lora, the midwife, had explained that breeding women often had dark moods and this was likely the cause of Cecily's woe.

But Edric knew better. Cecily did not want *his* child.

In spite of her pregnancy, she'd had his steward, Oswin, make a monthly request of her father asking to leave Braxton Fell and return home. She wanted an end to the marriage as badly as Edric did, but her father had refused every request.

The child was due in only a few weeks' time, and as soon after the birth as Cecily could travel, Edric was going to send her to the nunnery at Evesham Bridge. He was done with the marriage.

"Lord Edric." Drogan, a strong and sturdy warrior ten years Edric's senior, rode up beside the two brothers. As their father's most trusted retainer, Drogan was more an uncle to Edric and Bryce than a mere huscarl. Drogan was as close as family, as was Oswin, Braxton's steward.

"They rode this way," Drogan said, pointing ahead at the fresh tracks that were now visible in the midday light. "There was at least one wagon, but I doubt more than twenty-five or thirty riders."

"They cannot be far," said Bryce.

Edric looked ahead. "They'll stay to the path with their wagons. We can ride through the woods and get ahead of them."

Drogan grinned. "My only hope is that it's Léod Ferguson."

They took to the trees with all their warriors behind them. If Drogan's estimate of the Scots' numbers was correct, the Saxons would have the advantage. But their movement would be slow through the woods.

Still, they managed to make good time.

Edric and Bryce rode ahead, leaving Drogan in command of Braxton's fyrd a short distance behind. They moved stealthily, and when Edric heard the sound of voices ahead, he dismounted and signaled the men behind him to halt.

He stayed under cover of the trees and soon came to a narrow clearing just off the path. There, he sighted the Scottish raiding party. As suspected, 'twas the vile Fergusons, Léod and his son, Robert.

In all, there were only a few more than twenty Scots in the clearing.

Bryce joined Edric and spoke quietly. "There must have been another party. Looks like they split up from here."

"Aye. Ferguson never goes raiding with so few men," Edric replied in a hushed voice. "He must think he's safe now that he's so close to his lands."

Two male captives sat upon the ground together, their wrists bound behind them. There were two wagons in the center of the clearing, and Edric could not see if there were men posted beyond them, nor could he see what lay within them. Spoils of a profitable raid, he supposed, as his men gathered 'round, moving into position for their attack.

* * *

Shards of light cut to the back of Kathryn's eyes and she winced with pain. Her head hurt abominably, and nausea cramped her belly. Gingerly, she looked 'round, and saw that she lay inside a rough wooden cart.

What had happened to Geoffroi?

Kathryn feared the worst. He'd been without a sword when she'd pulled him away from the dancers in Kettwyck's courtyard. And 'twas *her* fault he'd been caught unarmed and unable to defend himself. Kathryn blinked away her tears, but a few still managed to slide down the sides of her face.

If only she and Geoffroi had stayed close to the festivities at her father's hall, he might have had a chance to take up a weapon. Instead, she'd followed a half-witted whim, and Geoffroi had been caught unarmed and away from the relative safety of the keep.

She stifled her tears and lay still, hoping not to draw the attention of the men whose low voices were audible nearby. Her hands and feet were still tied, but in the light of day, she was able to see the knot that bound her hands together. Using her teeth, she loosened it, then wriggled her wrists to and fro. Soon she managed to free them.

In silence, Kathryn shifted to her side and raised her knees to her chest. She reached down and pried the rope from her ankles, then considered what to do next.

She did not know how much time had elapsed since she was taken, nor how far from Kettwyck she had traveled. If she could escape unnoticed from the wagon, she might be able to run some distance from her captors. There was no doubt the Scots would come after her, but Kettwyck knights had surely been sent in pursuit of them. With luck, her father's knights would already be on the Scots' trail and would save her from a horrible fate.

A sudden burst of laughter startled Kathryn and she froze in place. An instant later, a grizzled Scot with wild russet hair and a thick beard jumped into the wagon's bed at her feet. He shouted something unintelligible to the other men, then bent over and grabbed Kathryn, roughly pulling her up by the arms.

She screamed, but her cries only resulted in more coarse laughter. The Scot was impervious to her struggles as he pulled her from the wagon, and Kathryn could only whimper when he threw her over his shoulder. Though she kicked and pummeled him as he carried her to a circle where his accursed men had gathered, he was impervious to her blows.

* * *

The lass in the circle was possessed of a soft kind of beauty that made Edric wish he'd not tied himself to such a harsh and brittle wife. He could easily lose himself in this woman's deep doe's eyes, could almost feel her lush, full lips upon his. Her clothes were in tatters, revealing more of her exquisitely rounded form than any gentle maid would willingly display.

He muttered a curse, aware that there was naught to be done for her. Hell's bells, she was a Norman wench anyway, and Edric had no love for her kind. She would suffer her fate here as his people had suffered at the hands of their Norman conquerors.

His men were still donning hauberks and helms, and getting into position. 'Twould be several long minutes before they were ready. Minutes the lass did not have.

Edric spat his disgust when Léod Ferguson pounced upon the poor woman in the circle, intent upon raping her. When she screamed, his stomach turned and prudence lost out. He raised his sword and shouted his battle cry, rallying Bryce and the rest of his men 'round him, unready as they were.

In a mass of confusion, they roared into the clearing, hewing every Scot who stood in their path, quickly reaching the circle where Léod Ferguson's bare arse rose obscenely above the captive maiden. Edric yanked the Scottish lord off the lass, and as he gained his feet, Léod grabbed a sword from the Scot nearest him.

"Ha, Ferguson," Edric taunted as he engaged Braxton's longtime enemy. 'Twas a rare and unexpected pleasure to have the upper hand with the wily worm. "Caught you with your trews about your ankles, eh?"

The Scot growled and used one hand to yank up his leggings.

"You'll note I didn't just slice you down, maggot." Edric dodged the first awkward thrust of the man's blade. "I just can't bring myself to kill a man with his arse flapping in the wind."

"As if ye could, lad," said the chieftain. He poised himself, sword at the ready, half crouched for battle. Balancing his weight upon the balls of his feet, Léod started to circle 'round Edric.

Edric moved likewise as the other Scottish raiders in the circle quickly took up arms and mounted their defense. Edric's warriors fought alongside him, preventing anyone from assisting Léod, making it a contest of one to one, man to man. Yet in the midst of it all, Edric was fully attuned to the clang of swords and the smell of blood and sweat around him.

"You've got a grizzled bum, even for a Scot, old

man." Edric glanced toward his brother as Bryce fought, then took quick note of the maiden whose soft brown eyes seemed huge now, providing the only color in her ghostly, pale face. What a fool he'd been to rush to her rescue.

"Edric!" Bryce shouted as he parried with Robert, the big, red-haired son of the Ferguson chieftain. "Get her away from here!"

"She can move herself," Edric shot back. Damn his brother for paying more heed to a comely face than to his own skin. A captive Norman, stolen from a nearby estate, was not his concern. Especially not now, not while he had Léod Ferguson within killing distance.

Edric barely needed to exert himself as he met every thrust, every strike of the older man's sword. 'Twas almost cruel, but no less than the bastard deserved. Edric grinned. "Won't any of your own women have you, Ferguson?"

"Ye're one to talk, lad! Word is that your own wife canna abide ye."

Edric felt his blood pulse in his forehead, but he did not allow his temper to distract him. No misstep would cause him to lose this battle against Léod Ferguson, the man who had caused no end of trouble at Braxton Fell. The whoreson would not escape this time.

Léod wielded his sword with two hands, raising

it high, then swinging down in one brutal blow in an attempt to split Edric's skull.

Edric sidestepped the blow and made a slash of his own, but the Scot managed to dodge it. "Very impressive, Ferguson!" he shouted. No doubt he could finish off the Scot right now, but that would be too easy a death for the bastard who'd caused the destruction of Edric's lands. At the very least, he wanted retribution for all Léod had done two years before, when Edric's attentions were elsewhere.

"Behind you, Edric!"

He whirled and slashed at once, killing a Scot who'd slipped through the barrier of Saxon fighters to assist his chieftain. Two more Scottish warriors came, brandishing sword and mace, but Edric evaded their attack and jumped to a nearby rock. He heaved a solid kick to one man's chest, knocking him to the ground, and parried with the other while Léod came 'round to attack from behind.

Edric gave a mocking laugh, quickly dispatching the Scot in front of him, then turning back to go head to head with Léod again. " 'Tis customary to face a man as you *try* to kill him, Ferguson!"

"Ye might try facing yer brother as Robert slays him, then," Ferguson shouted with a smirk upon his grimy face.

The Norman woman screamed as two Scots

tried to carry her off, distracting Bryce. The one second of inattention gave Robert the opportunity to strike, viciously hacking Bryce in his side. Edric roared and, without thinking, used the full force of his strength to spear Léod, just below his heart. He did not wait to see the result of his jab, but moved quickly to prevent Robert from finishing Bryce.

"Drogan!" he bellowed.

Naught mattered but getting to Bryce. Edric skirted 'round another small skirmish, dashing past his battling warriors, aware that Drogan was doing the same. He arrived at the spot where Bryce lay wounded, just as Robert realized that Edric had killed his father.

The Scot roared with fury and turned to strike madly at Edric while Drogan tended to Bryce. The burly huscarl pulled the younger man from the fray as Braxton warriors moved to surround them. Someone tripped Edric and he fell, but rolled quickly away from the ax blow that followed him down. The battle waned as the warriors tired, but Robert managed to flee. The Scots abandoned their dead, and ran from the clearing.

Edric let them go as he knelt beside Bryce.

Shaking uncontrollably, Kathryn somehow managed to crawl to the space under one of the wagons and draw her knees to her chest. Wrapping her arms 'round her legs, she quivered with cold and fright, and rocked back and forth as if the motion could shut out the brutal battle going on all 'round her.

She had as much to fear from these Saxon barbarians as the Scots who would have raped and killed her. In their rough woolens with their long hair, their axes and maces, they were as terrifying as the Scots.

Somewhere in the back of her mind, Kathryn realized that all had finally become quiet. The battle was over, and the surviving Scots were running away.

Though the Saxons were victorious, their mood was somber. One of them crouched before her, a seasoned warrior with an unruly mane of flaxen hair and a bushy beard. He stretched his hand out to her. " 'Tis over, lass. Come out."

Kathryn did not trust him any more than she would a filthy Scotsman. She gave no indication that she understood his words as she considered how she could possibly get away.

"You are safe now," the Saxon said, his voice grave. "No further harm will come to you."

Kathryn took a shuddering breath and felt a tear run down her cheek. Absently, she brushed it away. If only Isabel were here—No! She would not wish this terrible predicament on her sister, but wished she had a few of Isabel's talents. Her sister would know what to do.

"You don't understand what I'm saying, do you?" the man remarked. He pointed to his chest. "Drogan," he said. "I am Drogan of Braxton Fell. Come out."

What choice did she have? She could not stay under the wagon forever, nor could she run from these Saxons. She could only trust that this warrior, Sir Drogan, spoke truly. All seemed peaceful in the clearing now, as the Saxon warriors tended their wounds or dragged the dead Scots away. 'Twas quiet, too, with only the sound of the wind rushing through the dried leaves in the trees.

She took hold of Sir Drogan's hand, letting him ease her out from under the wagon. Her legs faltered, but Drogan supported her when she would have sunk down to the ground once again. He draped a thin woolen blanket over her shoulders to cover what remained of her clothes.

The fierce, dark-haired warrior who'd killed the Scottish chieftain approached Drogan, never allowing his icy blue gaze to rest upon her. He was tall, with shoulders broader than those of any man she'd seen in Normandy or England, and a comely face marred only by a narrow white scar that split the dark line of his brow. If the sight of his strong, masculine physique gave her pause, 'twas his rugged visage that caused her heart to trip. Even though he was unshaven, she could discern the strong line of his jaw, the corded sinews of his neck. His nose was thick and straight, his forehead creased with worry. Or mayhap 'twas anger.

"We'll carry my brother in the wagon." He gave a quick nod toward Kathryn, seemingly unwilling to show any particular interest or curiosity about her. A stubborn man. "Bring her," he said.

"What's your plan?" Drogan asked.

"The woman will have some skill with needle and thread," said Edric. "She can sew Bryce's wound."

"But I—" Kathryn blurted out the English words before considering that, by speaking, she'd given away her understanding of their language.

Edric's hand shot out and encircled her throat, his eyes cold and full of anger. He clearly understood her attempt to deceive them, yet he did not hurt her. There was power in his grasp but he did not hold her too tightly.

She yanked away from him.

"Do you refuse, woman?"

"No, I do not." But she felt shaken by the wrath in his tone, and even more so by his touch. He gave her a look of contempt before striding from her presence.

How barbaric! "Just because I am female does

26

not mean I can sew a man!" On the contrary, she was not a very good seamstress at all, and was quite squeamish, besides.

"We'd better go, lass. When Lord Edric sets his mind to something, 'tis not likely to change."

Kathryn took a deep breath and followed Sir Drogan to the spot where Edric knelt beside his brother. The wounded man lay insensible, his mangled hauberk lying open to reveal a growing bloodstain just under his arm. His face might have been as comely as his brother's, but it was deathly pale. Even his lips were devoid of color.

"*Jesu*," Drogan muttered.

One of the men placed a leather satchel beside Edric, who opened it and removed the contents. There were rolls of clean cloth and a piece of leather with two sturdy needles pierced through it. "Where is the thread?" Edric grumbled. His voice betrayed the worry and concern he felt for his brother, and as he searched through the bag, Kathryn watched the play of muscles in his arms and the frown of concentration upon his brow.

Drogan knelt beside Edric's brother and pushed the cloth of his tunic away from the wound. The sight of the gash made Kathryn's legs feel as mushy as gruel and she slid to the ground beside Drogan. "I don't think I . . ."

Her mouth went dry and her fingers felt like

icicles. She wiped her hands on the tops of her legs and looked up. The Saxon could not possibly insist that she sew his brother's wound.

He paid her no heed as he riffled through the contents of the satchel, finally pulling out a bundle of coarse thread. He tossed it, along with the needles, to her.

"See that you make the edges match."

Kathryn swallowed her indignation at the orders given by this uncouth Saxon. No one spoke to her thus. She was a baron's daughter . . . though the less he knew of that, the better. She did not want to be offered back to her family, insulted and dishonored, mayhap in exchange for a ransom. There was a very good chance her family would not pay it anyway, not for a daughter who'd been violated by Scottish raiders.

She took a deep breath. "Surely there is someone else who knows what to do. I have never . . ."

" 'Tis Graeme who usually does the mending for us," said Drogan.

"Graeme will be doing no mending tonight." Edric made a quick gesture toward a nearby warrior who'd bound his own hand in a bloody rag. "And since *you* were the cause of Bryce's distraction, *you* will be the one who makes repairs."

Kathryn bristled at his arrogant tone, but Drogan drew her attention back to Bryce before she could make the impudent remark that was on the tip of her tongue. "Look, lass. His wound is not as bad as it might be. 'Tis only a deep cut through the lad's thick muscle."

Kathryn shuddered and risked another glance at the wound in the young man's side. She considered refusing, but did not want to risk the Saxon lord's ire. Picking up the needle, she wondered how she could possibly do what Lord Edric demanded. Luckily, Sir Drogan took a clean cloth and blotted blood from the gash. "Start here, lass," he said. "Bryce won't feel it at all."

Kathryn doubted that, but she did not dare hesitate, not with the surly Saxon lord hovering so close, his demeanor so threatening. Besides, he was right. Bryce's wound was her fault, as was Geoffroi's fate. Would her culpability never end? She threaded the needle and leaned close to the Saxon's brother. Sir Drogan took the cloth away and held the wound together as Kathryn made the first pass with the needle.

She could do this. All she needed was to turn her thoughts elsewhere. She could think of one of her sister's many tales as she worked—stories of valiant heroes and their beautiful ladies.

Yet every hero that came to mind had the face of Edric the Saxon as he pulled the filthy Scot off her and fought him to the death.

Edric rubbed one hand across his whiskered chin and took a shaky breath. Though Bryce's injury was not a sucking wound of the lung, the younger man was not out of danger yet. Edric had seen many a battle wound go putrid, with death as a result. He would do all in his power to prevent that from happening to his brother.

In spite of her protests, the Norman lass sewed the wound and did a fair job of it. The blanket 'round her shoulders gaped as she worked, giving Edric a view of her full ripe breasts, tipped by pale pink nipples, a sight he'd sorely missed all through this miserable year of his marriage. Every drop of his red, male blood urged him to lay claim to this woman, to take her away from camp and quench his lust while he was far from Braxton Fell, far from Cecily.

'Twas some Norman trick—ensnaring a man with her beauty and the promise of sensual bliss, only to repel him when he would take action. But he would do naught with this woman. And he wanted nary a hint of his lustful thoughts to reach Cecily's ears, for they had naught to do with the poor state of his marriage.

The Norman woman had small, graceful hands. She'd tried to be gentle with Bryce, but it had soon become clear that more force was needed to stitch through his brother's flesh. She recoiled with every pass of the needle, but faithful Drogan talked to her, urging her to finish, as Edric stood and left them, pacing nearby until she finally completed the gruesome task and rested back on her heels.

Bryce moaned.

"Do you hear, my lord?" Drogan called to him. "'Tis a good sign. He's coming 'round."

The Norman seemed shaky and uncertain now, but Edric refused to feel any pity for her, and forced himself to tamp down the lust that surged through him at the sight of her. 'Twould be best to focus on his victory over Léod Ferguson and begin planning the destruction of the Scot's son, Robert. But Drogan distracted him as he questioned the woman.

"What's your name, lass?" he asked.

She appeared puzzled for a moment, as if she didn't understand the question. When she responded, it seemed to Edric that she was unsure of her answer. "Kate . . . I am . . . just Kate."

"From where were you taken?" Drogan queried.

"'Twas a place called . . . Rushton." Her French accent gave a softness to Edric's language and he could not help but think of his Norman wife, who'd learned no more than a handful of English words, most of them derogatory expressions that she used liberally upon him and the servants.

"Your people will be wondering—"

"*Non!* Er . . ." The muscles of her slender throat moved as she swallowed. "I have no reason to go back, not after . . ." She cast her glance toward the place where Ferguson had assaulted her. Rising to her feet, she pulled the blanket tight 'round her shoulders, clearly conscious of her ruined attire. Below her torn and filthy undergarment, her legs were shapely, her feet and ankles narrow and delicate.

Every muscle in Edric's body clenched when he thought of the feminine warmth that lay concealed beneath that thin chemise and he damned his unruly cock for reacting so strongly to the wench.

"It does not matter," she said. "I am no one . . . I will not be missed."

Edric narrowed his eyes as he looked at her. He doubted she was no one, not with those soft hands and her perfect command of his language. Yet if she did not wish to return to Rushton—

"Edric?" 'Twas Bryce, awake now.

He turned and answered his brother. "Aye, Bryce?"

"'Twas Robert . . . I'll kill him for this."

"No doubt you will. But you've got healing to do first." Edric gave his brother a sip of water and covered him with a blanket. Then he looked up at

Drogan. "Post a watch and have the men set cook fires. We'll sleep here tonight and make for Braxton in the morning."

Then he would decide what to do about Kate.

Chapter 3

As night fell, the men built small fires and broke out what food they had before making their beds under the trees, but Edric had no appetite. He took his post near Bryce, dismissing Drogan to take his own rest.

"I will relieve you in a few hours, my lord," Drogan said, placing a comforting hand upon Edric's shoulder.

"See to the Norman woman," Edric countered in spite of himself. "She will feel the night's chill."

The other two Norman captives had not survived. 'Twas possible Léod would have killed

Kate, too, after she'd served her purpose there in the dirt. Still, she was comely enough for Ferguson to have kept her for himself, or sold her to another rich chieftain.

She sat near the fire with Drogan's blanket tied securely about her shoulders, so there would be no further gawking at her pretty breasts. At least he was still able to admire her legs without being too obvious about it. Edric gazed at her, at the proud set of her shoulders and the stiff bearing of her spine, and watched the lass's eyes fill with tears. She tried to blink them away but they streamed down her cheeks, unchecked.

Edric wanted to feel no sympathy for her. He preferred not to think of the ordeal she must have withstood since her capture. He wanted to hate her. She was a Norman, by God. And had she not screamed as his men were donning their gear and preparing for battle, he would never have felt compelled to race into the clearing to rescue her. The skirmish would have been more organized and Bryce's hauberk would have been secured. Her scream in the midst of battle had been the distraction that made Bryce vulnerable.

Edric clenched his jaw and looked away. The woman was obviously ill at ease, but he refused to show her any mercy. He was not about to make her welcome here, or at Braxton Fell.

He'd had enough of Normans at his holding, *Norman women* in particular.

Drogan managed to find another blanket for the woman. Edric saw him make a place near the fire for her to sleep, then stood by as she eased herself down to the ground. A moment later, Drogan did the same, making his bed nearby.

Edric would have to speak to his huscarl about being overly soft with their Norman captive.

Kathryn would awaken from this horrible dream at any moment. Surely morning would soon come and she would hear the birds singing outside her window at the abbey. After dressing in her simple kirtle, she would join Soeur Agnes in the animal pen and help the old nun feed the orphaned lambs and throw grain to the chickens, just as she'd done most every day since she was nine years old. Then there would be prayers, and afterward, the nuns and all the lay residents of the abbey would break their fast.

There would be no Scottish raider's flat gray gaze to haunt her sleep, nor cruel arms that could crush her without a moment's thought.

Kathryn gasped for air as she pushed up from her earthen bed and looked 'round. 'Twas all true. Amid the death and disaster at Kettwyck, she'd been taken from her father's keep. She said a prayer of thanks that her family had been well guarded inside the keep, but could not help but worry about Geoffroi. She'd lured him away from the keep, putting him in danger, just as her scream during the course of yesterday's battle had caused valiant young Bryce to be so gravely wounded. No wonder his brother had looked at her with such hatred, clearly holding her responsible for Bryce's injury.

Kathryn's stomach turned. Her own people would view her with contempt, too. She could never return to Kettwyck with honor and dignity. Everyone on the estate would know she'd drawn Geoffroi away from safety. And they would assume she'd become a Scotsman's whore.

'Twas why she had decided not to tell Sir Drogan her true name, and why she had to convince these Saxons she was no one of consequence. Else they would be compelled to send word to Rushton, news which would soon spread to Kettwyck. Her father would come and return her to face her shame at home.

Nausea roiled in her belly as she forced herself to accept the reality of her situation. She could never go back, but only forward to whatever fate awaited her at the hands of the Saxon lord.

'Twas a bitter potion to swallow. Her sister had worked so hard at persuading their father to allow them to choose their own husbands and Kathryn had so looked forward to marriage and motherhood. 'Twas all she'd ever wanted—to be a wife and lover to a good man, and mother of as many bairns as God sent her. She went cold when she realized how irrevocably changed her future had become. She would either live out her days as a servant in a Saxon holding, or choose the alternative that had been abhorrent to her only a fortnight ago.

A nunnery.

Her heart seemed to stop beating in her chest. No honorable Norman would take her to wife now, not if her own parents would disown her. She risked a glance at the wagon where Bryce lay, and caught sight of the cold Saxon lord.

What if she spent the rest of her life at Edric's holding? Kathryn swallowed thickly. The Saxon had made his disdain clear enough. She had no future in his domain or at Kettwyck, either. She had come from a nunnery, and, as much as she despised that alternative, to a nunnery she would return.

Kathryn had heard of a religious house at Evesham Bridge and realized it could not be far from Lord Edric's estate. The abbess was known as a kindly and pious woman, and if Kathryn could find a way to get there, 'twould be the perfect place to seek refuge. Mayhap the kindly Sir Drogan would provide her an escort.

She wondered how Edric would react if he knew she was the daughter of Baron Henri Louvet. Though she knew little of politics, she supposed 'twas possible he would ask for a ransom to return her. Her father might be surprised to learn she'd survived her abduction, but would he pay for a daughter he believed had been despoiled by a Scot? The best Kathryn could hope for was that Lord Edric would forget about her once they reached his holding. She would slip away and somehow make her way to Evesham Bridge.

'Twas past dawn, and the Saxons put out their fires and began to pack the horses in preparation for leaving camp. Drogan came to her and helped her to her feet. "There is a secluded spot past that stand of rocks. If you're wanting a moment's privacy before we ride, you should take it now."

Kathryn made use of the short time allotted her. She was fortunate to be alive, and knew upon reflection that it was only right to devote the rest of her life to prayer and charitable works. In spite of her aversion to returning to the monastic life, it had to be better than suffering the scorn of her parents and the contempt of her peers for the rest of her days.

They carried Bryce in Ferguson's wagon and

rode slowly southwest, toward Lord Edric's holding. The Saxon lord wore his sword at his side and had an ax slung through a loop upon his saddle. His hair was loose again today, thick and black, worn much longer than the Norman style, with narrow plaits at the temples. He sat tall and straight in his saddle, and wore no cloak, leaving his arms bare to his shoulders. Never before had Kathryn seen muscles so thick or so well defined.

In spite of herself, she could not ignore the breadth of the man's shoulders and the tapering of his powerful torso to his hips. She'd seen him battle the Ferguson chieftain and been awed by his strength and agility. 'Twas partly Edric's fault that she'd screamed during the battle and distracted Lord Bryce. Had she not been so awestruck by the sight of him, so terrifying yet so compelling, she might have been prepared when the raiders had tried to drag her away.

As it was, she'd been startled, terrified, and nearly taken again. If not for Sir Drogan, who'd come to her aid, she'd likely have become a captive of the Scots once more. She shuddered at the thought. So far, none of the Saxons had threatened or mistreated her, if she discounted the gruesome task Lord Edric had forced her to perform the night before.

These men had fed her and given her their

protection overnight, though 'twas clear Lord Edric resented her. And he viewed her the same as every Norman would—she'd been debased and dishonored by the Scots, and could hardly call herself a decent woman, even though her virtue remained intact.

Mortified by her recollection of the Scottish chieftain's vile attack upon her, Kathryn shrank deeper into her borrowed blanket. Ferguson had exposed his thick man-shaft to her and had nearly assaulted her with it. Edric and Bryce had seen her with her skirts shoved indecently askew, with her bodice torn beyond what modesty required.

How could she face even these low barbarians without a blush of shame coloring her face?

Sir Drogan was the only one of the Saxons who showed her the simplest courtesy. Kathryn told him she was unaccustomed to riding, and so even though Edric kept their pace fairly slow to accommodate the wagon, the man stayed close, conversing with her to help keep her mind from the uncomfortable ride.

"Léod Ferguson and his men burned Braxton Fell's lands two years ago," said Drogan. " 'Tis fitting that he met his end at Lord Edric's hand."

"But Lord Bryce is so badly injured—"

"Robert will pay for that dark deed."

Kathryn did not doubt it. Edric seemed a man

who would take care of his own, no matter what the cost. She wondered how 'twould be to feel the protection of his strong arms and powerful body, but knew she would never experience such a marvel, not with any man.

"You've got a torn lip, lass," said Drogan. "Does it pain you much?"

"A little," she replied. " 'Tis naught when I think what might have happened."

"Aye. You were fortunate. Neither Edric nor Bryce can stand to see a woman mishandled. 'Tis why they rushed the Scots instead of waiting for a more prudent moment."

"I'm grateful for it."

"What of your other injuries? I saw a few bruises—"

Edric turned to call out to them. "Can we not ride in peace, Drogan?" His tone was one of annoyance and Kathryn regretted having his attention called to her. His eyes raked over her, taking in her disheveled appearance, no doubt remembering her shame the day before. He would never believe she was a lady and she quickly reminded herself she did not want him to. The less he thought of her, the better. Then, when she disappeared, he would barely notice.

"Aren't you the surly one today?" Drogan

laughed. "Léod Ferguson is dead, your brother is alive, yet you can find no joy in the day."

"There'll be joy once Bryce is out of danger."

"We'll give him over to Lora's good care and he'll fare well."

"Who is Lora?" Kathryn asked her question quietly, so as not to draw Edric's attention again.

"She is the healer of Braxton, and midwife," Drogan replied equally quietly, and Kathryn heard admiration for the woman in his voice. "She'll do well by Bryce."

Kathryn hoped so, though she did not intend to stay at Braxton Fell long enough to find out. 'Twould be best to travel on to Evesham Bridge right away.

They rode all day, stopping only once to water the horses and partake of a small meal. Sometime before dusk, they came to a narrow brook in a wooded area and Edric gave the order to halt and make camp. Then he picked up a bow and a quiver of arrows and left the camp, heading upstream.

Kathryn also took her leave, but went in the opposite direction. The man might have a fascinating face and form, but his scornful gaze intimidated her. She did not wish to encounter him in the isolation of the woods.

Staying close to the water, Kathryn eventually

happened upon a secluded spot where she removed Sir Drogan's blanket from her shoulders. She folded it and placed it upon a nearby tree stump, then knelt at the water's edge and began to wash the dust and dirt from her skin.

Sir Drogan was right—her lip did hurt, but 'twas the least of her worries. Everything about her situation was foreign and painful and she could only hope she had made the right decision about her course of action. Retiring to the nunnery was the only way to spare herself and her family from her shame. Or was it?

She thought of Edric again, of the controlled power she'd felt in his hand the night before, when he'd encircled her neck. He had not frightened her. On the contrary, she had felt defiant, even stimulated by his touch. He had not hurt her and Kathryn was certain he'd restrained himself intentionally, allowing the heel of his hand to rest upon her chest. Mayhap it hadn't entirely been anger in his eyes.

Kathryn's blood heated at the thought, but she shook her head in self-derision.

The idea that he'd looked upon her favorably was a mere flight of fancy. Even if there had been masculine interest in his eyes, Kathryn would never submit to a foreign barbarian. Theirs would be an untenable alliance, at odds with all she'd ever hoped for. Besides, he loathed her for being responsible for Bryce's wound, and most certainly for her Norman heritage.

And if Bryce died . . .

Kathryn shuddered, unable to finish the thought. She bent to the cold water of the stream, which did little to soothe the heat in her blood, though it helped to chase away the fatigue of the day's travels. They'd ridden slowly to keep from jarring Lord Bryce in the wagon, but after several hours in the uncomfortable saddle, every extra moment of riding was painful.

The quiet of the woods was suddenly broken by a low sound, almost like a voice, that startled her. She held still to listen, and when she heard it again, Kathryn realized 'twas the snort of an animal. Slowly, she turned toward the sound, and found herself staring into the biggest, blackest eyes she'd ever seen.

Edric had to get away from the Norman woman.

Hunting was the perfect distraction from his unwelcome awareness of her tempting body and her wary eyes. The sight of her split lip infuriated him, and far too easily, he could imagine touching it with his fingers, soothing it with his mouth.

He made a quiet growl of frustration and started to search the terrain for animal tracks. A deer or wild pig would serve his men well tonight, and what was left of the meat would be a welcome addition to his kitchen.

There were plenty of animal signs, from the smallest rodents to the tracks of a sizeable deer, and Edric followed the large animal trail. It took him to the riverbank where he stopped for a taste of the cool, clean water and attempted, once again, to force thoughts of Kate from his mind. Her haunted eyes meant naught to him, nor did her disheveled and vulnerable appearance, calling to mind a woman who has just been well bedded.

She was Norman. And Edric knew from experience that, in spite of their considerable beauty, they were coldhearted and icy limbed.

Edric picked up the trail of a wild pig and followed it past the point where he knew his men were encamped. He walked beside the riverbank as it curved to the south, and came to a place where the bank turned rocky, and the terrain on the far side of the water rose up to craggy cliffs. The trees grew thick near the water, but Edric had no trouble seeing the Norman wench.

The shreds of her chemise seemed to flow from her shoulders, molding to her breasts, her nipples puckering the damp fabric. Her chest rose and fell with rapid breaths and the only color in her face was in her eyes. The boar he'd been tracking stood only ten paces from her, snorting and pawing the ground.

In silence, Edric removed an arrow from his quiver, nocked it into the bow, took aim, and shot.

Kate gave a small cry when the pig fell and she sank to the ground, as if her muscles would not hold her up. The boar was not yet dead, so Edric moved in for the kill, as wary of the beast as he was of the woman.

He killed the pig with one stab of his sword, then looked at Kate. She'd been kneeling before, but sat on the ground now, with her arms wrapped about her. Tears filled her dark eyes and violent shudders racked her body.

Edric took a deep breath and tore his gaze from her vulnerable form. Her blanket-shawl must be nearby.

When he found it neatly folded on a tree stump, he picked it up and took it to her. She seemed not to notice him, so he shook it open and draped it 'round her shoulders.

He did not remove his hands, but rubbed her arms and shoulders in an attempt to warm her. "You are safe now," he said, and silently cursed himself for bothering.

Her body quaked with one muffled sob and he could do naught but crouch down and pull her into his arms. 'Twas only to give comfort to one who'd been frightened beyond her endurance, but when she leaned into his embrace and pressed her face to his chest, it became something more. 'Twas that soft, feminine need that he'd sorely missed since exchanging vows with Cecily, and Edric felt his body stir with awareness. He clamped his jaws together and forced himself to ignore the surge of lust that tore through his veins, but arousal hit him like a jagged finger of lightning.

'Twas impossible.

Hastily, he backed away. He stood and left the Norman where she sat, and composed himself before returning to the encampment. Giving orders for his men to go and collect the boar, he remained in camp and helped to get a few more cook fires started. They would feast tonight, and there would be a healing broth for Bryce to sip.

And Edric would forget the fierce lust roused by Ferguson's captive.

Now Kathryn knew. She'd felt the power and heat of Lord Edric's strong arms and knew what it was that she'd craved these past few years. A man's touch. The caress of a husband.

She'd seen Edric's prowess in battle, and now at the hunt. He'd saved her virtue and her life, and had rescued her yet again tonight. She closed her eyes and steadied herself. It could only be fear that made her react to the Saxon, for he did not appeal to her. Not really.

Yet the heat of his body had sent a flood of sensation coursing through her. *This* was what she'd hoped to feel at Geoffroi's touch . . . and what was lacking when he had. Kathryn had never thought 'twould be a bearded, long-haired ruffian who elicited such feelings.

She returned to the camp and approached the wagon where Sir Drogan sat with Bryce. On the other side of camp, Lord Edric threw a few branches into a fire circle, then crouched down and nursed it to life. Kathryn turned her eyes away. She could not possibly feel an attraction for the rude and coarse Saxon. He was nothing like the refined and courteous Normans who'd come to Kettwyck at her father's invitation, barbered, clean-shaven men like Geoffroi. Edric of Braxton Fell was certainly no candidate for matrimony.

She looked at the young man in the wagon and turned to Drogan. "How is Lord Bryce?"

Drogan shrugged, his expression fraught with worry.

Kathryn frowned with concern. "Will Lora be able to help him?"

The warrior sighed. "I hope so, lass. She is a

gifted woman." He lowered a cup of water to Bryce's lips and urged him to drink. "I understand you met with Master Pig near the river."

Kathryn nodded. "I thought 'twould be the end of me, but Lord Edric came along. He saved me yet again."

Drogan nodded. "The lad has a rare talent for being where he's needed."

Kathryn thanked God for it, if not for whatever quality he possessed that drew her to him.

"The day's kill will be welcome at Braxton Fell," said Drogan. "Our larders are in pitiful form these days."

"Is it not harvesttime, Sir Drogan?" Kathryn asked. Summer had waned and Kathryn felt the chill of autumn in the air.

" 'Twould be so, had the Fergusons not harried our fields when they attacked us two summers ago."

Kathryn did not understand. "Two years is a long time, is it not?"

"You've not much experience of war, have you, lass?"

She shook her head. "I only came from Normandy a few weeks ago."

"The Scots burned our fields and woodlands, and the land has not yet recovered. Very little will grow in the sooty ground. They killed livestock, scattered our sheep . . ."

" 'Twas not . . . Normans?"

"No, lass. You Normans are . . . allies. Now."

Kathryn suspected from his tone that he was not being entirely candid. She knew little of politics, but the English people could hardly approve of their Norman conquerors. In truth, of all the Saxons with whom she traveled, only Sir Drogan showed her the least kindness. The others simply tolerated her. Drogan was the only one who spoke to her, who saw to her needs. Looking 'round at these warriors with their swords and axes ready, Kathryn remembered hearing terrible tales of Saxons and their barbaric customs. She knew she must be wary until she found a way to get to Evesham Bridge.

She glanced in Edric's direction and saw him setting up a wood frame over the fire—a spit for cooking the meat. He betrayed no emotion as he worked, nor did he look to see if she'd returned to camp. 'Twas as if what had transpired between them at the river had not even occurred. Yet Kathryn could still feel the heat and strength of his hands upon her arms and shoulders.

"Sir Drogan—"

"I am not 'sir,' " he said. "Simply Drogan, though some call me Drogan the White. Saxon warriors

51

are not the same as your Norman knights. I am a huscarl in Edric's house and have been ever since I could wield a sword."

"Forgive me," Kathryn replied. "Then is it also wrong to say 'Lord' Edric?"

Drogan smiled. "Ah, no, lass. By your king's grace, he is eorl of all these lands, as his wife is lady."

"His wife?"

"Aye. Lady Cecily."

Chapter 4

Preoccupied with worry for his brother, and painfully lustful thoughts about the Norman woman, Edric entered the village and rode into the narrow lane leading to the gates of his fortress at Braxton Fell. He'd been ordered by William to build the stone-and-timber keep that was now his residence, but his father's hall still remained on the grounds of the ancient Saxon settlement. The new keep was a formidable structure, much better suited to a man of Edric's standing, with its three levels, its tower and crenellated battlements. The banner of his ancient house hung from the highest tower, proof indeed of his mastery here.

A high wall surrounded a goodly portion of the village, but much of it had been left outside the tall barricade. As impressive as it was, the wall had done little to protect Braxton Fell from the Fergusons' raid two years before, when Edric and Bryce had been required to join William's army in York, and the damned Scots had come burning and ravaging their lands.

The people of Braxton Fell had come much too close to famine last year, and many would have starved had Cecily's dowry not included barrels of grain, stores of beans and cabbage, leeks, and a hundred hens for laying. This year, Edric's father-in-law had refused to give any assistance. Oswin the steward had read Lord Gui's letter stoically, his voice level and emotionless, as though the Norman's decision to withhold his aid would not result in hardship at Braxton Fell.

Edric refused to beg. If Gui had suddenly decided to hoard his wealth, 'twas not only the Saxons of Braxton Fell who would suffer. The accursed Norman's own daughter would starve.

Leading his riders to the keep, Edric did not bother to glance up to the window of his wife's bedchamber where she'd been confined for the last weeks of her pregnancy. Cecily would not welcome him home, nor would she show any concern for Bryce. She would take her old nursemaid, Berta, and return to her father's lands at once if her sire would take her. But Lord Gui had refused her latest plea, just as he'd refused every one before that.

If Cecily gave Edric a son, he would have his heir and there would be amity between Braxton Fell and the Norman estates *without* his spoiled wife. She could spend her days upon her knees at the nunnery, praying for temperance and humility.

Grooms rushed to take Edric's reins while Drogan helped the Norman woman to dismount. The men gathered 'round Bryce's wagon, more than willing to carry the young lord into the keep, but Edric called for a litter.

Unreasonably annoyed by the attention Drogan was giving Kate, Edric sent his huscarl to fetch the steward. He and every man in the courtyard knew Bryce had been injured only because of the pathetic Frenchwoman who could not seem to stay out of trouble.

Now she was about to cause him no end of grief—once Cecily saw her.

Edric's lady wife would no doubt assume he had risked all just for a taste of the comely hostage, for Cecily was forever accusing him of sexual incontinence, when he'd been painfully faithful to her.

Carefully, he schooled his expression, taking care not to show any of the lust that had possessed him since laying eyes upon the Norman wench.

All seemed strangely quiet in the courtyard, but Oswin pushed through the crowd of warriors and caught up to Edric before Drogan had a chance to go in search of him. Edric cleared his mind of the plague of Norman women and turned his attention to Oswin.

"My lord." The steward's voice was shaky and he sounded much older than his years. When he looked into the wagon, his complexion turned gray, obviously reminded of the time his own sons had been carried home dead, both of them, in battle against the Normans. "Dear God. How . . . ? Not Bryce."

"He lives," said Edric. "But his wound is grave. We'll need Lora to tend him."

Servants brought the litter and the men transferred Bryce to it. With care, they took him from the wagon and carried him into the great hall.

Edric followed, not stopping as he spoke to the steward. "We came upon the Fergusons and engaged them. I killed Léod, but Robert wounded Bryce, then took to the hills with the rest of their cursed kin." He could still see the site of battle in his mind, as clear as if he still stood upon it, facing Léod and Robert and the rest of their murderous clan. He could almost hear Kate's distracting screams.

He reminded himself that this was the most important thing to remember about her—not the flare of female interest he saw on the rare occasions when he caught her glance, nor the warm feminine softness of her body. She was a Norman. And in his experience, they were a people with no conscience, no soul.

"My lord . . ." said the steward, his manner strangely uncertain for a man who'd served for many years as advisor to Lord Aidan, Edric's father.

"Send someone to fetch Lora. And get the priest, too," Edric said, even though he had no desire to face the disagreeable old cleric. Father Algar was as likely to blame this misfortune upon what he perceived as Edric's and Bryce's sinful ways as he was to condemn the damned Scot who'd actually cut Bryce down. Yet he kept the old man in his service since he'd been here as long as Edric could remember. Algar generally kept to his tasks, peddling religion as was his wont, and keeping his nose out of the affairs of Edric's estates.

Edric entered the hall and climbed the steps, barely aware of anything but Bryce's plight and the somber gray of the day, yet an unfamiliar, discordant cry managed to pierce through his haze of worry. 'Twas the mewling of some small animal, caught in a trap.

"My lord," said Oswin. "I must speak to you before—"

"What the . . ." Dread pooled in Edric's belly when he realized the sound came from Cecily's bedchamber. He'd heard her vicious cries many times before, but this was different. Trusting that his men would see to Bryce, Edric took the stairs two at a time until he reached the gallery on the second floor. Cecily's room was at the far end, and Edric reached it quickly, pushing open the door.

'Twas Berta, Cecily's old Norman nursemaid, keening loudly as she crouched over the bed. She wore a voluminous black kirtle and hood that shielded all but her hands and face from his gaze. She blocked Edric's view of the bed as well, and his wife in it.

The flame-haired midwife, Lora, stood in front of the old woman, speaking quietly as she tried to get 'round her to the bed. Edric narrowed his eyes as he turned slightly and spoke to the steward, who'd followed him. "Oswin?"

The steward cleared his throat. "Bryce's injury is not the only traged—"

The old woman's shrill cries filled the chamber once again. She seemed unaware of Edric's presence, but fully occupied with her own wrenching grief, ignoring Lora's attempt to draw her away.

"My lord," said the steward, "Berta will not leave her mistress. Lora and I have done all but remove her bodily—"

The old woman's cries intensified, suddenly sounding as though her voice split in two. A crowd of servants began to gather in the gallery outside the room, but Drogan managed to push his way through them to come inside. Their Norman captive followed close behind, her doe's eyes large and round and troubled.

"My lord . . ." said Oswin.

"Speak up, Oswin," Edric said roughly. "What is amiss here?"

Berta did not move away from the bed, guarding her charge as though Satan himself were trying to steal her mistress away. Lora continued to cajole her, using an awkward mixture of Norman French and English, trying every word she could find to coax the old woman away from the bed.

Oswin touched Edric's arm and spoke in a hushed tone. "Lady Cecily's labor began just after you went off to pursue the Scots. Lora told us there was bleeding . . . exhaustion. Your lady wife delivered her child last night—midnight."

Edric narrowed his eyes. Too much was happening and Cecily was ominously quiet. "What are you saying, Oswin?"

He felt Drogan's hand upon his shoulder, a consoling gesture between comrades, but he felt no comfort. In spite of all that was wrong between him and Cecily, he'd had expectations for their child. Hopes. To have lost the bairn in childbirth . . .

Berta's lamentations intensified, making his temples throb painfully. He wished for a few brief moments of privacy to compose himself, but Lora seemed unable to quiet the woman.

"Do whatever is necessary to get her away from here, and leave me with my wife," he said to Drogan.

"Aye, my lord."

Firmly, but with care, Drogan placed his hands upon the old woman's shoulders and pulled her up from her crouch. Once the bed was visible, Edric's eyes locked on Cecily's quiescent form. His beautiful wife lay in the center of the bed, devoid of color and unnaturally still. His throat went dry and his faculties suddenly failed him, making him speechless. Though there had been no affection between them, she was his wife . . . the woman to whom he'd pledged his loyalty and his life. And she was . . . gone.

An odd sense of unreality assailed him. This could not be happening . . . No matter what their differences, Edric would never have wished Cecily dead.

There was movement beside her, something squirming under the linen sheeting. Edric approached warily, afraid to hope, closing the distance between himself and the bed.

"You!" Berta cried, raising one gnarled hand to point an accusing finger at him. She spoke, even as a tortured mewling sound came from the bed. "*You* are responsible for my poor Cecily's death! She wanted naught to do with—"

"Berta," said Drogan, drawing the woman away from the bed. "You must come away now. Lora, give a hand here."

And as Berta moved away, Edric pushed aside the sheeting, revealing a tiny, squirming bairn, his son.

Kathryn felt shaky inside, and brittle, as though she would splinter into pieces with one wrong step. Her legs wobbled with fatigue, and her mind still reeled with all that had happened in the past few days. Unsure what to do with so many Saxons pressing 'round her, she'd followed Edric and Drogan up the steps to a large chamber and found herself pushed inside.

She winced at the shriek of an old woman dressed in black, and wondered what was amiss.

Then Kathryn saw her—the beautiful lady who lay in the bed and the bairn beside her.

Edric's wife and child.

The old woman screeched inconsolably, and 'twas only through the efforts of Drogan and the comely young woman they'd called Lora that they managed to pull the crone away. "Stay away!" she cried. "You Saxon dog—you will destroy *him*, too!"

"Begone, hag!" shouted the tall, bearded steward who'd spoken so quietly to Edric. But the woman ignored him, crying out invectives in Kathryn's native tongue. She winced at the woman's words and hoped no one could understand her.

Edric turned to the bed, his expression raw with grief. Quickly discerning the situation, Kathryn could well imagine his shock at finding his wife dead in childbed.

As Lora finally managed to draw the old woman away, Drogan took advantage of the moment and lifted the tiny bairn from the bed, his weathered swordsman's hands seeming out of place as they handled such soft innocence.

"You cannot take him!" the crone wailed.

Quickly, Drogan turned and handed the bairn to Kathryn before she could even consider what he was doing. As she swallowed her alarm and took the infant into her arms, his tiny body went rigid with his cries, inconsolable.

"Lora," said Edric, his voice clear and distinct

above the cacophony made by the old woman and the bairn. "I don't understand. 'Tis weeks before her time."

"Aye. This is why I ordered her to bed a fortnight ago."

"But—"

"But Lady Cecily went into labor in spite of my precautions," said the midwife, and Kathryn was amazed at her brazen reply. She had no fear of Lord Edric and spoke to him as though she were a trusted advisor. "Your wife's labors began long before she called for me . . . Had started even before you left Braxton Fell, my lord."

Drogan took charge of the old woman, who continued to weep uncontrollably. When he drew her away, Kathryn wrapped the bairn in a soft woolen blanket. She noticed a small earthen crock on a nearby table with a thin nipple made of sheep's gut beside it, just like the kind she'd used to feed Soeur Agnes's lambs. The crock was full of milk.

Taking a seat on a wooden chest near the window, Kathryn tied the false nipple over the mouth of the crock and began to feed the tiny infant, who sucked greedily.

The bairn's sudden silence was remarkable, and everyone turned to gape at her, even the old Norman crone. Uncomfortable under their scrutiny, Kathryn cast her eyes down.

"'Tis impossible," said Lora. "The wet nurse has no milk and no one else has been able to coax the bairn to drink."

"Mayhap he feeds from her because she is Norman," Drogan suggested, "as his mother was."

"Mayhap," said Lora. "Though 'tis more likely the bairn likes her soft breast against his cheek. With the wet nurse ill, none of us thought to do that."

Kathryn felt her face heat when she realized the blanket had fallen from her shoulder, leaving her breast all but bare. 'Twas only the little bairn's body that shielded its fullness from the gaze of all who stood watching her.

Too embarrassed to look up at the Saxon, Kathryn continued to feed his child, even when he ran one thumb across the bairn's soft cheek, then traced the curve of his ear with one finger. Her heart sped up and her nipples tightened, though he had not touched her.

"Lora, you are needed in my brother's chamber," he said, half turning to speak to the others. "Drogan, clear the room and take Berta to her chamber. Then go find the priest."

"What will you do now, Edric?" Drogan asked.

"I'll remain here and acquaint myself with my son," he replied coldly. "And his new nurse."

The steward spoke next, his tone gruff and hostile. "Who is she, my lord?"

"Ferguson's captive."

"Another *Norman*?"

Fumbling to pull the blanket back over her shoulders, Kathryn managed to continue feeding the tiny bairn in spite of the steward's obvious disdain. Their harsh language made her head throb, so she shut out their voices and gave her full attention to the infant in her arms.

'Twas heaven, and likely the closest she would ever come to mothering a child. Her heart tripped as she looked into the bairn's bright blue eyes and felt his perfect hand upon her breast. This was nothing like feeding one of Soeur Agnes's lambs. He was so tiny . . . with skin red and wrinkled, and a shock of black hair that seemed too thick and unruly for his newborn head. He sucked hungrily and Kathryn felt a surge of maternal protectiveness for this bairn, for this son of Lady Cecily.

Kathryn recognized Edric's wife. The abbey de St. Marie was a prestigious religious house, and many of the daughters of King William's vassals spent months or years there for one reason or another—usually for safety, or as a punishment. Cecily was one who'd come more than a year ago, before her marriage. Though Kathryn had barely spoken to her, she had a clear recollection of Cecily and the reason for her banishment to the abbey. The lady had been exiled there until she'd consented to marry the man chosen for her. Apparently, Cecily had finally capitulated to her father's command, since Kathryn had not heard of her since.

Until now.

No doubt Lord Edric had been besotted with Cecily from the moment he'd laid eyes upon her. She was tall and stately, easily the most graceful and comeliest of maidens.

Edric stood with his feet braced solidly on the floor, his thick, muscular arms crossed against his chest as he spoke to the steward. Kathryn could not fathom how he must feel, with his brother lying gravely wounded somewhere within his hall, his wife dead, and a tiny new son holding on to life by a tenuous thread.

When he finished with his steward, the man departed the chamber, leaving Kathryn alone with the formidable lord of Braxton Fell. Crouching down before her, he watched his child drink from the false nipple.

In spite of the thick whiskers that shadowed the Saxon's jaw, Kathryn could see that his mouth was pressed into a hard line, and a muscle in his jaw flexed tightly. His loss touched Kathryn deeply, but she felt ridiculous sitting there beside poor, dead Cecily, nursing the woman's child . . . feeling the unexpected and unwelcome pull of attraction for the woman's husband. She had to get away from there. Away from Braxton Fell.

"He is so . . . small," Edric muttered to himself, as if Kathryn weren't even there. He touched the bairn's forehead.

"Aye," she whispered. Edric's hand was huge and dark against the child's wrinkled skin. His awe at the sight of his son was nearly palpable. A spike of pain pierced Kathryn's breast when the realization struck her once again that she would never share such a moment with her own husband.

Lord Edric startled her by standing abruptly and walking to the opposite side of the room. Kathryn blinked away tears she knew he would not want to see. 'Twas presumptuous of her to grieve for his loss, being little more than a stranger here, and an unwelcome one at that.

The oaken door suddenly crashed open and a fierce little man entered the bedchamber. With eyes as black as his hair was white, he took no notice of Kathryn, but strode with purpose directly to the far side of the room to face Lord Edric. Sir Drogan followed right behind him, an expression of consternation upon his face.

"Edric of Braxton Fell, you who scorn tradition, God will avenge and cast you into a pool of fire!" cried the old man.

"Cease, priest," said Edric, his voice low and threatening. "Prepare for my wife's Requiem upon the morrow. In the meantime, offer intercessions for my brother's recovery."

"Look at the disasters you have wrought," replied the white-haired priest in a venomous tone. " 'Tis your unholy alliance with all that is evil—"

Edric held up one hand, palm out, effectively warding off the priest's words. "Father Algar, I am of no mood to listen to another of your tirades. What's done is—"

The priest whirled away from Edric so abruptly that he startled Kathryn, and she gathered the bairn closer to her heart. The old man pointed one bony finger at her. "You! *Norman* offal again!"

Kathryn's throat went dry, but she raised her chin defiantly, even though she possessed no confidence whatsoever. The priest's curses frightened her, for 'twas true that the young lord's injury was upon her conscience.

"Father Algar . . ." Drogan's tone was one of warning, but the priest ignored him.

"Even this bairn is cursed by—"

"*I said enough!*" Edric roared. "You know naught of what you speak, priest."

Father Algar kept his silence for the moment, but his beady eyes shifted between Kathryn and Lord Edric, then to the bairn.

"Drogan," Edric said, "take the Norman maid to the nursery."

"Aye, my lord."

"And get her some clothes."

Chapter 5

~~~ OC ~~~

E dric's eyes burned as if he'd spent the day toiling over a smoky cook fire. He tried to focus his sights upon Bryce, who lay deathly quiet in his bed, but he could barely keep his eyes open.

"My lord, mayhap you should seek your own bed and sleep some," said Drogan. "With Lady Cecily's funeral upon the morrow, it might be best if you had some rest."

"They say it comes in threes."

"What does, my lord?"

"Death." Edric rubbed his eyes. "First Cecily.

With Bryce so sorely wounded, and my son so small and fragile . . ."

"So, Father Algar is not the only superstitious one?"

"Do you think either of them will survive?"

"You heard Lora yourself," said Drogan. "Bryce's wound is the kind every warrior should pray for—Robert's sword sliced through muscle and not much else. As to the bairn . . ."

"He has no name, Drogan," Edric remarked, aware that his thoughts were jumping from one subject to the next. He'd never felt so scattered in his life, except perhaps during the weeks after Siric and Sighelm, Oswin's sons, had been slain in battle.

It seemed a lifetime ago that he and Bryce had run freely as lighthearted lads with the steward's sons. Siric and Sighelm had been like brothers to Edric and Bryce. They'd been inseparable throughout their early years, and their deaths in battle against the Normans had hit Edric nearly as hard as it had their father. Now Bryce lay near death, and Edric's son's life was in the balance, too. If the bairn died, Edric's year of marriage to Cecily would come to naught.

Was he to lose all that he cared for?

"Give him your father's name," said Drogan. "Lord Aidan was a powerful warrior and a fair-minded lord. The lad could do worse for a namesake."

Edric gave a vague nod. Aidan he would be, but the bairn seemed too small to survive. Edric had been certain that Cecily, with her Norman stubbornness and foul disposition, would deliver a hearty child, in spite of Lora's warnings. The woman had never missed an opportunity to berate him for his barbarian ways . . . and for causing all her misery.

"Never again." Edric rose to his feet, went to a window and opened a shutter to gaze upon his ruined lands in the twilight.

"My lord?"

He turned to face Drogan. "I will not marry again." He had no use for a wife—certainly not another Norman wife, the only kind King William would permit. Edric was going to rebuild Braxton Fell and take no Norman help to do it. "If the bairn survives, he will be my heir," he said coldly. "If not, then Bryce will inherit my father's lands."

Drogan nodded. "Your son has taken to Kate. 'Tis fortunate he will feed from her hand."

How easily Edric could imagine her feeding the bairn from her breast. "Aye, but 'tis the only Norman assistance we will accept."

"I don't under—"

Edric shook his head and went to the door. He

knew he was making no sense. Drogan was right. He needed sleep.

Braxton's keep was as new as Castle Kettwyck, and Kathryn thought it might even be somewhat larger. Its great hall was huge, with bare floors and walls, and a massive fireplace carved into one wall. In the flickering light of the wall sconces, 'twas a cold and cheerless place, a fair match to its cold and cheerless lord.

The keep rose three levels above the ground, and there were multiple staircases, a maze of rooms, and servants in every direction Kathryn turned. In spite of them, there were no rushes upon the cold floor, nor wall hangings to insulate the chilly stone walls. 'Twas an empty shell, certainly not home to a Norman lady.

Kathryn had been given a bedchamber on the second level near the room where Lady Cecily lay dead, and now she had all the peace and privacy she could want. Yet what was she to do with the bairn? She'd had little exposure to children, but since this one seemed content to sleep in her arms, she went to the only chair in the room and sat down.

When a light knock sounded at the door, Kathryn arose to answer it, afraid the noise might wake the child. A young maid entered, with red-haired

Lora right behind her, carrying a bundle of clothes and blankets. The midwife was a much younger woman than Kathryn had supposed when Drogan had first mentioned her.

"Lay the fire, Wilona," Lora said, then turned to Kathryn. "I brought you a few things . . . You must have had quite an ordeal, being stolen from your home. Rushton, was it?"

Kathryn nodded, but could not speak of her abduction. Not yet.

"I brought some clothes for you, and some things for the bairn. If you're to be his nursemaid, you'll need—"

"But I am no nursemaid. I . . ." What could she tell of herself? She knew 'twas best not to let anyone know who she was or where her true home was, for they would send her back to Kettwyck to face the scorn of her family and her peers.

Lora looked at her quizzically, but did not press her to continue. When she spoke, her words were firm, but not unkind. "You must serve as nurse to Edric's son until we can find another. The bairn was born too soon . . . and he refused all sustenance until you arrived. You are his only hope, at least for now."

Kathryn nodded, coming to grips with what she must do. Besides, how could she object? The bairn was as helpless as he was beautiful. And if

Kathryn was the only one who could feed him, who was she to argue? A few days at Braxton Fell would change naught.

Lora took the bairn from her and placed him in the small cradle next to the bed. "Now let me look at you." She became the healer then, placing her hands on either side of Kathryn's head and turning her this way and that, feeling her scalp for cuts and bumps. "You have a nasty abrasion here. Any other injuries? Did they . . . did any of the Scots . . . rape you?"

Kathryn shook her head. She wrapped her arms 'round herself and turned away. "But it was a near thing. The Saxons—your Lord Edric and his men—appeared just in time. The leader—"

"That would be Léod Ferguson. He's a measle, but his son is worse. Drop the blanket and let me see your back."

Kathryn did as she was told and when Lora had finished examining her, she picked up a canvas pouch containing some salve, and placed it upon a table. "I thought you might need this. Use it after your bath."

"Bath?" Kathryn's heart nearly leaped at the word.

Lora laughed. "Aye. Wilona will bring the tub, and grooms have already been ordered to carry water for you."

Tears welled in Kathryn's eyes at the woman's kindness. She gestured toward the plain blue kirtle and bliaut, the woolen hose and shoes, and the undergarment lying on the bed. No noble princess could have had finer attire. "My thanks to you. You've been very kind."

As promised, the bath was provided. When Kathryn was finally alone, she let Sir Drogan's blanket slide to the floor, removed the filthy rag that had once been a delicate chemise, and stepped naked into the tub near the fire. All her various cuts and scrapes stung as she sat down in the water, but her bruises practically sang with joy.

Closing her eyes for just a moment, she leaned back and let herself drift in the heat and comfort of her bath. Her hips and thighs were sore from two days on horseback, but she felt the tension ease from them as she reclined in the hot water.

It had been naïve of her to think Lord Edric might be unmarried, and to have entertained such wild musings about him. She'd gawked at his muscular form and his glossy hair, had daydreamed about his big, square hands and the masculine sprinkling of dark hair upon them. Cecily was easily the comeliest woman in all of England and France. And though she might be dead, Kathryn did not doubt her husband would compare every other woman to her.

Her eyelids fluttered closed and she sank down in slumber, only to be shocked awake some time later by a piercing wail and freezing cold water. She had no idea how long she'd slept in the tub, but the infant's cry was enough to wake all who dwelled in the keep. Quickly, she climbed from the tub and wrapped herself like a sausage into Drogan's blanket. Tucking one corner of the wool under her arm, she bent over and picked up Cecily's child just as the door to her chamber burst open.

"What commotion is this?" Edric demanded.

Kathryn felt her cheeks flood with color. She walked to the door, flustered at being caught in such dishabille. "Please, sir," she said, holding the bairn to her breast, pushing the door wide open as a broad hint for him to leave. "'Tis not necessary for you to—"

"'Tis my son's cries that brought me here."

"He is just . . . just hungry, my lord." She curled her toes as though that would help to cover her naked legs, yet it was strangely thrilling to feel his gaze upon her.

And entirely indecent.

"I will feed him and all will be well."

Lord Edric did not make his exit, but closed the door behind him and glanced 'round the room. "Is that my son's milk?" He went to the hearth, picked up the crock of milk Lora had placed there earlier, and poured some of it into the bairn's cup.

"It might be too hot." Kathryn attempted a demure mien, one that a simple maid would affect. "I'll just—"

"Show me how this is done."

The room felt much too small with the Saxon lord in it. His attire was the same battle-stained tunic and hose he'd worn the past two days. He was stunningly male, impossibly intriguing. In perfect detail, Kathryn recalled how safe and secure she'd felt after he'd killed the boar, when he'd held her against his strong chest. She knew now that it had been naught but a reflexive action, for he'd believed that his comely wife awaited him here.

Steeling herself against the influence of his male potency, she picked up the false nipple and joined him near the hearth. Surely, once she quieted the bairn with his milk, Edric would leave and she could breathe easily again. "I'm to tie this to the crock, then shake a few drops upon my hand."

His expression turned dubious. Kathryn took note of the deep circles under his bloodshot eyes and realized the man was so weary he probably did not even realize she was undressed, or that it was wholly improper for him to be in her chamber.

Or that he hated her.

"This is what Lora said I should do to be sure of the temperature."

Edric proceeded to tie the nipple onto the cup. When Kathryn held out the back of her hand to him, he took it and turned it over, shaking a few drops of the milk upon the inside of her wrist. "Is this not a more sensitive spot?" he asked.

"'Tis p-perfect," Kathryn replied, though she felt an arrow of heat shoot up her arm. And 'twas not the milk that caused it.

Ignoring her racing heart, she took the cup, gathered the bairn close to her breast, and drew away. She sat down on the soft chair at the opposite side of the room while the child cried for his meal. Reaching for the blue kirtle, Kathryn drew it over her legs and wished she could crawl into the bed and cover herself completely.

"*Merci*, er . . . Thank you for your assistance, my lord," she said, waiting for him to go. "We'll manage now."

But he did not leave. Instead, he took a seat upon her bed. She should be outraged at his incursion here, but she could not muster any anger, not when he leaned his elbows upon his knees and let his hands dangle between his powerful legs.

"I . . . I apologize for letting the bairn wake you."

"He did not wake me." His voice was as blunt as the thick veins that lined the backs of his hands and arms. His feet seemed huge, encased as they were in soft leather boots. He watched her intently, waiting to see if the child quieted, and Kathryn felt inept and clumsy under his harsh scrutiny.

She put the nipple to the bairn's mouth, but he rejected it and turned toward her breast, finding only the wool of the blanket she'd wrapped around herself. He let out a series of heartrending whimpers.

" 'Tis your soft skin he seeks."

Embarrassed and conscious of her own awkwardness, Kathryn fumbled with the cup, trying to get the child to accept the nipple. Soon he began to bawl again, and in the midst of the clamor, Edric leaned close. He slipped one finger under the edge of the blanket.

And pulled.

Everything went silent in Kathryn's ears. No longer did she hear the infant's squalls, but only a faint humming as the blanket came loose, pulling away just enough for the bairn's cheek to rest against her bare skin while her own nipple remained concealed beneath the soft wool.

She dared not look up at Lord Edric, but managed to slip the false nipple into his son's mouth this time. The child suckled greedily as Kathryn savored the sensation of Lord Edric's touch against her sensitive skin. She doubted the intimate touch meant anything to him, but tension gathered in her loins, nonetheless. Her pulse pounded in her throat as he caressed his son, inadvertently stroking the fullness of her breast. Kathryn closed her eyes, and and 'twas all she could do to hold in a wanton whimper of pleasure.

Edric suddenly withdrew his hand. He made a gruff sound of annoyance, then stood and left the chamber without another word, closing the door behind him.

Kathryn took a shuddering breath and looked down at the beautiful, tiny bairn in her arms. "We both know I am a pale substitute for your poor *mère*, do we not?" The child broke away from the cup and trained his eyes upon her, and Kathryn wished she had her own child to love and nurture.

And a husband who could make her quiver with longing. A man like Edric of Braxton Fell.

'Twas well past dawn, yet the workmen who were charged with making Norman improvements at Braxton Fell were quiet, out of respect for Lady Cecily.

In the early morning light, Edric looked out over his lands. Ever since the fires set by the Fergusons, more than half his woodlands resembled stands of white-gray sticks. The fields were still black and sooty, their autumn yield paltry. The mill at the river's edge stood silent, its wheels quiet without sufficient grain to grind.

Had Edric and Bryce remained at home two years before, rather than haring down to York with half of Braxton's fyrd, Léod Ferguson would never have had the opportunity to cause such damage. Oswin was right. With their excessive demands, the Normans had brought naught but death and destruction to Braxton.

Disgusted by the sight of his ruined lands, Edric turned away, clasping his hands behind him. It seemed a lifetime since life had been good at Braxton Fell.

Mayhap the priest was right, too, and Braxton Fell *was* cursed.

Edric surely felt cursed every time he looked at the Norman wench. Though he knew better, he wanted her.

'Twas no more than his wayward cock demanding female attention. It had naught to do with the way her breath quickened when he touched her, or the enticing beading of her pretty nipples when she fed his son.

She was a delicate beauty, her lips full and enticing, her eyes dark and expressive. Hers was not the conventional but brittle beauty of Cecily's face and form, but a gently rounded comeliness that had no sharp edges.

It had been pure torture to watch her nuzzle Aidan's head, to see his son cradled upon those plush breasts. Her virginal embarrassment at her lack of proper clothes in his presence was beyond appealing. Edric had wanted to unwrap the woolen blanket from Kate's body and sample the feminine secrets that had been denied him for much too long.

Now that there was no longer any reason for him to abstain, he would take her to bed. Soon.

The sound of footsteps caused Edric to turn. Oswin approached him from the far end of the escarpment, his expression grim, as usual. The man was dressed severely in unrelenting black—robes, tunic, and hose. His beard was only partially white, and his body just as powerful as in the days of his prime when he'd fought at Edric's father's side. He was still a vigorous man. "Wulfgar of Tredburgh is coming to Braxton Fell, my lord. I did not mention it yesterday—"

"What reason could Wulfgar possibly have for coming here?" Edric asked the question, but he knew the answer. Wulfgar was an old Saxon thane who had lost his lands to King William. He'd spent the last year trying to garner support for a Saxon rebellion, and he'd not been entirely unsuccessful. The man had the sympathy and support of several Saxon families, gaining him a growing number of followers. He'd made it known he wanted Braxton Fell behind him.

Wulfgar was trouble that Edric did not need.

"Dissuade him."

" 'Tis too late, my lord. I do not know his location, so there is no way to deliver a message to him."

Edric cursed under his breath. As soon as Baron Gui received news of his daughter's death, he would come to Braxton to visit her tomb and see his grandson for himself. 'Twould not do to have a band of rebellious Saxons present when the Norman baron arrived. "I want him gone, Oswin," said Edric. "Quarreling with King William is pointless now."

"You cannot know that, my lord. You and Lord Wulfgar could raise a powerful Saxon fyrd."

"I have naught to gain by doing so." But much to lose. Braxton Fell needed time to recover from the damage of the Ferguson raid. 'Twould not do to rekindle Norman animosity now.

Oswin made a rude noise. "Normans have made life here a misery."

"I will not argue that point, but our lands are still under Saxon control—*my* control."

"When does the price of your enfeoffment become too great, Lord Edric?"

"Enough, Oswin." Edric would not take offense at the steward's condescension, for the man had advised the lords of Braxton Fell long and well. However, he was mistaken in this instance. "Send Wulfgar on his way when he arrives here."

Kathryn awoke early. She dressed, combed her hair, and put it in a neat plait. Taking care not to awaken Edric's child, she picked him up, cradled him in her arms, then left her chamber to go in search of Drogan. The burly huscarl was the only one she knew who might escort her to Evesham Bridge. 'Twas imperative to leave as soon as possible, before she developed any stronger attachment to the bairn.

She did not go far before she saw Lora and two other women leaving Lady Cecily's chamber. Several men followed, carrying Lady Cecily's body on a bier. Edric and Drogan were among them.

Edric wore a clean gray tunic with elaborate stitchery at the neck and wrists. In such finery, and with his hair neatly tied at his nape, he looked impossibly regal. And though his face was still unshaven, Kathryn could see that his expression was understandably grim. His glance brushed over her once quickly, as though he found her entirely unremarkable, then rested upon the infant in her arms.

Church bells suddenly began to peal and Lora came to Kathryn's side. "Come, we depart for church."

Edric did not look again in her direction, but Drogan gave her a polite nod as the men balanced Cecily's bier upon their shoulders and followed Edric's dignified lead. Kathryn followed the women down the steps and through the hall. The church bells continued to clang as they went outside where a number of Lord Edric's retainers joined them.

The steward approached and blocked Kathryn's path, his expression dark and forbidding. "Lora," he said, "take the child. There is no need for this one to attend Lady Cecily's funeral."

Except for her Scottish captors, no one had ever spoken in such a rude manner to Kathryn before, and she didn't understand why the steward was so irate with her. Except that he, too, must blame her for Bryce's injury.

"She comes, Oswin." Without turning, Edric spoke from his place at the head of Cecily's bier. "She will bring my son."

"My lord—"

"Aidan will attend his mother's funeral with his nurse."

Edric said no more, but resumed his walk

toward the church. The steward glowered at Kathryn before turning away, and she pressed her lips to the bairn's head. *"Aidan,"* she whispered. " 'Tis a fine name you've been given."

She felt a quickening in her heart as she watched the proprietary manner in which the Saxon lord led the procession to church, and thought of what he must feel as he carried his dead wife to her burial. Cecily had borne Edric's child, but thinking of the intimacies they must have shared as husband and wife gave Kathryn an odd, unsettling feeling.

Moving closer to Lora as they walked, she let her eyes wander. They passed cottages that were surprisingly quiet. There were no pigs rooting in the dirt, and few chickens pecking at the ground. People were scarce as well, with only a few of the villagers joining the procession to the church.

Much of the village was enclosed by an unfinished wall of timber and stone, though she'd seen a good number of cottages outside. Cecily's procession passed shops—the chandler's, a blacksmith's forge, a glazier's, the shoemaker, and many more—but all were quiet due to the somber occasion. It occurred to Kathryn that mayhap the inactivity of the village was partly related to the state of Braxton's lands.

The malevolent little priest met them at the

church door and led them inside. The old Norman woman in black was already there, weeping loudly as she sat upon a bench at the back of the church. Her sorrow touched Kathryn, especially since there seemed to be no one here to comfort her.

"Lora, will you hold Aidan?" Turning the bairn over to Lora, she made her way to the back of the church. She took a seat beside the old woman and spoke to her soothingly, hoping to console her.

Cecily's nursemaid turned into her arms, and Kathryn patted her back as she wept, calming her and assuring her that Cecily's soul was surely in heaven now.

The men stayed close to the bier all through the Mass. Edric's attention stayed fully focused on the ritual, while Kathryn's gaze was torn between watching Aidan sleep in Lora's arms, and Edric, kneeling with his head bowed in piety and sorrow.

Kathryn looked away from his powerful physique, and offered prayers for Cecily's soul, for Lord Bryce's recovery, and for poor Berta, even as she prayed for her own flight from Braxton. She had to speak to Drogan soon, before she fell completely in love with the lord's tiny son.

Or worse, with his father.

* * *

Edric felt tense and restless when they returned to the hall for Cecily's wake. He could not mourn the woman who had made his life a misery these past months, but she'd been his wife, had borne his child, and had died in the process.

What he felt was certainly not affection, nor was it grief. 'Twas more like regret for what had never been, what could never be. Cecily had been a beautiful woman, and he'd wanted her fiercely in the first few days of their marriage. He'd quickly learned that in all the ways that mattered, she was as cold and uncaring as a fish swimming in one of Braxton's many lakes. Still, 'twas not every day a man lost his wife.

Oswin's voice drew him from his reverie. "Care must be taken with the ale, my lord." He joined Edric, who stood alone near the fireplace in the great hall. "Our stores are not what they should be."

"See to it, then," Edric said, although he did not anticipate much toasting of Cecily's grand life. She had insulted or alienated everyone she'd touched here at Braxton.

'Twas not to say that the hall was empty, either. The men of his fyrd and many of the villagers had come to pay respects. Though they had little affection for Lady Cecily, they had respect for Edric and for the son who would be eorl after him, providing Edric managed to continue holding his estate from the Norman king. That could easily change, depending upon William's whim.

"They come for what food you will provide," said Oswin. "Not for any fondness for your Norman wife."

Edric shrugged. That much was obvious, but tradition would be observed. He did not condemn Oswin for his hostility toward the Normans. They had caused untold damage to the man's family, but Oswin had to understand that no amount of hatred would bring back his sons, and rebellion was useless. The reign of the Saxons in England was done.

Musicians stood near the staircase, tuning their instruments, and the aroma of roasting pig wafted through the hall. Yet Cecily's wake was conspicuously subdued. 'Twas nothing like the sorrow shown by raucous song and loud weeping that had followed the funerals of Siric and Sighelm. Instead, the servants went quietly about the hall, pouring mugs of ale and placing platters of meat and bread on the tables. When Oswin left, no one approached Edric, all apparently uncertain what to say to him.

He caught sight of Kate, wearing the blue gown she'd tossed across her legs the night before for modesty's sake. He'd taken note of her at the funeral, giving care and consolation to the old Norman nurse, a woman she did not even know.

To Edric's knowledge, Cecily had never shown kindness to a stranger . . . But mayhap he was giving too much credit to Kate. The old woman was Norman, and the only other one of her kind at Braxton. 'Twas possible they were conspiring together, planning to wreak havoc somehow on the man responsible for Cecily's pregnancy and death, and for her unhappiness this past year.

Yet as Kate made her way toward the stairs with Lora, he felt a pressing urge to go to her, to take hold of that thick plait of rich, brown hair and bury his face in it. It seemed impossible that she could be just as alluring fully dressed as when he'd burst unannounced into her chamber. She was fresh from her bath, and he'd been struck yet again by her feminine perfection.

He should not have lingered in her room. His brain must have been addled when he touched her, when he slid his fingers across the fullness of her breast while she fed his son.

God's blood, she was Norman, and he'd vowed to have naught to do with any of them, beyond what was utterly necessary. There was no point in entertaining any thoughts about taking her to bed.

"Many condolences for your loss, my lord."

Edric turned away from Kate's retreating figure

to the first person to approach him. 'Twas Felicia, daughter of Wilfred the tavernkeeper. Many a time had Edric sported with this lusty blonde, but those trysts had ended as soon as he'd said his marriage vows and Cecily had made her demands. Even so, Felicia had always made it known she would welcome him back to her bed at any time.

" 'Tis said your lady wife bore you a son."

"Aye." He wondered where Lora was taking Kate. Mayhap 'twas time to feed Aidan and they were going to a place with fewer distractions. She would loosen her bodice and—

"Things have been quiet at the Silver Dragon, my lord." She gave him a wicked smile and leaned into him, pressing her body against his. "I won't be missed if I disappear a while."

Edric had thought of this so many times during the past year, he could not believe he was hesitating now. But this was not the time. With all that had recently transpired, Edric was in no mood to frolic in Felicia's bed.

"My lord?"

Edric looked into her eyes. She was as comely as any woman in the town and knew how to satisfy a man's lusty appetites. Yet she smelled of cabbage and sour hops.

"Once my brother is out of danger and things

are settled here, I'll send someone for you." When he finally bedded her, he wanted no worries to detract from the moment.

He disengaged his arm from her grasp. Taking his leave, he headed toward the stairs. 'Twas past time to check on Bryce.

"Come, Bryce wishes to see you," said Lora.

"He is awake now?" asked Kathryn.

"Aye, and complaining of being confined to his bed."

Kathryn could scarcely believe it had been only three days since she'd sewn his terrible gash. She'd been at Braxton Keep only one night, yet it seemed as if weeks had passed since she'd first set eyes upon Lord Edric, since she'd first felt the swell of arousal in her breast.

She'd had no chance to speak to Drogan about going to Evesham Bridge. She had to do so soon, before the stirrings of motherly affection for Aidan became any stronger. Even now, 'twould be difficult to leave the bairn.

No one had ever needed her so desperately before.

Kathryn tucked his head under her chin and followed Lora down the dim corridor of the second floor. Lora walked past Cecily's bedchamber and down another long passageway.

The healer's manner reminded Kathryn of her sister, Isabel. Gifted, confident, and striking in her appearance, she had many talents. Kathryn doubted Lora would have allowed herself to be abducted. Surely she—like Isabel—would have found a way to escape the raiders.

"Where is Berta?" Kathryn asked, concerned about the old woman.

"In her chamber. She took to her bed after the burial and will not come out."

"Where?"

"On the floor above. She seemed to take comfort from you. You might visit later."

"Does she have a maid or anyone to attend her?"

"Oh, aye," Lora replied. "But I understand 'tis not a satisfactory arrangement. There is no Saxon who can satisfy the old crone."

Kathryn was silent for a moment. She felt pity for the poor woman, who must have been taken from all that was familiar to follow Cecily to Braxton Fell. Now that Cecily was gone, there was nothing here for her.

"Will Lord Edric send her back to Cecily's family at Lichford?"

"Aye. 'Tis likely."

"Mayhap I'll take Aidan to her chamber to visit her from time to time," Kathryn said.

" 'Twould be a kindness, I'm sure."

They walked on, and Kathryn became curious about Lora, who seemed so much at home as they walked up steps and through dark corridors. She liked the young woman, who was so forthright and friendly. "Do you live here in the keep, Lora?"

She shook her head. "No, my cottage is in the village, outside the walls."

"Your family did not join you in church."

Lora gave a brief shake of her head. "I have little family. I am a widow."

"Oh! I am sorry . . . I should not have—"

" 'Tis naught. My husband has been gone more than twelvemonth. 'Tis no longer painful to speak of him. But what of you?" Lora asked. "Who waits for you at Rushton?"

Kathryn did not want to perpetuate the lie about Rushton, but she could think of no alternative.

"No one." Though Geoffroi might still be at Kettwyck. She wondered again whether he'd survived the attack and knew she could never face her family—and his—if he had not. Outside of what anyone thought of a Scot's captive, her behavior on the night of the fete had been shameful. She had led Geoffroi to his . . .

Dear God, she hoped he had not been killed.

"I—I cannot return home."

95

"What of your family? Will they not be glad to know—"

"My people would condemn me for what happened," Kathryn replied. "I cannot go back."

"Condemn you for *what happened*?" A deep furrow appeared between Lora's brows. "Do you mean they would hold *you* responsible for being abducted?"

Lora could not possibly understand Kathryn's culpability. She'd drawn Geoffroi away from the festivities at Kettwyck, which might very well have resulted in his death. She prayed to God that he had survived, but regardless, she had heard every word spoken by the ladies at Kettwyck. She knew exactly how she would be received if she returned. "Aye. I am outcast."

Lora gave her a sidelong glance. " 'Tis just as well, for Aidan needs his nurse."

"I cannot stay here, either."

"But here you are, thanks to Edric and Bryce. If the Fergusons had succeeded in taking you to their holding . . ." Lora shuddered visibly and left the thought unfinished.

Kathryn took a deep breath. Edric had truly been her savior and hero, preventing Léod Ferguson from assaulting and perhaps even killing her. Even so, Kathryn had no future here, nor at Kettwyck, either. Evesham Bridge was her only option.

She bit her lip. "I plan to ask Drogan to escort me to the nunnery at Evesham Bridge."

Lora looked at her curiously and Kathryn realized she'd misspoken. If she wanted this household to believe she was a simple maiden, she could not ask for such special treatment. No peasant maid would ever ask for a knightly escort.

"Evesham Bridge?" Lora asked. " 'Tis a two-day ride from Braxton Fell."

" 'Twas a foolish thought," said Kathryn, hoping to cover her mistake. She would find some other way to leave Braxton Fell. "I . . . I saw no other alternative besides the nunnery."

They passed a narrow, curving staircase that went up to the next floor, but did not stop until they came to an open door. Pausing outside, Lora said, " 'Tis sure Lord Edric will order you to stay, at least as long as you're the only nursemaid his son will accept."

"Aye," she said quietly. "I'm sure you're right."

Inside the room, a fire burned low in the grate, casting a small amount of heat and light. One long-legged Saxon warrior named Alf sat on a chair within, but he exited the room to stand guard outside when Kathryn and Lora entered.

Bryce lay quiet in the bed, but he was awake. The corners of his mouth lifted in a smile when Kathryn and Lora approached him. "Ah, 'tis our

Norman guest. And my nephew." His voice was low and pitifully weak for a man of his size. Kathryn wondered if he remembered the part she'd played in causing his injury . . . and the sewing of it. "Come close," he said.

Aidan was awake now, and content for the moment. Bryce raised his uninjured arm to touch him. "He's a homely wretch," he said with a wan smile. "Looks just like his sire."

Lora placed one hand on the young man's forehead. "Your eyes must have been affected by your injury, you impudent dotard. For your brother is far from homely."

Bryce started to laugh, but grimaced with pain instead. "Have mercy, Lora. What think you, Kate? Is my brother not the homeliest lout you've ever seen?"

What was she to say? That a glance from Lord Edric seared her blood? That his touch made her breasts tingle and her womb contract with the kind of awareness she'd never hoped to experience. "I . . ."

A sound at the door made them turn.

"Leave the Norman alone, Bryce." Edric stepped through the doorway and came into the chamber to stand beside Kathryn. He did not look at her, but she felt the heat of his body and a tightness rising in her throat.

"Lord Bryce is a tease, Kate," Lora said. "He has not changed since he was a small lad hanging on to my skirts."

"I beg to differ," Bryce scoffed. "I never held your skirts."

Lora turned to Kathryn. "Young Bryce was my charge as a lad, and a wee hellion he was, too."

"Don't listen to her, Kate. I was a well-behaved—"

"Lout."

Kathryn lost track of their banter as Edric turned his attention to the bairn in her arms. He smelled of the incense Father Algar had used in church, and of the cold air at the cemetery. He touched Aidan's mouth, and the infant started to suckle the end of his finger. Kathryn closed her eyes and swallowed, appalled at the direction of her thoughts.

Edric did not take his eyes from his son, letting his thumb brush over the child's chin. Aidan soon started making the small sounds that came just before a full-blown screeching, so she shifted the bairn's position, holding him upright against her shoulder, bouncing him softly, the way Lora had shown her. Oh, so gently, Edric cupped Aidan's head in the palm of his hand. The infant quieted even as Kathryn's heart thundered in her chest.

"You have the touch, my lord," said Lora. She poured water into a mug, then stirred in a fine, white powder from a small vial on a nearby table.

"The touch?" asked Bryce.

"Aye. Same as your father."

"And how would you know, wench?" Bryce mocked playfully as Lora helped him raise his head to drink her potion. But Edric's hand was so close to Kathryn's cheek that she could hardly follow the playful teasing between the other two.

"I was nearly twelve years old when you were born, sapling. And my memory is flawless. There were times when neither your mother nor your nurse could calm you. 'Twas your sire who stepped in a number of those times. He did not care that child-rearing is women's work."

Bryce drank, making a sour face as the concoction went down. "What is this rubbish anyway?"

"For your fever. And I'll have a look at that wound now."

Bryce pushed the blanket from his chest to give Lora access to the injury. Kathryn did not look away quickly enough, and the sight of that terrible gash with its thick, black stitches made her stomach queasy and her knees weak.

She staggered. Edric reached out and took

Aidan from her as he placed an arm 'round her shoulders.

"Take a deep breath," he said as he guided her to a nearby chair. "Better yet, put your head between your knees."

Chapter 6

Immediately, Edric thought of something he'd rather place between her knees, but quickly closed that line of thought. Felicia would soon quench his lust. Mayhap not this eve, but soon he would seek her out and take her to bed. She was skilled in every possible way to please a man, so there was no good reason to consider the pleasures Kate's lush mouth could give, or how her nipples would taste upon his tongue.

She raised her head and Edric watched as a bit of color returned to her lips. He'd never seen anyone go so totally pale, so quickly. The Norman was the most squeamish woman he'd ever seen, and her delicacy reminded him he'd intended to send someone to Rushton on her behalf. She was much too gentle and well spoken to be a peasant maid. Her English was nearly flawless, and he'd noticed that the shreds of her ruined chemise had been of a fine, elegant cloth. 'Twas certain she'd be missed from Rushton, though Edric did not understand why she would not admit to her elevated status there.

Lora brought a glass of water and handed it to Kate to drink. "You'll be all right. 'Tis not everyone who can stand the sight of such an awful thing." She flashed a teasing grin at Bryce. "Or a bloody wound like that, either."

Edric did not share in their lighthearted jesting. He'd seen the wound, and naught but a miracle would see it healed. He would make sure every Mass at Braxton Fell's church was offered for Bryce's recovery and for the survival of tiny Aidan.

"You are a saucy wench, Lora," Bryce said. "Edric, tell me why we tolerate such impudence."

Drogan came into the room just then. "So this is where you've all gone." His eyes alighted upon Kate. "What ails our Norman nursemaid?"

Kate's embarrassment was plain on her face, and her discomfiture roused protective instincts

Edric did not know he had. 'Twas no one's concern if the lass had a weak stomach. "What of the wake?" he asked Drogan. "Is the meal served?"

"Aye, and the company awaits your return," the huscarl replied. "You have not yet raised your glass to Lady Cecily."

"Aye. 'Tis past time for me to return."

Gingerly, Kate came to her feet, and when she spoke, Edric was struck again by the pleasing cadence of her speech. "I am fine now, Lord Edric. I apologize for keeping you from your duties."

Aye. His duties, the most onerous of which had been marrying Cecily. He reminded himself that he wanted no part of this newest Norman wench, and that he had no business taking note of the intriguing blush that colored her cheeks when she took Aidan from him. He was no raw lad to be paralyzed by his first surge of lust, but a full-grown man, a discerning man of twenty-six years.

"Come, my lord, and we can put Lady Cecily to rest." Drogan turned to Lora and went pink to the ears when he addressed her. "I've saved a place for you at my table, mistress."

Lora did not notice Drogan's blush as she concentrated on Bryce's wound, answering offhandedly. "Aye. I'll be down soon."

Drogan and Edric returned to the hall together.

"You'll need to be more direct with Lora," Edric said, rather than dwelling upon thoughts of the gentle swell of Kate's breast or the sweet gaze she cast upon his son.

"Oh. And I suppose you're the master seducer?" the huscurl retorted, obviously sensitive about his feelings for Braxton's healer.

"Don't get into a furor, Drogan. I merely state that Lora hasn't yet taken notice of your subtle hints."

Drogan grunted and started down the steps. "What will you do about the Norman woman?"

Edric gave a shrug, not ready to discuss the woman who wreaked such havoc on his own composure.

" 'Tis obvious she's no serving maid. Someone will be missing her. Mayhap searching for her."

" 'Tis not our concern." Edric was curt. "Whoever she is, Aidan needs her."

Drogan inclined his head slightly. "Aye. But she could be the daughter of Rushton's lord or some other high-ranking knight. Will you jeopardize your relationship with the Normans by keeping her here?"

"Only until my son will take his feedings from another."

"Then we must search for someone to do so."

"Even if I sent men with a letter to Rushton, it could be weeks before we receive a reply."

"So why not—"

"Lora will inform me when another wet nurse becomes available. In the meantime, Aidan's life depends upon Kate. I won't jeopardize his well-being by getting rid of the wench."

In all Kathryn's years at the abbey, she had not learned any of the more feminine skills of needlework, preferring the study of numbers and mathematics, and gaining fluency in the languages their priest could teach her. These would not serve her, or anyone else, now. If she'd wed Geoffroi, she might have used them to help manage his estates.

Mayhap those skills would be useful at Evesham Bridge, but if not, there would be animals to tend in the nunnery's barns.

Kathryn realized that her chamber was meant to be Braxton's nursery, but it was surprisingly bare. Cecily must have been quite ill during the last weeks of her pregnancy, else she'd have made the room more pleasant for her child and his nurse.

When evening came, Kathryn was hungry, but she was loath to leave the chamber and join the gathering of Saxons in the hall. Most of them had given her a cold reception, while the priest and steward were downright hostile. She did not care to encounter any of them again, but she seemed to have been forgotten.

A light tapping at the door interrupted her thoughts. She opened it to two young serving maids.

"I'm Rheda. I'm to show you where to get milk for the bairn," said the taller of the two girls. "Gwen will stay here and mind him while we're gone."

Kathryn had not thought she would be required to fetch and carry for herself and Aidan, but of course she would. Why would anyone serve *her*?

"Lora sent us," said Gwen, as though that explained everything.

"Do you . . . Lora said you would understand our words."

"Aye, I'll come with you." Kathryn pulled her shawl 'round her. "Aidan should sleep a while, for I just fed him."

'Twas clear neither girl knew how to treat Kathryn—as a servant like themselves, or as someone of a higher rank. She could easily understand their dilemma since her position at Braxton Fell was ill-defined. She was Norman, too, as Lord Edric's lady had been, but neither of them showed any particular respect or friendliness.

On the contrary, she felt some hostility from Rheda.

Saying naught, she went with the tall maid. They went down a back staircase and Kathryn soon found herself in a poorly lit passageway. She knew they were somewhere behind the great hall, for she could still hear the muted tones of the music and voices of those who had gathered for Cecily's wake.

They walked past a number of smaller rooms, some with closed doors and others open, but too dark to see inside. They reached the kitchen, where there was a lot of activity, with maids scrubbing pots and young boys carrying hot water to pour into the washtubs. The cook directed each task, which slowed somewhat as Kathryn walked past, following the maid to a dark entryway.

They exited the keep and descended a set of steps to the ground, walking through the kitchen garden. Kathryn had no difficulty finding her way, for the night was clear and the waxing moon bright, but there was a wicked wind that whipped at her skirts. They came to a barn where an old man who smelled of sheep awaited them. He held out a large earthen crock.

"Here, Rheda," he said.

" 'Tis sheep's milk?" Kathryn asked.

"Aye. What else would it be? We've got three

ewes that give milk." His tone was harsh and Kathryn drew back a step. "They've more than enough to share with the lord's son."

Kathryn felt so much the stranger here . . . unexpected duties, a strange language that often made her head hurt, and a master who made her ache for all that she could not have. But when she felt the warmth of the animals inside the barn and heard the low baaing of several lambs, she felt a pang of homesickness for the abbey.

Her decision to go to Evesham Bridge was the right one. "Do you keep them penned?" she asked.

"Never did in years past, but after war with the Normans"—he turned and spat upon the ground—"and with our flock nearly ruined by the Fergusons, we must be more careful with the wee ones."

"There's a cold edge to the wind tonight, Beorn," said Rheda.

"Aye. Now you'd best take yourself back to the keep before the storm breaks." His expression went neutral as he turned and spoke to Kathryn. "One of the lads will have a crock of milk ready for you twice daily—once in the morn and again at dark. If it's not enough—"

"I'm sure 'twill be sufficient for now."

Kathryn took the crock from Rheda and started back to the keep. She tried to make allowances for the man's rude attitude toward her, and wondered if Cecily had met with such enmity when she'd come here. Even though they were Norman, they were merely women, and had naught to do with the bloody battles fought for England.

While the old man had been impolite, he'd spoken truly—the weather was about to change. Clouds started to move in, obscuring the light of the moon. Kathryn watched her step as she hurried up the stairs, holding the crock securely with both hands. 'Twould not do to trip and drop the milk she'd been given.

But as the sharp wind whipped wildly at her skirts, she stopped short when she saw Lord Edric waiting inside the door at the top of the stairs.

"Where is my son?" Edric asked. He'd caught sight of Kate leaving the keep with the young maid, and wondered where she would go—and who had charge of the bairn.

"He is with Gwen, my lord," Rheda replied. "Lora sent us to show the Norman where to find the bairn's milk."

He leveled his sternest glance at the servant while he took the crock from Kate's hands and handed it to her. "I assume you have other chores?"

"Aye, my lord," she said, taking the milk and hurrying away.

Kathryn started to take her leave as well, but Edric took hold of her arm, keeping her with him. Rheda went on without her. "One of the maids will fetch Aidan's milk. You need not take him out in the cold for his food."

He did not release her arm, nor did he step back. Thick, dark lashes framed her beautiful dark eyes; their expression was wary, but oh, so alluring.

"I do not m-mind going, my lord. And I can wrap Aidan warmly."

If he moved one step closer, the tips of her breasts would brush against his chest. He'd seen their pink-tipped peaks as she'd bent over Bryce to sew him. Even then, his hands had fairly itched to touch them, to weigh their fullness in his hands, to draw the nipples into his mouth. Her exposed legs had been sleek and feminine, and Edric could almost feel them wrapped 'round his waist, hear her gentle voice panting with arousal.

She leaned back against the cold stone wall, putting space between them, but Edric could not let her slip away so easily.

He placed one hand upon the wall next to her ear. With the other, he touched her jaw where it met her ear, sliding his finger to her chin and down to her throat. She moistened her lower lip, then bit down on it, nervously letting it slide back.

Edric's cock rose with arousal but he somehow

managed to speak coherently. "You said there is no one at Rushton who will miss you."

She hesitated the same way she'd done when first telling Drogan her name. Edric leaned slightly toward her, allowing her skirts to brush against his exquisitely sensitive erection. He could almost taste her.

"No, my lord. No one." Her accent was as soft as the rest of her, her voice sliding seductively through him, like the honey-sweetened morsels Cook had given him as a lad.

"No husband?" He realized he had whispered the question when she gave a slight shake of her head. And found himself decidedly glad of her answer. "Then I prevented Léod Ferguson from deflowering a . . . an innocent?"

He heard her swallow. "Aye. I am virginal, my lord."

Edric's heart thundered in his chest. He had already decided he would have naught to do with this Norman, yet his body refused to listen to reason. He slipped his hand 'round her waist and pulled her fully against him. He groaned with arousal or frustration—he knew not which—and dipped his head. His lips were a mere breath away when he heard footsteps and voices behind him.

"Lord Edric!" 'Twas Drogan calling, searching for him.

He released Kate and backed away from her, and she raced away from him as if the room were afire.

It was, he mused as Drogan reached him. He didn't believe he'd ever burned so hot for any woman.

"My lord, you must come quickly."

"What's amiss?" Edric replied as he hastened away with Drogan.

"The ale cellar . . . the kegs are leaking, spilling ale all over the floor."

"How can that be?"

"I do not know, my lord, but Oswin sent up a call for assistance only a few minutes ago."

They hurried to the opposite side of the kitchen. Edric took a torch from one of the wall sconces and led the way through the cellar door. The scent of ale was stronger than usual, and when they reached the bottom, there were half a dozen other men, toiling to collect the spilling ale into buckets.

"Oswin, have we any spare barrels?"

"Aye, my lord. In the storage shed behind the stable."

"Drogan, get more buckets from the kitchen or

wherever you can find them," Edric said. "I'll get the barrels."

It took another hour, but they salvaged what they could, and when all was done, servants mopped the floor.

Edric summoned his two chief advisors, Oswin and Drogan, to the room where he conducted business. 'Twas his study, a chamber in the back passageway where he went over his accounts with Oswin and discussed matters of the fyrd with Drogan. The estate records were stored there, as well as every one of the letters containing King William's demands and Lord Gui de Crispin's refusals of assistance. "This was no accident," he said.

"It couldn't have been. Not with every one of those corks pulled and destroyed," Drogan remarked.

Edric sat down upon the chair behind his desk. "Why would anyone want to waste our ale?"

Drogan scratched his head while Oswin paced.

" 'Twill make the winter a misery, my lord," Oswin said, "as if it weren't going to be bad enough."

"How will we find out who did this?" Edric asked. "Half the village passed through here tonight. Anyone could have gone down to the cellar and ruined the corks."

Oswin shook his head in puzzlement. "I can

question everyone who attended the wake, my lord. See if anyone saw anything suspicious."

"Aye. It seems the only course to take."

Aidan was still asleep when Kathryn returned to her chamber. So was Gwen. She roused the girl and sent her on her way, glad of the quiet solitude of her chamber. *Lord Edric had nearly kissed her.*

With shaky hands, she hung her shawl over the back of the chair, then stoked the fire while she tried to settle the flames that burned within her. Merely standing so close to the Saxon lord was more arousing than Geoffroi's kiss had been. Kathryn could hardly imagine how it would feel if their lips had actually touched.

She pressed a hand to her chest as though she could slow her pounding heart. If Drogan had not interrupted, there was no telling how far Edric's advances would have gone.

Kathryn's face heated with belated embarrassment when she considered what she'd told him . . . that she was a virgin. 'Twas hardly decent discourse between a woman and a man who was all but a stranger to her. What could she have been thinking?

More to the point, why hadn't she taken her leave of the man before he'd had a chance to corner her?

'Twas more likely he had *not* intended to kiss her. He had just buried his beautiful wife, and was still angry about Bryce's wound. Mayhap he'd had something else in mind when he'd stopped her by the door, when he'd touched her face and drawn her close to him. Might it be a new punishment . . . humiliation?

She had no experience with the ways of men and was likely mistaken in everything Edric made her feel. She reminded herself that she must get away. Her only reason for staying here was Aidan, but she could not remain at Braxton Fell much longer, or Lord Edric would succeed in punishing her for her part in Bryce's injury.

Besides, tales of her survival would surely reach Kettwyck. Then all choice would be removed from her. She would have to return and face society's scorn.

And that was something she was not willing to do.

Edric was just about to mount the stairs to sit with Bryce once again, when he caught sight of Lora coming into the hall with a small bundle in one hand. "I heard what happened in the cellar, my lord."

Edric raised an eyebrow. "Word travels fast."

"Aye, it does. In every way," Lora said. "Which

is why you should find out who Kate really is, before her kin comes looking for her."

He did not like to think about changing anything now, especially with regard to his son's nursemaid. "Who she really is? She is Kate of Rushton."

"She is no serving maid, as well you know it."

"So?"

"She told me she intends to go to the nunnery at Evesham Bridge."

"What? She is a nun?"

Lora clucked her tongue. "Edric—think."

There were few at Braxton Fell who could speak to him so familiarly, and Lora was one. Daughter of one of his father's huscarls, she had grown up in the old keep with him and Bryce, much like an older sister. Oft were the times when she had been given charge of Edric and Bryce as young lads, though she was only a few years older than Edric.

"Kate—if that is her true name—believes she was disgraced by her abduction and cannot return home."

"Absurd."

"She is Norman, Edric. You know how they—"

"Aye. You needn't remind me."

She handed her bundle to him. "Here. I'm sure Kate has not eaten since early in the day. Mayhap you can take this to her and see what you can learn about her while I go and put a new poultice on Bryce's wound."

"Likely Rushton assumes she is dead."

Lora shook her head. "If her father survived, he will do all that is earthly possible to find his daughter."

Which was a complication Braxton Fell did not need. Not when Wulfgar of Tredburgh was on his way, and Cecily's father likely to arrive at any time. Edric took the parcel of food and started up the stairs just as Drogan came into the hall.

"Mistress Lora, you were missed this afternoon," Edric heard him say.

"My apologies," the healer replied as the two followed Edric up the stairs. " 'Tis not my intention to disappoint."

"Do you plan to see young Bryce?"

Edric knew he should give the food back to Lora and tell her to deal with it, but Drogan would not thank him for interfering with his moment with her. He found himself heading toward the nursery, drawn to the feminine softness he knew he would find there.

His own chamber was not far from the nursery, the room Cecily had left so bleak and bare. She had taken little interest in the cradle made especially for their child, nor had she sewn any tiny clothes or blankets for her bairn. She was an unnatural woman. A Norman.

All was quiet at the nursery door, so Edric gave a gentle knock, rather than barging in as he'd done before. There was no answer, so he eased the door open and stepped inside.

The shutters were closed against the sudden rain, but Edric heard it pattering outside. The fire had burned low, but there was enough light in the room to see Kate, lying sound asleep in the bed. Edric had come upon her undressed once again, though this time she wore a thin linen undergarment that left her arms bare to the shoulders.

Aidan was not in his cradle, but lay beside her in the bed, against the fullness of her breast. He, too, was fast asleep with his empty milk cup nearby. Edric took an unsteady breath at the sight of the two of them lying together, and fought the urge to slide in beside them.

He muttered a curse. He should have sought out Felicia at the Silver Dragon. A quick lay would have drummed this lust from his loins and he would be able to think rationally once again.

He turned his back and placed Lora's food on the table where Kate would find it if she awoke before morning. After adding wood to the fire, he banked it for the night. He worked in silence so as not to wake either Kate or the bairn, but when he turned to take one last look at her, he saw that her eyes were partially open, unfocused.

Edric knew when his presence registered in her mind, for her nipples beaded against the thin linen of her shift. She was as aware of him as he was of her. As she looked at him with a sleepy gaze, there were questions in her eyes.

"Lora sent you a meal. I brought it." His throat felt raw and he cleared it.

Her hair was loose and covered the feather bolster. Her eyes were heavy-lidded, giving her an expression of sensual awareness. Edric took one forbidden step, and then another. He crouched down beside her, his attention fully caught when she moistened her lips. Aidan made a small sound and Kate lightly stroked his forehead.

Edric felt a pang of nostalgia rather than the punch of lust he expected. As a young lad he'd once blundered into his mother's bedchamber and discovered his parents lying contentedly with their limbs entwined in the aftermath of loving. He'd always hoped he'd share the same kind of moments with the wife that was chosen for him.

But he had never counted on marrying a Norman shrew.

Kate kept her eyes upon Aidan as she touched

the bairn. " 'Tis sad that your son will never know his mother."

Edric's mind returned to the present, to who and what she was—a Norman wench, no more, no less. He stood and walked to the door. "Sad? The woman did him a service by dying. Never has anyone been more despised than that Norman harpy. He is far better off without her."

Chapter 7

Kathryn had never felt so lonely. She missed Isabel and the abbey, and the friendly smiles of those who served her family at Kettwyck. Here, no one spoke to her unless 'twas absolutely necessary. With the exception of Lora, Drogan, and Bryce, Kathryn felt most unwelcome here.

She felt little satisfaction at being right about Lord Edric's attitude. 'Twas clear how he felt about Normans, and Kathryn realized he tolerated her only because of Aidan's needs. That encounter at the rear door of the keep had been intended to make a fool of her, to make her feel more vulnerable than she already was.

She would not be so susceptible to him in future.

When morning came, she fed Aidan, then carried him down to the kitchen where she was given a bit of bread and honey, and a cup of cider. She saw Gwen, whose manner toward her was cool and aloof.

Clearly, she could not go on this way. She had to speak to Lora about other arrangements, and tell Lord Edric she was leaving. One way or another she was going to make her way to Evesham Bridge.

Hoping to find Lora in Bryce's chamber, she returned to the second floor, but saw that Edric was already there, standing alongside Drogan. Anxious to avoid him, she turned to leave, but Bryce stopped her.

"Ah, 'tis Kate. You just can't stay away from my comely face, can you?" He smiled warmly and Kathryn hesitated. She would ask about Lora and not be intimidated by Bryce's scowling brother.

"Take a seat, lass," said Drogan before she could pose her question. "And show us the bairn."

The chair beside the bed was vacant and Kathryn sat down, much too aware of Edric's ice-blue eyes upon her.

"He's grown, hasn't he?" asked Drogan.

"What would you know of it, old man?" asked Bryce jovially.

"Er . . . His cheeks are fuller." The huscarl was clearly out of his element with the bairn, but Kathryn appreciated his attempt at easing the tension in the room.

Bryce gave a weak laugh, but Edric still said naught, turning his back and stepping away to the window. He opened the shutters and looked down, an obvious snub of Kathryn.

"How do you fare, Lord Bryce?" she asked, annoyed for feeling so flustered. She had done naught to incur Edric's wrath. On the contrary, if Lora was to be believed, Kathryn had saved Aidan's life.

"If Lora would allow me out of this bed, I'd fare much better." Bryce glanced in his brother's direction. "I'd find out who ruined our ale supply."

"You can leave it to Oswin. We'll soon know what happened," Edric said without turning.

"The ale supply?" asked Kathryn.

"Someone went to the cellar and pulled all the corks during the wake," Drogan explained. "We lost more than half our ale."

"What has Oswin learned?" Bryce asked.

"Naught." Edric put his hands upon the window frame. "He will be questioning all who attended the wake. Mayhap someone saw something suspicious."

"What will we do, Edric, without enough ale to get through winter?" asked Bryce.

" 'Tis the least of our problems. Though we still have most of the hens sent by Cecily's father," he replied, "the rest of her dowry is gone."

"Cecily's dowry was . . . food?" Kathryn asked incredulously.

When Edric turned, his hard gaze bored straight into her. "What other reason would I have for tying myself to a Norman?"

Kathryn swallowed.

"Our fields were ruined, so many of our people would have starved had I not negotiated with Baron Gui for food."

"What will we do this year?" asked Bryce.

Edric crossed his arms against his chest. "We will raid the Fergusons and take what they have."

Bryce let out a low whistle as his brother began to pace.

"He owes us . . . for our fields and forests, and for your injury."

"More warfare? Has there not been enough?" Kathryn said. "So many will be killed. Or wounded as Lord Bryce was."

All three men stared at her in disbelief. "You, of all people, should not question our desire for revenge against the Fergusons," said Edric.

Lora swept into the room just then and looked at Edric and Drogan with irritation. "Did I not tell you both that Bryce needs his rest?"

Drogan's face flushed with color as he took the tray she held and placed it on a table near the bed. "Aye, lass. We were just going."

But Kathryn was not finished. Now was the time to ask for an escort to Evesham. War against the Scots was Edric's business and she wanted naught to do with it. She preferred to be far from Braxton Fell when news of more injuries—and deaths— came from the battlefield.

She held Aidan against her shoulder like a shield. "My lord, I have a request."

Edric turned, his gaze resting first upon his son, then on her. When he spoke, 'twas with impatience. "What is it?"

"I wish to . . . to take my leave of Braxton Fell," she said, stepping back a pace. "Is there someone who might escort me to the nunnery at Evesham Bridge?"

"Not until we find a new nurse for Aidan," Edric replied. "Besides, 'tis too dangerous." He dismissed the subject out of hand, unwilling to dwell on any other motive he might have for wanting to keep her at Braxton Fell.

"If you're concerned about my safety—"

"I'm not. But the man who escorts you would be at risk. 'Tis forty miles through dangerous country."

Lora gave a wry laugh. "You might teach her—as you did me—to defend herself if she comes upon any Scots or other brigands upon the road."

Edric shot Lora a look of pure aggravation, willing her to remain silent. He had no intention of allowing Kate to go, even though he knew it would be best. The attraction he felt was absurd, knowing what he did about Norman women. Cecily had been a beauty, too . . . All outward loveliness, but possessed of a soul as cold as the blade of his sword in the darkest days of winter. The farther removed she was from Braxton Fell, the better. Yet . . .

"I've already said she is not going."

"On the contrary, my lord, I will not stay here."

"Will not?"

The wench did not cower at his raised voice, but her full lips tightened into a straight line and a small crease appeared between her eyebrows.

"She should know how to defend herself in case of trouble even here at Braxton Fell, my lord," said Lora.

"You're our best at hand to hand, Lord Edric," said Drogan. "I'm sure you can teach the lass a few tricks."

"No he can't," said Bryce. "My brother may know how to fight, but he's the worst tutor I ever had."

"Well, you may be right about that," Drogan interjected. "Mayhap I should do it. We can—"

" 'Tis not necessary," said Kate. She raised her chin in a defiant gesture that made Edric want to press his lips to the rapid pulse in her neck while he explored every womanly curve of her body. "I'm sure I can avoid trouble until I arrive at the nunnery."

Edric dropped his arms to his sides and headed for the door. What did any of them know about it? As a Norman, she could very well be subject to a hostile act here at Braxton Fell. His people were decidedly unfriendly to her kind. "Meet me in the solar in the southwest corner, in one hour."

He left Bryce and the others, angry that he'd allowed himself to be goaded into teaching Kate what he'd taught Lora years ago. He had more important matters to attend, starting with meeting with his steward. He went to his study, where Oswin was writing in a large, leather-bound ledger, and decided to forgo the Norman's lesson in defense. Let her stay within the keep and there would be no trouble.

"What have you learned?" he asked the steward.

"So far, no one I spoke to saw anyone but me near the cellar door."

Edric took a seat at the desk as Oswin pushed aside the ledger. To Edric's knowledge, his steward kept impeccable records, being one of the few on the estate who had learned to read. Oswin's son, Sighelm, had had a talent for it, too, and Oswin had been preparing him for the stewardship sometime in the future. Edric sometimes thought that these quiet moments in the study reminded Oswin too much of all he'd lost to the Normans. 'Twas better when he was out scrutinizing the fields and assessing Edric's other estates.

"Who profits by our loss of ale?" Edric asked.

"Wilfred the tavernkeeper."

Edric shook his head. In his wildest imaginings, he could not see Felicia's father causing such trouble. The man liked Edric and wanted his favor, which was the primary reason his daughter had been so available to him. "I don't think so."

"Then I can think of no one," said Oswin. "What of the Norman wench? You know naught of her."

"Kate? How would she manage such a thing while she was caring for Aidan?"

"Mayhap she does not keep the bairn with her constantly."

"To my knowledge, she's left him only once in the charge of another." It had been the evening

129

before, when he'd stood so close to her he'd been able to smell the scent of the previous night's bath on her.

"She is Norman, my lord. You know better than to trust her."

"Aye." She hadn't been truthful about who she was. In fact, he wasn't even sure *Kate* was her true name.

Oswin began to pace. "Mind that she doesn't set fire to the keep while she's here."

"Oswin, I hardly think it would be in her best interests to do such a thing." For as much as he distrusted Normans, she'd shown naught but true affection for Aidan.

The steward came back to the desk and sat across from Edric. He spoke with urgency. "My lord, you should meet with Wulfgar when he comes. With our fyrd behind him, we could unseat the Normans in Northumbria. We'll carve out our own kingdom. Wulfgar's daughter, Odelia, could be your queen."

"Never again will I take a wife, as well you know, Oswin. Besides, it's all pointless now. We haven't the resources to fight the Normans. Remember, I've seen their king in battle. He is a formidable leader."

"And so is Wulfgar."

Edric had never seen anyone as powerful as

King William. He and Bryce had witnessed the wrath of the Norman monarch when he'd put down the rebellion in York and did not want to risk bringing the same down upon the people of Braxton Fell. There was no point to it, and his people had suffered enough.

But the Fergusons were another matter altogether. War against them was a matter of honor. And survival.

He pushed the ledger toward Oswin. "Tell me about the harvest. How bad is it?"

"Let me carry Aidan," Lora said to Kathryn as they left Bryce's chamber. "I'll keep him while you're having your lesson with Lord Edric."

Kathryn turned the bairn over to the healer and took the crock of milk she carried. "I have no intention of going."

Lora stopped. "What?"

"He can wait all day for me in the solar, but I will not be there."

" 'Tis not wise to defy the man, Kate."

"I want to leave Braxton Fell."

"But there is no one else to care for Aidan."

Kathryn tried not to feel quite so desperate. "Surely you can find *someone* to take my place. Help me, Lora."

The healer considered Kathryn's words. "There

are two women in the village who will soon deliver their bairns. One of them will likely suit."

"You will tell me as soon as—"

"Aye. Though Aidan could not want for a better nurse."

And Kathryn could not imagine anyone else loving the bairn as she did, but she was not going to end up like Berta, completely devoted to her charge, with no life of her own.

"Edric taught me a few effective maneuvers . . . and they came in handy more than once before I had my husband to protect me. What's the harm in letting Edric teach you, too?"

What harm, indeed, Kathryn wondered. Her clumsiness had been a source of embarrassment all her life. She knew not what Edric's lesson would entail, but she had no doubt 'twas likely to demonstrate how awkward she could be.

And how he would enjoy that.

"I know what it is to be attacked by a man . . . by *men*. There was naught that I could do against them," Kathryn said.

"Even the strongest man can be brought down. Don't you want to know how to do it?"

"Of course." She never wanted to find herself as helpless as she'd been when the Fergusons had carried her from Kettwyck. "But Drogan is likely a more patient teacher. Mayhap we can summon him—"

"He will not go against Lord Edric's wishes."

Kathryn did not understand why Edric would want to bother wasting his time with her, if not to humiliate her.

"You're not afraid of him, are you?"

"Of course not," Kathryn retorted. "'Tis just that . . . Tell me about Lady Cecily. Why was she so despised here?"

Lora glanced sharply at her. "Who said she was despised?"

"Her husband."

Lora led her into a large, cold chamber. 'Twas furnished, but there was no fire in the grate, and no signs of recent use. Kathryn sat down upon a long settee that spanned the space in front of the fireplace and Lora placed Aidan on the cushion beside her. "Let me get some heat in here."

Lora laid wood on the grate and soon had a fire going, and Kathryn wondered if she would speak freely. She dearly wished to understand what had happened to make Edric—and his people—despise not only Cecily, but herself, as well.

Lora returned to sit beside Kathryn. "Why must you hurry to Evesham Bridge?"

"I am not welcome here, Lora. The servants

ignore me or they're deliberately unfriendly. Though it may be because of my part in Lord Bryce's injury, I fear it has more to do with my being Norman."

Lora tapped her fingers on her knee. "Did you know Lady Cecily?" she finally asked.

Kathryn nodded. "But only briefly when she came to the abbey de St. Marie in Normandy."

"And do you know why she was sent to that place?"

"Because she refused to wed the bridegroom who was chosen for her."

"The *Saxon* bridegroom."

Kathryn lowered her eyes. She had already realized 'twas Edric whom Cecily had refused to wed.

"Lord Edric fought for your king," Lora explained. "His 'reward' was Braxton Fell—his own lands were granted him by King William. The pact was to be sealed by marriage to a highborn Norman wife."

"Aye. 'Twas said Cecily did not care to wed."

"The truth was that she did not care to wed a Saxon."

"But she came and they married . . ."

"Lady Cecily was . . . unhappy here," said Lora. "I did not know her character before her marriage, but in the past year she was demanding, overbearing, and disagreeable."

Kathryn recalled Cecily's petulant expression every time she'd seen her at the abbey and realized the girl had never been lighthearted or happy. It never occurred to her that Cecily had been merely mean-spirited. "So she did not endear herself to anyone here."

"To say the least," Lora said offhandedly. "'Twill take some time for our people to accept you, but soon they will. They'll see that you are nothing like the lord's late wife."

Kathryn doubted that Lord Edric's attitude would ever change. Nor would that of the priest and steward. Their hatred for their Norman conquerors was too strong.

Kathryn gave a slight shake of her head. "No. I must go."

"Do you think they will accept you at Evesham Bridge?"

Kathryn felt her face heat. Usually, 'twas only the widows and daughters of well-to-do men who were able to afford entry to a nunnery. She hoped to gain admission on the mere promise of her dowry. Eventually, she would have to notify her family that she'd survived the Scots' attack and had taken herself to Evesham Bridge to avoid the derision of her peers.

"Under the circumstances, I . . . believe they will have mercy and take me in."

Lora's expression made it clear that she did not accept Kathryn's assertion.

"Please, Lora. I cannot say more. Believe me when I say I cannot return home. The nunnery is my only choice."

"Look at Aidan," the midwife argued. "He needs you."

Emotion tore at Kathryn's throat and she shut her eyes against the tears that had begun to form. She closed her heart against a surge of motherly love, aware that she must distance herself from him. She lifted the bairn and handed him to Lora. "Take him. I—"

She fell silent when Edric strode into the chamber. Lora stood. "My lord . . . has it been an hour?"

"You betrayed me!" Kathryn whispered when she realized they'd been sitting in the designated southwest solar. Lora knew how she felt about the proposed lesson, yet she'd brought her here.

"No—I acted as a friend," Lora replied quietly. "'Tis best that you learn what Edric can teach you."

"Take Aidan," Edric said. "The Norman will find you when we're finished here."

"My lord," said Kathryn, feeling cornered once again, "I assure you this is not necessary."

Lora quit the room while Edric circled 'round Kathryn. She stood before the settee, as anxious now as she was the time she'd stared down the boar in the woods. Edric had come to her rescue then, but he seemed the dangerous predator now.

Edric came directly to the point. "When the Scots stole you from Rushton, what happened?"

Kathryn's breath caught at the memory of that horrible night. "I do not wish to speak of it."

"You *will* speak of it, so that I can show you how you might have avoided capture."

He wore a plain tunic that matched the deep blue of his eyes. His leggings were black, but the dense muscles of his legs were clearly delineated through the wool. With his hands on his hips, his shoulders seemed even broader, his arms thicker. Kathryn rubbed her damp hands together and turned toward the window.

"Two men singled me out," she said. "They chased me and trapped me in a storage building."

"What did you do?"

She glanced back to look at him. "I—I don't remember."

"Of course you do," he said, dropping his hands to his sides and taking a step toward her. "They split up, did they not?"

She nodded.

"Did you run?"

"Aye. But first I threw a wooden box at one of them."

"Did it help?"

"No. It had no effect. They came at me and knocked me down." Emotion welled in her throat as the memories of that horrible night flooded her mind. "They tore my clothes and I thought . . . I thought . . ."

"That they would rape you."

"Aye," she whispered.

Chapter 8

❧ ❧❧ ❧

Edric's blood burned with anger as she told of the attack, of how the Ferguson men had hurt and abused her. No woman should have to endure such treatment, not even a disagreeable wench like Cecily. But surely not gentle, delicate Kate, who looked at Aidan with such motherly affection. Her bruises were fading and there was only a hint of the cut on her lip, but that did not diminish the brutality of the attack upon her.

"When you kicked him, did you aim for any particular spot?" he asked.

A familiar crease appeared above her brow. "N-no. Why?"

He came close enough to see the gold flecks in her eyes and the thick, black lashes that framed them. "Do you know a man's most vulnerable part?"

He saw her throat move as she swallowed. "His nose?"

Edric laughed. "Lower."

She blushed and it was Edric's turn to swallow. He'd done his best to ignore the womanly curves she'd inadvertently shown him, but it was no use. He should never have come up here, should have ridden out with Oswin as he'd planned.

Kate's features tightened in annoyance, and when she started to walk 'round him toward the door, Edric blocked her path. "Use your knees or elbows—strike him where it hurts and he will be immobilized for a few moments, mayhap long enough for you to run."

Crossing her arms, she nodded. "Thank you, my lord. I'll do that. Now, if you'll excuse me, I'm sure Lora has other—"

"I want you to try it."

"Try it?"

"Aye. I'm going to grab you. Try to do me some damage and get away."

" 'Tis not necessary. I'll remember what you told me."

"You're too small to overpower a man who would attack you. You must use your wits. Be unpredictable. Do the thing he would least expect." She started to go 'round him again, but he slid his arm across her waist and pulled her against him.

She stiffened and clawed at his arm.

"No—try to turn so you can—"

She kicked his shin and started to struggle, blindly lashing out at him. She used all four of her limbs to fight him, and soon Edric had no choice but to lift her and hold her against him. He heard her whimpers and realized she was not simply trying to get away from him.

She was frightened. Truly afraid. And it occurred to him that she might be feeling the same kind of terror as when the Scots had abducted her. He knew of seasoned warriors who relived battles in their dreams . . .

"Kate, stop."

She flailed against him, her legs kicking ineffectually, her arms swinging wildly with no target.

" 'Tis only me. You are safe."

He shifted his weight and leveraged her to the floor between the settee and the fire, taking hold of her wrists and quieting her kicking with his own legs. Her breath came out in rapid, shuddering bursts and her eyes were fixed on some point beyond him. Edric was certain she did not realize where she was.

He immobilized her legs with his own, but let go of her wrists to take her head in his hands. "Look at me! There isn't a Scotsman within fifty miles."

Her struggles diminished slightly, but he could see that she was still deep in the throes of her recent memories. "Kate. Easy, now." Edric continued to speak soothing words, but he didn't know if she heard or understood him.

When she finally focused her gaze upon him, she stilled, but confusion clouded her eyes. She trembled and took a few whimpering breaths. *"Mon Dieu . . . Je m'excuse. Je ne sais pas ce que j'ai . . ."* She closed her eyes and breathed deeply. "I don't know what happened to me. I . . ."

Edric barely heard her. Not while he lay half on top of her, fully aroused by Kate's feminine body beneath him and her beautiful, puzzled eyes that sought an explanation for what had just happened. Her lips were full, moist, and inviting. He could feel her heart beating in her chest, beneath those soft breasts that his son so favored. He placed his palm against the center of her chest. Gently, tantalizingly close to heaven, he felt her pulse racing.

"Kate." He heard himself say her name again as her body seemed to swell and soften beneath him. Her gaze touched upon his eyes, then his mouth.

He slid his hand down to her waist and caressed her there, then moved to her hip and leg, pulling her closer, slipping one of his legs between hers. He closed his eyes and savored the fierce arousal he felt. Stifling a groan of pleasure, he lowered his head and touched his lips to hers, restraining his urge to plunder her mouth, wary of frightening her again.

He felt her tremble, and then her eyes drifted closed once again. Raw sensation rippled through him, like the sun's heat on a warm day. He deepened the kiss and she responded to him, her lips soft and welcoming. When he folded her into his arms, her breath quickened, then her hand touched his shoulder and rose to the nape of his neck. She arrowed her fingers into his hair and he leaned into the caress. He parted her lips and slid inside.

She was utterly feminine. He tasted sweet cider on her tongue, and sucked it into his mouth. He feasted on her, like a man who couldn't recall his last meal. She shifted beneath him and Edric moved to cup her breast.

Kate broke the kiss and drew in a deep, shuddering breath. "Edric . . ."

He loosened the laces of her bodice and shoved the cloth aside. "Beautiful." Full mounds were tipped by nipples the color and texture of a ripe peach. Kate arched her back when Edric circled one with his tongue. Sighing, she took his head in her hands and held him in place.

With his free hand, he moved her skirts aside and ventured into that feminine territory above her stockinged legs. He moved tentatively, touching the responsive indentation behind her knee, then sliding up the smooth flesh of her thigh.

Gently, he touched the juncture with his knuckles and she closed her legs against him. "Open, sweeting." He drew her other nipple into his mouth and teased it with his tongue; her legs dropped apart again.

Edric was as hard as a lance and aching for her touch, but his exploration of her feminine attributes was nearly as pleasurable. Using his thumb, he traced a circle 'round the nether passage he so yearned to explore. He slipped one finger inside her while he fondled the sensitive nub at the apex.

A feather-light sound came from the back of Kate's throat, and Edric kissed her mouth as he imitated with his fingers the act he craved. She moved against him, opening for him, greeting his

144

foray with innocent abandon. Her breath quickened and her breasts rose against his chest. When she shuddered and tightened, he knew she'd found the essential fulfillment he also sought.

"Aye," he whispered, loosening his belt. "'Tis nearly perfect, is it not? The only thing missing is me. Inside you."

Oblivious to the muted sound of voices outside, Edric pushed aside his braies, took one of her hands and placed it upon his cock. Her eyes were heavy-lidded and dazed, but she encircled him with her fingers and instinctually guided him toward her portal.

The door of the chamber crashed open and the vague, distant voices became louder.

"Damnable Norman giglet!"

"Father Algar!" 'Twas Lora's voice now, but Edric did not waste time listening to their argument. With more haste than he'd ever thought possible, he drew Kate's skirts down her legs and righted his own clothes before Father Algar could get 'round the settee and see just how far they'd gone. Fortunately, Lora impeded the priest's passage into the room.

Edric pushed up from the floor and helped Kate to a sitting position. "What business have you to barge into a man's private quarters?" he demanded.

He felt Kate trembling under his hand, and knew she was fumbling with the laces of her bodice.

" 'Tis an offense against nature—Saxon and Norman mix with ruinous result," Father Algar cautioned. "Disasters will follow you, Edric of Braxton Fell!"

Kathryn did not dare look at Edric, standing with his hands upon his hips as he faced Father Algar. What the Saxon lord had done to her was more astonishing than anything she could ever have imagined. As much as she'd hoped, she hadn't known that a man could give such pleasure to a woman. She wondered if he'd felt the same.

"Send her away!" cried the priest. "We were well rid of pestilent Normans but you brought yet another into our midst!"

"Take care, priest. The Norman you are 'rid' of was my wife."

"But your *wife* brought naught but—"

" 'Twas not your concern while she was alive, and it is not your concern now!" Edric spoke the words low and dangerously. "State your business and take your leave!"

The priest clasped his hands behind his back and turned 'round. "Your brother refuses the Last Sacrament."

The priest's words gave Kathryn a queasy

feeling in the pit of her stomach. All of Braxton Fell believed Bryce's injury was her fault, and should he die without the Sacrament, he would spend eternity in hell.

Because of her.

"Come, Kate," said Lora. She took Kathryn's arm and drew her toward the door. "Let Lord Edric deal with Father Algar."

In her confused state, Kathryn was glad to leave the two men. She barely understood what had just happened with Edric, and needed time to clear her head. Lora took the lead and drew her down the corridor to the nursery where she found Gwen watching over Aidan. They collected Kathryn's shawl and a blanket for the bairn.

"Are you all right?" Lora asked when Gwen had gone.

Kathryn remained silent, but nodded her head.

" 'Tis a pleasant day . . . A walk outdoors will be good for . . . for Aidan."

"If only we'd done so before," Kathryn muttered, her legs still weak from the experience she'd just shared with Edric. "Why did you take me to that room, knowing I preferred not to meet with Lord Edric? You betrayed me."

Lora's expression was one of sisterly concern. "I hope you do not truly believe that. A woman needs to learn all she can to protect herself, and Edric is best qualified to teach you."

"I'd rather he just gave me a weapon," Kathryn muttered. "If I had a knife, no man would ever assault me again."

Lora reached under her skirt and took out a blade with a dark handle. "I keep this strapped to my leg. You might do the same." She handed the dagger to Kathryn, who took it gingerly.

"I . . . I cannot take your—"

"I have another. We'll have to fashion a strap for you. For now, just keep it in your garter."

"Is there no end to your abilities, Lora?"

The woman grinned and headed for the door. 'Twas certain Kathryn could not lose her head again as she'd done earlier. If she were attacked again, she would need to keep her wits about her. Later, in the privacy of the nursery, she would fashion a strap to hold the knife, and practice reaching for it.

And she would think about the suggestions Edric had given her . . . before he'd ravished her with just a kiss and a touch of his hand.

Wrapping herself and Aidan snugly, Kathryn followed the other woman down the stairs and out of the hall. They took the main path toward the church, but Lora and Kathryn turned south and walked across a grassy courtyard.

Lora gestured to the tall building ahead, smaller than Edric's keep, but larger than any cottage. 'Twas a structure made of timber with a high tower that had long, shuttered windows on its three sides. "'Tis the old keep, where Edric and Bryce were born and raised."

"Might we go inside?"

"I don't see why not."

Kathryn tucked Aidan into the blanket for the walk across the courtyard.

"What did Edric teach you?" Lora asked.

Kathryn nearly choked at the question, but quickly realized Lora was asking about the lesson in defense. She cleared her throat. "'Twas odd . . . I don't know what happened to me. One minute we were talking, and suddenly I felt as if I were reliving the raid at . . . er, Rushton. I fought him. I couldn't think, but only tried to get away."

"Well, that must be a good thing. No doubt he intended to teach you to get away. Did he show you where to kick? Or how to shove your knuckles into a man's nose to break it?"

"Break his nose?" Kathryn's stomach turned at the thought of it.

"No? Well, mayhap next time."

Feeling overwhelmed by what had happened in the solar, Kathryn wondered if she should ask Lora about the things Edric had made her feel, and whether he'd felt the same. Lora was a mid-wife, and she'd once had a husband. She would have knowledge of these things.

"I'm sure it's perfectly natural to experience the same fright you felt at Rushton," Lora said. "It hasn't been so long since you were attacked, has it?"

Kathryn shook her head. "Seems like weeks."

"I'm sure it does." Lora pushed open the door and stepped inside. Kathryn followed and watched as Lora went to each window of the great hall and pulled open the shutters. 'Twas dark and dusty inside, with old wall hangings and furniture shrouded in shadows. The hall was smaller, more intimate than the one Edric now used, with space for only one large table on a dais in the center.

"My father was huscarl here," said Lora, "before Drogan."

Kathryn walked the length of the hall. "He spoke of you before, when Bryce was wounded."

Lora smiled. "He fancies me."

Kathryn had suspected as much. Drogan's blushes were hard to miss, and she'd noticed the softening of his voice when he spoke of her. He kept Lora in his sights whenever she was near.

"My husband was his closest friend."

"Did you love him very much?" Kathryn felt compelled to ask.

"Aye. Every woman should love and be loved as we did."

Kathryn wondered if husbands and wives often engaged in the kind of intimate behavior she'd just shared with Edric, and wished there'd been a man at Kettwyck as besotted with her as Drogan was with Lora, a man who would not have minded that she'd been taken by the Fergusons. Then, mayhap she'd have been able to return to him, and all would be well.

Such things were beyond her grasp now.

Kathryn cuddled Aidan in her arms. "Why is the new keep so cold and bare?"

"Lord Edric thought his Norman bride would furnish it to her liking."

"But she did not?"

"Cecily wanted only to return to Lichford, her father's holding," Lora replied. "She cared naught for her new home, nor her husband."

"Do you think she would have changed once she saw her child?"

Lora found a lamp and lit it, then started up the stairs. Kathryn followed. At the top of the stairs was a large gallery. "The boys often played here— Edric and Bryce, along with Oswin's sons."

Kathryn noted that Lora did not answer the question about Cecily, but she respected her silence on the matter. 'Twas not seemly to speak of the dead, especially when it seemed there was not much good to say.

"What's in these trunks?" Kathryn asked.

Lora went to the one in the farthest corner and opened it. "Toys." She smiled. "A leather ball and some glass marbles, dice . . . chess pieces . . ." She laughed. "Here's a slingshot. Edric was a terror with this in his youth."

He was a terror now, to Kathryn's peace of mind. She opened another of the trunks and found a stack of woolens. There were blankets and clothes, all small. She did not doubt they were the garments Edric and his brother had worn as children. "Look," Kathryn said, holding up a small linen sherte. "The ones on top are moth-eaten, but down below . . ." She pulled out the rest of the items, which seemed to be in good condition. "Aidan should have the use of these. Do you think Lord Edric will mind if we take some of these back to the keep—the clothes and toys?"

"I cannot imagine that he would."

"What about the steward? If he learns I am responsible for making changes, he will be angry. He despises me."

"'Tis nothing personal," Lora remarked. "His sons were killed in battle against your king's armies and Oswin holds every Norman responsible."

"And the priest?"

"Has never been fully sane. 'Tis a wonder that Edric has not retired him and sent for a new cleric to replace him."

Kathryn opened one of the shutters and looked out over the hilly countryside and the mountains in the distance. The forest in this direction was intact, although she had seen large areas that had been burned. The fields she saw through the window were recently harvested, but on the northern side of the estate, they were barren.

"It must have been a beautiful landscape," Kathryn observed.

"Aye. The richest, most handsome estate in all Northumbria," Lora remarked. "The fells and valleys were sacred to the ancient people who once inhabited these lands."

Kathryn could well imagine that was so. There was something ethereal about the mountains in the distance and the closer hills. There'd been a mist hovering about them early this morn, and Kathryn could almost believe 'twas a magical place. "What will happen when winter comes?"

Lora shrugged. "I do not know."

"Mayhap Lord Edric should take a bride. Another one with a generous dowry."

The midwife shook her head. "'Tis said he has vowed never to marry again. Especially—"

"Not a Norman," Kathryn interjected. She was

not witless. "But you, Lora . . . You have been kind and accepting, in spite of my heritage."

"We are women," Lora said. "What have we to do with the death and destruction of war? We make homes, tend the sick, and bear the children."

Kathryn agreed, but she had no doubt that if Edric ever learned that her father was one of King William's most powerful barons, a soldier who'd fought against Saxons and been given a dozen Saxon holdings as his reward, he would not think her so harmless.

She made her own vow that he would never find out.

"This is Aidan's legacy," she said. "Should we not take some of these furnishings to the new keep?"

Lora smiled. "Of course. But Edric's servants can do it. Come. Let's go back down to the hall and choose the things we should take."

"And rushes for the floor. 'Twill not be good for Aidan to learn to walk upon a cold, bare floor," she said, though she knew she would not be there to see it.

Edric took his practice sword from the armorer and headed to the field where a large number of swordsmen battled one another to hone their skills. He joined them, hoping that with hard exercise, mayhap he would be able to sweat the Norman woman out of his system.

Jesu, no woman had ever responded to him as Kate had done. He had no doubt of her innocence, for her actions had been tentative and shy . . . and all the more alluring. She had none of the cold rigidity of Cecily's bed habits, but had reacted to his touch, and even come to completion. He could not help but think of the pleasure she would give when he took her to bed and they had the whole night to explore the limits of her passion.

He muttered a curse, knowing full well 'twould only complicate matters if he bedded her.

"My lord!" called one of his warriors. "I challenge you!"

Edric put thoughts of seduction from his mind and stepped up to the men who were parrying in the field. The sounds of battle drew his attention and he deflected the first blow from Toothless Tostig. Far better to work out his frustrations here, in practice with his men. They all knew they were to stay in condition and battle-ready, for 'twould not be long before Edric led them in a raid against the Ferguson clan.

And with luck, Edric would bring Robert's head back to Bryce.

Gildas tossed him an ax, and Edric used both

weapons to fight the men, sharpening his proficiency, keeping his arms and shoulders strong, his legs taut and agile. He needed no one to tell him he was the most powerful of all the Braxton Fell warriors, and he wanted never to discover that any of his men could beat him.

He fought fiercely, giving no quarter and expecting none in return. He worked up a sweat, and with barely a ripple in his rhythm, threw down his ax, whipped off his woolen overtunic, and resumed the fight. A crowd gathered 'round to watch, but Edric was nearly oblivious to it. He took little note of Felicia, who gave rapt attention to every move he made as she carried two heavy buckets well out of her path to gawk at him.

Felicia was the one whose bed he should visit. 'Twas muddle-brained to dwell upon the charms of a Norman virgin, especially one who had decided to enter a nunnery. He wanted no part of chaste, inexperienced females. The tavern wench needed no gentle seduction, and though her bed skills were well practiced and premeditated, she would suit him well enough.

Redoubling his efforts against Tostig and Gildas, Edric battled fiercely. They baited him and circled him, each taking a side, neither one gaining the advantage as Edric parried with his sword and swung his ax. He was well into the rhythm of the fight when Lora and Kate walked past, neither one paying any heed to the men in the practice yard.

Edric lost his footing and went down on one knee. Tostig and Gildas each delivered what would have been killing jabs, had this been a real battle.

The confounded wench had done it again. She'd provided a near-fatal distraction.

Chapter 9

❝❞

"**W**e can leave the bairn with Gwen," said Lora, "and walk through the village."

Kathryn averted her eyes from the sight of Edric wearing only a thin linen sherte and hose. Every line of his powerful chest was delineated through the damp sherte, and the muscles of his neck and shoulders strained with effort.

She felt a quickening deep inside her belly when she looked at him, and the same liquid warmth that had suffused her earlier, when he touched her.

Quickly averting her eyes, she went along with

Lora to the keep. Standing beside the healer, who was well known and respected by Edric's household, Kathryn gave instructions to have some of the furniture and the trunks from the old building brought here. She would go through everything later, and see that it was laundered and made ready for Aidan's use.

"Thank you for coming with me to speak to the servants . . . They did not seem quite so unfriendly this time."

"I had little to do with it. 'Tis your affable manner that wins them. They are coming to see that see you are nothing like Cecily."

They returned to the village streets, stopping along the way, lingering to speak to housewives and shopkeepers. The Saxons gazed at Kathryn with suspicion, but Lora introduced her and included her in conversation as though she would be staying at Braxton Fell.

"They do not care to have me in their midst," said Kathryn as they walked farther, through a postern gate at the eastern end of the wall.

They went over a small bridge. "'Tis only because you are Norman." They skirted a flock of geese pecking at the ground. "Look. 'Tis no secret that Lady Cecily was not popular here. We came to know Normans through your king's vicious conquest and Lord Edric's spoiled wife. 'Twill take some time, but our people will come to accept you. They will see that you are nothing like the only other Normans they ever knew."

They came to a neat cottage where Lora greeted a tall woman with steel-gray hair and a stern expression. "Kate, this is Elga, Braxton's most gifted weaver, and mother of my late husband. We share lodgings."

Kathryn exchanged nods with her and Elga invited her into the cottage. The older woman was not hostile toward Kathryn, but reserved in her manner.

Lora took her mother-in-law's arm and said, "Show us the cloth you're working on, Elga."

The woman took them past a heavy curtain that divided her workroom from the rest of the cottage. There was a large window to give adequate light to see, and two looms that held a magical combination of colorful threads forming a handsome cloth in the center. Several baskets contained colorful balls of wool, along with long, wooden sticks for knitting.

"Once the wool is spun into thread, Elga chooses her colors and has them dyed," said Lora. "Then she weaves them together."

" 'Tis beautiful," Kathryn remarked, gazing with interest at the looms and the cloth that was emerging from each. "I've always taken for granted the cloth of my clothes."

Elga nodded, but said naught.

"May I see how you do this?" Kathryn hoped she did not offend Elga by asking, but this process was one she'd never seen. The woman obliged her, and Kathryn took a seat where she was able to watch Elga at work.

"So, you are the only wet nurse the lord's bairn will accept?"

"Aye," Kathryn replied.

"He will grow to be a stubborn lad if he lives so long," said Elga.

"Like his sire," Lora added, and Kathryn felt a pang of worry for the bairn in her care. He *would* survive. She was sure of it. Soon they would find someone who could feed him, and she would leave Braxton Fell, confident that he would grow and thrive. "Do you remember the time when Edric and Sighelm burned down the storage shed and Edric took full blame for it?"

Elga nodded. "He took his whipping and never told of his accomplice."

"No one would ever have known Sighelm was just as guilty, had he not owned up to it himself."

"Aye. Stubborn. He will never give in to the Normans again."

"Elga, what choice has he?" Lora asked. "To keep his fief, he must obey all of the Norman king's commands, no matter how absurd they might be."

"What commands?" Kathryn asked. She'd heard that King William was demanding, but fair.

"Tributes," said Elga. "Grain, wool, warriors."

Kathryn was surprised. "Does the king know the dire situation here?"

"Of course," Elga said.

"Oswin has sent a number of letters to Winchester, but the king's missives are harsh in return," Lora explained. "The only command that is not resented here at Braxton Fell is the order to keep the Scots at bay. Our people have done so for generations. 'Tis nothing new."

"But the task sours with a Norman flavor to it," Elga said.

Kathryn could well imagine the resentment of being ordered to do what they'd done for many years past. Of course Braxton would protect its own lands. But under Norman rule, Edric's estate was considered to be King William's own property . . . *granted* to Edric for certain duties in return.

Their discussion was interrupted by a man's voice outside, calling to Lora. Kathryn followed her to the door and saw Drogan standing in the yard with a barrow full of cut wood. His hair was combed and his beard neatly trimmed. It looked as though he'd cleaned himself up and put on a fresh tunic for his visit to Lora's cottage.

Kathryn's breath caught as she thought how grand it would feel to be so loved. The man had no pretty words for Lora, but his high regard was obvious for all to see.

"The nights are cool now." Drogan turned and pointed toward the wood. "You'll need this."

"Aye." Lora's voice took on a quality Kathryn had not heard before. 'Twas softer somehow, and less certain than usual. " 'Tis full autumn already. Thank you, Drogan."

"I'll . . . just . . . stack the wood for you."

Lora's face was flushed when she closed the door and came inside.

"The man more than 'fancies' you, Lora," said Kathryn.

She nodded. "When Hrothgar courted me, I did not know his friend was smitten. Drogan stood aside because he saw how I felt about Hrothgar. I never knew . . . not until Elga told me a few months after Hrothgar's death."

"He is a good man, Lora. You could do worse." Elga stood at the curtain of her workroom, her arms crossed over her narrow chest. Though her words struck Kathryn as true, 'twas clear the older woman was reluctant to say them.

Lora nodded and sat down. "He is kind, and he

still loves me. But after Hrothgar . . . I want to be sure before I encourage him."

"What would make you sure?" Kathryn asked. Her own test had been Geoffroi's kiss, and he had failed.

Edric had not.

Lora shook her head. "I don't know . . . Hrothgar and I . . . We had something that is not easily replaced."

"Mayhap not replaced," Elga said. "But different, and just as good."

"You were my husband's mother," said Lora. "Are you saying I should forget him?"

"Of course not," said Elga. "But 'tis possible Drogan can give you the children you wanted with Hrothgar. Would you spend the rest of your days pining for my dead son and wishing for something that can never be?"

Sensing the gravity of the discussion, Kathryn stayed out of it. But she knew Elga's words would stay with her, for they were true of her own situation, too.

When it was time to return to the keep, Lora packed her old canvas satchel with healing herbs and potions for Bryce and they headed back, using a different route. 'Twas one that did not take them past Edric's practice field, but on toward the mill beyond the main gate and the river that ran beside it. In the distance, Kathryn saw a man who looked much like Lord Edric dive into the rushing water, and her heart beat a little faster at the sight of his brawny form.

A dunk in the river was just what Edric needed to wash off and cool down. The battle practice had done little to relieve the tension he felt, but surely a vigorous swim would do it.

Taking long strokes, he swam across the river and tried to force away thoughts of Kate from his mind. 'Twas not only lust that plagued him, but his infernal sense of protectiveness. She'd been badly frightened by the Scots, so badly that when he touched her, she relived her ordeal with them.

He cursed himself and decided to seek out a cure for what ailed him at the Silver Dragon. Felicia was a simple woman with no secrets. She was wise to the ways of the world, and a man had no need to be particularly careful with her.

He swam until his shoulders burned, then pulled himself up onto the riverbank. Grabbing his shoes, his tunic and sherte, he was glad the sun was still bright enough to cast some warmth to the air. He squeezed the water from his hose and braies and returned to the keep, slipping his sherte over his head as he walked.

A raucous crowd met him when he entered the

hall. Instead of the usual quiet, two housemaids were sweeping the floor and taking down cobwebs that had formed in all the corners. Oswin had returned from his ride and was scrapping with a family of beggars at the door, attempting to send them away, telling them there was naught to spare from the lord's kitchens.

"Hold, Oswin," Edric said. "Surely we have bread. And perhaps a pottage on the fire?"

"My lord, we are short—"

"Aye. We are all short of stores, Oswin. But what we have, we will share." He headed for the steps, turning back toward the steward as he walked. "I'll see you in my study after I've changed."

Catching sight of trunks and piles of cloth lying near the dais, Edric changed course to explore them. Four chairs had been set up before the fireplace. They were the chairs from his father's keep, and beside them lay the old cradle that his mother had used for him and his brother.

"Oswin, explain."

The beggars quit the doorway and went 'round to the kitchen to ask for their bread, leaving Oswin to approach Edric. Anger darkened his brow. "That Norman wench ordered these to be brought here. And all the rest." He gave a broad sweep with his arm.

"These were my father's."

"Aye."

Edric had thought 'twould be best to have new furnishings here, but Cecily had refused to have anything to do with making the hall habitable. She spent most of her time in her own chamber, or in the small chapel at the back of the keep, while Edric often stayed in the barracks with his men, coming to the hall only when he had business to attend in his study.

Bemused, he watched three grooms enter the hall carrying baskets. They tossed the contents of these baskets—rushes—on the floor, and the maids spread them out evenly with their brooms.

Standing with his hands upon his hips, his clothes damp from the river, he heard voices at the top of the stairs and wondered what would be next.

'Twas Kate, talking quietly with Lora, who turned and went her own way. When Kate descended the stairs, Edric felt a kick behind his knees. He tried to tamp down his memory of the full breasts he'd nuzzled just hours ago, and the liquid heat of her feminine center. She'd touched him, too . . . had felt the hard pulse of his arousal.

"My lord, say the word and all this will be removed," said the steward. "The woman has no right to—"

"No, leave it, Oswin."

She must have spent some time outside, for her complexion was robust, and her expression easy and relaxed. Her arms were free, but Edric barely considered where his son might be. He was much too enthralled by the foreign maiden and the way her hand lifted her skirts for her descent; by the sway of her plaited hair, come loose now from its bindings; by the heightened color in her cheeks; by the swell of her breasts above the bodice of her gown.

"She is Norman, my lord," said Oswin, clearly aware of the direction of Edric's thoughts. "No different from your late wife."

The steward's words seared through Edric's erotic thoughts. Oswin was right. The Norman was welcome here only until they found another who was able to feed Aidan. Where she went after they found a replacement nurse was no further concern to him.

Yet when she spoke to the grooms who were spreading the rushes, they listened attentively to her, then bowed slightly before resuming their task. She directed two housemaids to take the neatly folded cloths outside, and surprisingly, they obeyed. Something had changed.

It puzzled Kathryn to see that the steward was ill-tempered with everyone, and not only with her.

She did not understand how the man could turn away the hungry, when she knew there was sufficient food to be had at the keep.

Edric's reaction had surprised her, too. She'd not thought of him as the kindest of lords, yet without hesitation, he shared his stores of food with those who needed them most.

When he looked up at her, she nearly faltered in her descent. But the hateful steward made some quiet remark to him, and he looked away.

'Twas something like defiance that kept her moving down the stairs, toward Edric who was still wet from his dunking in the river. She wanted to demonstrate that their earlier interlude meant naught to her, that she was not some shameful varlet who would faint away at his touch, who would look at him with calf's eyes, hoping for a scrap of his attention. She was not so susceptible to the man's allure.

Averting her eyes from his damp form, she decided not to approach him and the forbidding steward, but went to speak to the grooms she and Lora had engaged earlier. A moment later, she directed the maids to take the old wall hangings outside to beat the dust out of them.

Lora's patronage had done much to improve the servants' attitude toward her. Ever since her tour of the village with Lora, they seemed to view her as more than a simple servant, even though they remained unsure of her rank.

Still avoiding Lord Edric, she knelt next to the larger of the trunks. Inside were blankets and small shertes, hoods, and linen swaddling. She chose the items she thought would be useful and made a neat stack beside the trunk.

Fully attuned to Edric's every move, she felt him approach her from the other side of the hall.

He picked up a small moth-eaten blanket. "You do not plan to use this with Aidan," he said.

"No, my lord," Kathryn replied, much too aware of his male scent and the heat of his body. She wanted to forget what had transpired between them, not relive it every time he was near. Truly.

Kathryn lifted a small sherte by the shoulders and held it up for him to see. "I cannot believe you were ever small enough to wear this," she said, then regretted her words, for they called to mind the size of his shaft and the smooth hardness she'd felt as she'd wrapped her fingers 'round it.

A muscle in Edric's cheek flexed once and Kathryn knew he was remembering the same moment. The activity in the hall seemed distant as Edric dropped to one knee beside her. "I have never been . . . small."

Kathryn's hands trembled slightly, so she put them to good use once again, sorting through the items in the trunk. 'Twas far better to ignore his seductive words, but when he lifted her plait of hair and pulled it carefully from her shoulder where it rested, her body quaked with awareness. She closed her eyes and swallowed, aware that encouraging any further congress between them would be a mistake. The heat that passed between them would burn her up if she let it, and leave her with naught.

"L-lord Bryce was asking for you." 'Twas the only ploy she could think of to make him go. And it wasn't exactly untrue. When she and Lora had returned to the keep a while ago and visited Bryce, the young man had asked if they'd seen his brother.

Edric's hand stilled. "All is not finished between us, wench. We will continue what we started."

"No, my lord. We cannot. I am a chaste maid and soon I will enter the nunnery."

His eyes bored into hers. "'Tis a mistake, as well you know. You were made for my touch."

Jesu, what had he been using for brains? Certainly not the contents of his head.

In the quiet of the bedchamber that Edric had hardly visited during the past year, he removed his wet clothes. Standing naked beside the bed, he was still partially aroused. 'Twas no difficult feat to imagine Kate lying upon the mattress, her eyes darkened with passion. He muttered a curse for engaging in such senseless whimsy, and forced her from his mind.

He drew on clean, dry clothes and quit the room, anxious to find something else to occupy his attention. 'Twas but a short walk to Bryce's chamber, and he found the guard outside and Father Algar within. The room smelled of incense and was cloudy with smoke. The priest knelt beside the bed, muttering Latin prayers, even though Bryce was asleep. At least, his eyes were closed.

"Father Algar, 'tis time you gave your knees a rest." 'Twas an irreverent suggestion, but the less Edric saw of Algar, the better. Besides, the man had fouled the air with his cloying smoke. Edric did not know how Bryce could breathe.

The priest pushed himself up to his feet and pierced Edric with an accusing glare. "You will pay for your sins, lad. Cast out the Norman and repent your unholy alliance."

Edric put his hand upon the priest's shoulder and ushered him to the door. "Will my repentance put food on our tables, old man? Will it replace our trees and repair our fields?"

He did not wait to hear the priest's reply, but closed the door behind the man and opened the shutters, letting the sweet smoke drift outside.

"God's eyebrows, I thought he would never leave," said Bryce, opening one eye a crack.

"I didn't think you were asleep." Edric took a seat beside his brother. "How do you fare?"

"If Lora would stop putting this putrid slop on the wound and allow me out of bed, I would be fine."

"I trust Lora."

"What of the other one? Kate?"

Edric ran the palms of his hands down his thighs. "She is a Norman. We'd be fools to trust her."

Bryce furrowed his brow. "I like her."

"'Tis all right to like her. Just don't trust her."

"Come now, Edric. You trust your son with her."

Edric stood and went to the window. "She is more a mother than Cecily would have been, I'll give you that."

"'Tis more than that."

"No it isn't. She is only enjoying her time with a bairn who needs her before she goes to Evesham Bridge."

"Ah. The nunnery. Is she a nun?" Bryce asked.

"No." He could not imagine a nun alive who would react to his touch the way Kate had done.

"Then I don't understand."

Of course Bryce didn't understand. He hadn't

spent enough time with her to know the inconsistencies she presented. And if Edric sorted out her true story, he feared he might be compelled to act on it, mayhap even depriving his son of the one woman who had succeeded in nurturing him. "She is Norman, and that is all we need to know."

"No need to get into a temper over it. I've just never before heard of a serving maid gaining entrance to Evesham Bridge. Won't she need a dowry?"

Edric nodded slowly. Yet another unanswered question.

"She'll stay here as long as Aidan needs her, won't she?"

"Aye," said Edric. "She'll stay."

"Did you teach her to protect herself once she leaves here?"

Edric gave a slight shake of his head. He did not want to speak of what had transpired in the solar—not with Bryce, not with anyone. 'Twas obvious his passionate encounter with Kate had merely been the result of his long abstinence. It meant naught. He sat down once again and spoke with Bryce of his plans to raid the Fergusons. Bryce would not be well enough to go, for Edric intended to attack soon, but 'twas best to include his brother in the planning. The younger man had a keen mind for strategy, and Edric intended to make use of it.

"Robert Ferguson keeps a mistress in a cottage west of his father's keep," said Bryce. " 'Tis outside the village at the base of a small fell near the river."

"How do you know this?"

Bryce smiled. " 'Tis called knowing your enemy. I thought we would be raiding Léod's holding weeks ago."

"Now that Léod is dead, Robert's arrangement with his whore may have changed. Mayhap he brings her into his house."

"Mayhap, but 'tis best to anticipate all the possibilities. When do you plan to go?"

"I'd intended to go right away, but Oswin advised waiting until the moon is full."

"He thinks the Fergusons will be occupied with mourning Léod?"

Edric nodded. "I'm not so sure—"

"He's known the Fergusons far longer than you, Edric."

"Aye. So we follow his advice and leave two days hence, our best time for traveling at night."

"If the weather holds," Bryce remarked.

"We'll go regardless. Even waiting these two days grates on my nerves."

When he left Bryce to his rest, Edric concentrated

on their discussion of battle plans, glad to have something that fully occupied his attention. He was distracted, however, by the pleasant smell of lavender.

Following his nose, he went to the stairs and looked down, only to spy Kate dropping small twigs of the aromatic plant over the rushes in the hall. He watched her move all alone about the room, happily chatting in French. Edric wondered who her audience was, since she appeared to be alone, then he noticed the old cradle from his father's keep. Aidan lay within it, aimlessly kicking his tiny hands and feet at the air.

Edric's knowledge of French was rudimentary. He'd managed to communicate with Cecily only because she took great pains to make her demands understood, and Berta was somewhat fluent in English. So he did not know exactly what Kate was saying to Aidan, only that his son seemed to enjoy the sound of her voice.

As did Edric. It was soft and melodic, and sounded almost like a language entirely different from that which Cecily had used. 'Twas arousing to see her in this unguarded moment, and when he closed his eyes and let the sweet sounds wash over him, he found himself growing painfully erect. The dunk in the river had done naught to ease his arousal.

Kate gave out a startled gasp when she saw him.

"What's all this?" he asked.

She hesitated at first. "Your hall is cold and unhealthy, my lord. Some changes were necessary."

Edric went down the stairs and met her in front of the fireplace where Aidan cooed contentedly. He could not deny the hall was a more pleasant place with the alterations Kate had wrought, although 'twas not her place to cause such changes.

"To my recollection, you are a servant here, Kate of Rushton." His cold words were tossed out like a challenge, but she did not deny them.

" 'Twas not done for my own comfort, my lord."

He loomed over her, tall and dark, with his powerful arms folded across his chest. "How do you know I have no other plans for my hall?"

Kathryn gritted her teeth and decided she could be just as unpleasant as the Saxon lord. "I beg your pardon, my lord. 'Tis my understanding that your hall has been barely habitable since its completion."

"I suppose Lora told you that."

"Oh, think you that only Lora has noticed the state of your residence?"

A muscle in his jaw twitched at her brazen reply, and he lowered his arms and came closer.

177

Kathryn stood her ground, even though she knew he could order her whipped for her insolence. He took her shoulders in his hands and she waited for him to shake her.

She felt his breath upon her forehead, and when she looked up, she saw that his expression was not one of anger. His eyes had darkened to a much deeper blue, and his chest seemed to grow immeasurably with each of his breaths, touching the peaks of her breasts, and rendering them exquisitely sensitive.

She should step away and put some distance between them, but she could not.

"I need no Norman wench telling me how to arrange my hall." His voice was low and threatening, but Kathryn felt no fear, only a shuddering awareness of his body.

"Mayhap it takes a Norman to carry out the task." Her words came out in barely a whisper as she felt the same kind of melting heat that she'd experienced with him in the solar. She should run, should escape as fast as her legs would carry her, yet when he increased the pressure of his hands upon her shoulders and pulled her toward him, she was immobilized.

"Since this is a Norman keep," Edric said as he lowered his head, "you may be right."

Kathryn gazed up at him as he touched his

mouth to hers, brushing his lips gently across her mouth. Her eyes drifted closed and he drew her even closer, pressing her breasts against his chest. Kathryn forgot where they were standing and returned his kiss with all the ardor of their earlier encounter.

Edric sucked her tongue into his mouth as he tipped his head and deepened his kiss. Kathryn slipped her arms 'round his waist and felt his hands slide down her back. She trembled when he cupped her buttocks and pulled her against the solid ridge between his legs.

Kathryn felt a raw yearning for what he'd done to her earlier, yet she wanted more. She wanted to feel him inside her, to know she could give him the same pulsing pleasure that she'd felt earlier.

'Twas sinful, but she could not deny him, or the potent feelings he aroused in her. She moved against him, brushing her breasts against his chest, cradling his hard arousal against her pelvis.

When she felt the vibration of a low sound he made in the back of his throat, Kathryn pushed back slightly. He slipped his hands up her sides until they reached her breasts. Somehow, they were even more sensitive than before, and when he cupped them fully, then toyed with her nipples, her knees buckled.

Edric managed to keep her from falling, but he

broke the kiss, growling, pressing his forehead against hers. He took her hand and started to lead her away, but at that moment, Aidan started to cry.

Kathryn felt momentarily disoriented, but regained her senses when Edric spoke. "I must be insane," he muttered.

Taking note of the savage heat in his gaze, Kathryn thought he might truly be mad.

But the madness was not only his.

Edric stalked out of the hall. He walked across the courtyard to his stable, dismissed the groom who offered to assist him, and saddled his own horse. A few minutes later, he was riding through the cobbled lanes of the village toward the Silver Dragon.

The tavern was in the farthest corner of the village, a prosperous building with two stories—a public room and kitchen on the main floor, and guest bedrooms abovestairs. Many a time had he taken his pleasure in one of those rooms on a soft feather bed, with the lusty Saxon wench who lived and worked there. Edric intended to finish his day in one of those rooms, with that same Saxon female riding him until he could no longer think.

The aroma of onions, beans, and cabbage assailed him as he entered the public room. He had not expected the place to be so crowded, but it was dark and noisy, with every table filled. The evenings were cold now, so there was a fire in the grate, and smoke hovered near the ceiling.

Wilfred the tavernkeeper shoved some men aside to make room for Edric, but Edric spied Drogan sitting with his hands cupped 'round a tankard, looking dejected. He picked his way through the crowd toward the huscarl, and sat down across from him.

"What ails you?" he asked, feeling as miserable as Drogan looked.

When Wilfred brought the mug of ale and set it before him, Edric wondered where Felicia was. She usually took pains to greet him and find him the best place in the house. And she'd said all had been quiet here recently.

"Lora," Drogan said.

"What?" Edric had already forgotten what he'd asked. He searched the crowd and saw Felicia enter from the kitchen, carrying a large tray laden with a platter of food, mugs, and a pitcher. She'd tied up her golden hair, but limp strands had escaped their bindings and hung down her back.

"The woman will not consider my suit."

"The wom—? Ah, Lora. Well, consider yourself

fortunate," Edric groused. "Respectable women are not for the likes of us."

Drogan growled and did not reply, preferring to swill his beer instead. Edric watched Felicia move among the crowd, her raucous laughter sounding quite harsh to his ears. Had she always been so strident?

She set down her tray and distributed meat and ale among the men before returning to the kitchen. Edric did not mind that she didn't notice him right away. He had all night, and he intended to take his pleasure slowly, starting now, by anticipating the carnal amusements he would soon enjoy in one of Wilfred's soft beds upstairs.

Darkness fell and Kathryn felt restless, more pent up than she'd ever felt before. 'Twas Edric's touch, his kiss, that had done it, had made her feel as though tiny moths were fluttering at her skin and in her belly. Pacing did not help. Finally enlisting Gwen's assistance, she left a sleeping Aidan with the housemaid in the nursery and went in search of Lora.

Kathryn hoped to find her in Lord Bryce's chamber, so she went to the young man's room and found him awake with his guard napping in a chair beside him. But Lora was not there.

Bryce waved her inside. He woke the guard and sent him away. " 'Tis past time for you to relieve yourself, is it not, Alf?"

The guard took his leave and Kathryn sat in the chair beside the bed, glad of a diversion. She had to put all her yearnings aside for they were mere foolishness. "How do you feel?"

"As though someone ran me through with a steely blade," he quipped.

"Aye, but are you improved at all?"

"Are you worried about your handiwork?" Bryce asked.

Kathryn gave a nod, but when Bryce threw off his blanket and started to lift his sherte, she looked away. "I'd rather not see it, my lord. I would be satisfied with *hearing* how it mends."

He gave her a wicked grin. "I forgot about your delicate stomach."

Kathryn doubted it, but knew he was just toying with her. "So . . . how is it?"

"Sore. Hot. Sometimes Lora makes a face when she tends the wound, and I know she's concerned about the fever that comes and goes. She worries too much." He shrugged and covered himself again. "But tell me—have you no faith in your own handiwork?"

"Since I'd never sewn a man before . . . No."

"Truly?"

She shook her head. "Your brother bullied me into it."

"Edric? Bully you?"

She heard the sarcasm in his tone but refused to play his game. "Is it true you refused last rites?"

Bryce looked down.

"My lord, if your condition should change—"

"Do not preach to me, Kate. I have enough with the damned priest and my overbearing brother."

"I apologize. I did not mean to lecture you. 'Tis only that I fear for—"

"I am not close to death, Lady Kate."

Kathryn's breath quickened. "What did you call me?"

"Merely jesting with you," he said, brushing off her question. "Lora said you ordered our furnishings brought here from the old keep."

She felt her face heat. "Was I too presumptuous?"

"Not at all, though Edric might be opposed at first. But since he does not intend ever to wed again, there will be no wife to order new furnishings. He'll soon see we need to make use of what we have."

Kathryn winced. "Was his marriage so very bad, then?"

"Bad? The only time the two of them conversed

was when Cecily screamed at him in her god-awful gibberish. Oh, sorry."

"And did he shout back?"

"Not usually. He spent as much time as possible away from here. Fortunately, Aidan was conceived quite soon after the nuptials."

Kathryn felt her face heat. She did not like to think of the intimacies Edric must have shared with his wife, even though he'd been far from enamored with her. It only demonstrated that a man—that Edric—might have no feelings at all for the woman in his bed, yet perform the act that should bind them together in affection and respect, if not love.

She stood and walked away from the bedside. It had grown cool in the room, so she added wood to the fire.

"So, you're going to Evesham Bridge?"

"Aye. 'Tis what I intend to do as soon as another nursemaid can be found."

Bryce said naught, but Kathryn felt him scrutinizing her. She felt vastly uncomfortable.

"I cannot return to Rushton." The name of the estate rolled off her tongue as though it were not a lie. 'Twas not a good sign that she was becoming so accustomed to telling falsehoods.

"Being abducted makes you . . . unacceptable?"

She nodded, and when he looked at her, Kathryn had the oddest sensation that he knew more about her than she'd said.

"I will never understand Normans. Your king, for example, has squeezed us until we can barely squeak."

"What do you mean?"

"In spite of the attacks upon us, he has never sent assistance. He has refused to lighten our burden here, and even continues to change the terms of Edric's enfeoffment."

Kathryn knitted her brows together in concern. "He knows of your difficulties with the Fergusons?"

Bryce made a rude noise. "Oswin has penned many a letter, but they are answered rudely, if at all."

Kathryn had never realized how coldhearted King William was. Her father had spoken highly of him, telling of his prowess in battle and his generosity toward his Norman barons. Apparently, his largesse did not extend to a Saxon holding—of which she knew there were very few.

Was it possible that King William exploited Edric? Used the Saxon lord and his men for his own purposes with little in return? This was not the same king of whom her father had spoken so highly. Or mayhap she was being naïve.

" 'Tis no wonder your steward hates me."

"He will come 'round . . . if you stay."

"I cannot." Not if she wanted to retain her chastity, for she had no doubt that if she stayed, Edric would succeed in seducing her. The idea of which both terrified and intrigued her. She longed for the experience Edric could give, but knew 'twould mean naught to him, while her own heart was at risk.

She returned to the bed and placed her hand upon Bryce's ankle. "I should go back to Aidan. I'll bid you good night and send your guard back to you."

"He'll be waiting outside my door."

But Alf was not there. Kathryn stuck her head into Bryce's chamber and informed him of the guard's absence.

"Not to worry. He's probably at the privy and will return soon."

Kathryn decided to pay a short visit to Berta before returning to the nursery. Carrying one small candle for light, she climbed the stairs and easily found the woman's bedchamber by the sound of quiet weeping within. After a light knock on the door, one of the housemaids opened it.

The old woman saw her and tearfully beckoned her to the bed where she lay with the curtains open, wearing a long-sleeved bed gown and a hood. Kathryn did not believe the woman had left the bed since the funeral. Her face was unwashed, her hair a mess . . . "Oh, praise be to God. I thought I was alone here." She dabbed at her nose with a bit of cloth and resumed her quiet weeping. "My poor Cecily."

"Are you all right, Berta?"

"Of course not. My poor child is dead . . . Dead and buried, and I've nowhere to go."

Kathryn came close and crouched beside the bed. "Have you thought of returning to Cecily's family?"

Berta looked sharply at Kathryn. "But of course. Do you think the Saxon dog will send me back?"

"I'm sure he will," Kathryn replied, "though it might be best if you avoided calling him a dog."

"Bah! He does not understand us. He cared naught for Cecily and all her delicate needs."

How could he, when Cecily apparently did not know how to make her requirements seem like anything but unreasonable demands. "I understand she wanted to return to her father's estate."

Berta's weeping began anew. "Her father admonished her to make her peace with her husband, that d— scoundrel."

Kathryn sighed. "Are you well enough to travel, Berta? If so, I will ask Lord Edric to provide you an escort to Lord Gui's estate."

Berta clasped her hands around Kathryn's. "Oh,

please! If you would do so, I will be eternally in your debt!"

"Think naught of it," Kathryn said. "Lying here despondent serves no one. 'Twill be better for all if you return to Norman lands."

Kathryn picked up her candle and took her leave. She made her way down the stairs and headed toward the nursery, quickening her step when she heard strange sounds coming from inside. When she pushed open the door, Kathryn was met by the sight of a man in dark clothes, pulling Gwen around to face her as he held a knife to her throat.

He looked at Kathryn, grinning, his red hair blazing in the flickering light, and Kathryn recognized the face of Robert Ferguson.

Chapter 10

❦

Carrying a small lamp to light their way, Felicia led Edric up the back stairs of the tavern, her warm hand pulling his as they searched for a likely chamber for their tryst. "I've missed you, my lord," she whispered.

And Edric had thought of her a thousand times during the past year. He could not help but remember the hard, peaked tips of her nipples as she fed them to him, nor could he forget the sensations she aroused when she closed her dark, red lips around his cock.

He put Kate from his mind and began to heat

up at the thought of sliding into this tavern maid, of taking his ease within her warm body.

She opened the door to one of the bedchambers and pushed him inside, giggling, trying to keep her voice quiet. She set down the candle and Edric let her take charge, closing his eyes and leaning back against the wall as she kissed him. She opened her mouth and shoved her tongue into his while she pushed her body against him. Squirming, she worked hard to elicit a response from him.

She tasted of onions.

Edric separated his mouth from hers and waited for the flurry of arousal to come over him as Felicia's hands slid down his chest to his crotch.

"Has it been so long, my lord, that you've forgotten how to use it?" Felicia cooed.

Edric moved his hips, letting her work him, picturing her pretty breasts and the way they would fill his hands . . .

But they would not . . . at least, not the way Kate's breasts did. The Norman's were tipped by nipples of the palest pink, the texture of a ripe fruit. The aroma of lavender had enshrouded her when last he'd kissed her mouth, and Edric had no doubt that she would have willingly yielded if he'd taken her to his chamber.

Felicia slipped her hand into his braies. "Remember our last tryst beside the river, my lord?"

Edric barely heard her. The alluring French cadence of Kate's speech was so much more seductive than anything Felicia could say. Kate was the one he wanted, and Felicia a poor substitute.

He took hold of Felicia's wrist and removed her hand from his body. "I should not stay away from Bryce for so long." 'Twas a lame excuse, but he saw no reason to pursue this empty assignation.

"But my lord, we've only just started."

"Mayhap another time," he said, though 'twould not be soon. He righted his clothes and left the chamber, fully intending to make Kate his mistress and show her how unsuited to the nunnery she was.

"Don't hurt her," Kathryn whispered.

Robert laughed and tossed Gwen aside, knocking her to the floor where she fell against the wooden frame of Kathryn's bed. His eyes were the same flat gray of his father's and the coldness of his gaze made Kathryn shudder. Gwen whimpered once but did not move from the floor.

"I'll scream for help!" Kathryn was so frightened that her knees shook, making her aware of the knife that she'd strapped to her leg. If any of them were going to survive this encounter, she would have to use her wits.

"Screaming will do you no good."

She feared that was true. Alf had not returned to his post and there could be only one reason for his dereliction. No one else would be nearby at this hour, except Bryce. "What do you want?"

"Edric's son."

"No!" Horror made Kathryn's cry come out as a mere whisper. "Take me instead! I'll make a better hostage than this innocent bairn."

Robert laughed again and placed his foot upon the rocker of the cradle. He pressed down, rocking the small bed in a parody of parental care. "I'll take the brat, and when Edric comes for him, 'twill be my pleasure to put an end to both father and son."

"You would not harm an innocent child."

"Wouldn't I?"

"You cannot possibly think you'll get away with this. Not alone."

"Ha. My men are outside the gates, waiting to see my torch on the battlement. When they see my signal they'll know I have the bairn. They'll attack, and nary a stick of Braxton Fell will remain standing."

"Why go to such trouble here? Can you not leave the child with me—"

"No! 'Tis the only way to assure that Edric dies."

Kathryn shuddered and risked a quick glance

at Gwen who lay insensible with a bloody gash on her head, and she knew she would have to do something drastic to divert Robert from his purpose. She wiped her damp palms on her thighs and wished Edric had taught her something she could use now.

Mayhap he had.

On trembling legs, she approached the man before he decided to grab Aidan. "Take me, Robert. My father is a wealthy Norman baron. You could demand any ransom." Terrified of what might happen if she did not distract him, she clenched her teeth and loosened the laces of her bodice. "I will be most cooperative . . ."

His eyes flickered over her and his foot stopped moving on the rocker. Kathryn wondered if she was going to be able to move fast enough to grab her knife and jab it into the Scot's heart before he hurt Aidan . . . or herself.

She swallowed, and as she thought of the things Edric had told her, she let her eyes drift down—to the man's most vulnerable part—and considered how she could do him some damage. Edric had asked if she'd aimed her blows when she was attacked. This time, she intended to inflict as much damage as . . . Oh! 'Twas growing. Under her scrutiny, the Scot's private part became a large bulge behind his tunic.

Whether 'twas caused by the loosening of her bodice or her gaze upon his crotch, Kathryn did not know. She took another step toward him, and started raising her skirt on the side where the knife was hidden. If she could make him believe she would welcome him under her skirts, mayhap 'twould give him a moment's pause, and her a quicker access to the dagger.

Gwen moaned just then, and started to rouse herself, drawing the Scot's attention for a mere second. Kathryn moved fast, hurling herself toward Ferguson, raising her knee as she did so, and jabbing as hard as she could between his legs.

He did naught but grunt and clutch her arms.

Aidan awoke and started to whimper. In a panic, Kathryn kicked frantically at Robert, but he stayed clear of her feet and knees. Even so, he was unable to wield his knife effectively while holding onto her with both hands.

With Kathryn's struggling and the noise of Aidan's wailing, the Scot did not see Gwen rouse herself. Stealthily, the maid crawled toward Robert, and when he noticed her, 'twas too late. She sank her teeth into his ankle, eliciting a roar of pain from him.

Kathryn took advantage of the moment and drew her knife. Using both hands, she plunged it into the Scot's chest. For one terrifying moment, she thought the blow had had no effect. Robert stood still, his gaze locked on her, unwavering.

Then his knife fell from his hand. A stain of red began to spread upon his chest and the blood dripped onto the floor, but Robert's astonished gaze held her fast.

"You've killed him," Gwen said, though Kathryn could barely hear her over Aidan's loud cries. She stood as if paralyzed and her stomach roiled with nausea.

The Scot finally fell and she was able to turn away. She picked up Aidan from his cradle and crushed him to her chest.

"Come, Gwen."

"Where?"

"You must take Aidan and go lock yourselves in with Lord Bryce. I'll see if I can find Lord Edric and Drogan."

"Y-your knife."

Kathryn steeled herself to look down at Robert, at Lora's knife that protruded from his chest. "I think I'm going to be ill," she said.

"Here." Gwen bent down and pulled it from the man's body. She wiped it on a nearby cloth and handed it back to Kathryn. "You saved my life, Norman . . . Kate."

"Aye, well, we'd best get help, or none of us will be saved."

Quickly, they made their way to Bryce's chamber. Pushing inside, Kathryn was not surprised to see that Alf had not returned. Bryce was asleep until Aidan's wailing woke him. "What is it?" He squinted his eyes against the torch light.

"The Fergusons are about to attack," Kathryn said, rocking the bairn to quiet him. "I must go find Edric and Drogan."

"What! How do you know? Where's Alf?"

"I fear he's been killed," she replied. "Robert Ferguson sneaked in with the intent to steal Aidan."

"Kate killed him," Gwen announced.

Bryce pushed up in bed as far as his wound allowed. "Kate?"

Kathryn laid the sleeping bairn on the bed with his uncle. "There is no time now. I must go. Bar the door when I am gone and do not let anyone in unless you are certain it's safe."

"Wait. Hand me that sword," Bryce said.

Kathryn saw the weapon lying in its scabbard upon a trunk and handed it to him. "Keep the door barred," she reiterated. "Let no one in."

"Kate—where is Edric?"

"I do not know." The last time she'd seen him, he'd just kissed her senseless. "But I promise you I'll find him before it's too late."

She exited the room and heard the bar drop against the door frame. Haste was absolutely vital, for Kathryn did not know how long Robert's men would wait for his signal. If it did not come soon, she feared they would attack without it.

Afraid to take any light with her, she made her way to Edric's bedchamber. Knocking as she pushed open the door, she called his name. When he did not reply, she hastened to the farthest end of the hall to the solar.

No one was there.

A moment later, she was moving down the stairs to the great hall. She picked up one of the lamps and poked her head into every room, afraid to call Edric's name for fear of alerting some lurking Scot. But she found no one skulking in the dark hall, not even Oswin.

The kitchen was quiet, too, though she found a few maids asleep on low cots in their quarters nearby.

Running back to the hall, she went for the door, hoping to find a groom or some other servant who might know where to find Edric. She put her hand upon the door latch, but before she could pull, it slammed open, nearly knocking her down.

"Edric!" She was breathless now, and close to tears. *"Grâce à Dieu, tu es revenu! Je ne savais pas comment je pourrais jamais te trouver."*

He took hold of her upper arms. "I don't understand you. What is it? Is Bryce—"

"Non. Mon Dieu." She caught her breath and forced herself to speak clearly in Edric's language. "No, he is all right for now. 'Tis Robert Ferguson."

"What about him?" His voice sounded rough and impatient.

"His men are gathering outside Braxton's walls and they're waiting for his . . . er, his signal to attack."

"What? Explain!"

"I cannot! There is no time! You must gather your men and—"

"How do you know this?" He pulled her outside, drawing her toward the practice field.

"He came to the nursery, intending to take Aidan."

Edric drew his sword and started back up the stairs. "Where is Robert now?"

"In the nursery. Dead."

Edric had never known such fear before. He gathered his thoughts and asked the most pertinent question. "What of Aidan?"

"He is safe with Lord Bryce, my lord. The door is locked against any intruders."

"Come with me."

He let out the breath he'd been holding as they hurried to the barracks where he roused his men, telling them to prepare for battle, for he did not doubt Kate's words. He cursed himself for failing to anticipate Robert's desire for revenge, for failing to attack Dunfergus before Robert could come to Braxton Fell, for failing to overrule Oswin.

He ordered one of the men to go to the Silver Dragon for Drogan and to raise the alarm, then turned back to Kate. "Tell me about Robert."

"*Juste ciel* . . ."

In the light, he could see that her face was streaked with tears. Her hands were red . . . bloodied. She was trembling.

"Robert . . . He came to the nursery while Gwen was staying with Aidan. He threatened to take him hostage—to draw you out." She took a shuddering breath, and for a moment Edric did not think she would be able to continue, but he took hold of her upper arms and bolstered her. "I—I did as you said. I aimed my kick at his . . . his most private parts."

One of the grooms brought Edric's helm and armor. He released Kate's arms and started donning his battle gear, preparing himself for battle. "Go on."

"It did not work as you said."

Frustrated with her lack of speed in telling the tale, he urged her to continue. "How did the bastard die?"

" 'Twas only because of Gwen. She crept close while he was shaking me. She bit his leg and I was able to pull out the knife Lora gave me."

He slid his sword into its scabbard, ready now for whatever awaited. "Lora?"

"Aye. For protection." She raised her skirt to her knee to show him a dagger that was strapped there. "I stabbed him with it."

"And killed him."

She nodded, dropping her skirt. Edric took her shoulders in hand once again. This time, he pulled her close, and kissed her soundly. "You saved my son, and mayhap this entire holding. Go and find safety in the keep. I will come to you when all is—"

Suddenly, they heard shouts and the rumble of horses' hooves. He turned Kate and pushed her gently toward the keep. "They must have killed the guards and scaled the walls. Go back to the hall. Go quickly."

Flames shot up near the gate and Edric feared for the safety of the cottars. Mounting his horse, he joined the ranks of men who were riding swiftly toward the gate, but gave a look back to see Kate rushing toward the keep.

As Edric watched her move swiftly through the courtyard, he saw that no Scots had breached the inner grounds, giving him confidence that she would make it safely into the hall. She would surely bar the doors and see to it that his son and brother were kept safe within.

Amazed at the resourcefulness of the lass who'd panicked when he'd tried to teach her to defend herself, there was no doubt left in his mind that she was not a simple maid.

Kathryn climbed the steps to the keep and turned 'round. There was fire in the distance and horrible sounds of battle. Men's voices carried on the wind, and the crash of steel meeting steel made her tremble with dread.

She started inside, but realized the battle could easily spread, making Lora and her neighbors vulnerable to attack. Someone needed to get them, and bring them to the safety of the keep.

But there was no one who could go. All the men had gone to battle, and the serving maids . . . Could Kathryn waste precious time to send one of them on such a perilous errand?

Swallowing her own fears, she went back down the steps and headed in the direction of Lora's cottage. Staying in the shadows as she hurried down the path, Kathryn refused to let her fear paralyze her. She reminded herself that this was nothing like the raid on Kettwyck. Edric's men had been warned in time, and had quickly met their enemies at the gates.

But Edric was involved this time, and as a leader of his men, he would be in the thick of it. She'd seen him in battle, and knew he was a master swordsman.

Such knowledge did not keep her from worrying. Taking no time to consider the significance of her fears for him, she banged on the doors of every cottage in her path, running and shouting for all to seek shelter in the keep.

Circling 'round to Lora's cottage, Kathryn saw the two women arguing. "Elga, we must go," Lora pleaded. "Your life is more important than your looms!"

"Lora! Elga! Come with me to the keep!" Kathryn cried. "The Scots have attacked the gate!"

"Do you hear, Elga? We must go!" Lora had hold of Elga's arm, but the older woman showed no fear, only confusion. She clung to a basket of colorful yarn, as if letting it go would be disastrous.

"'Tis my son's house," cried Elga. "I cannot leave it!"

"If you cannot reason with her, Lora," Kathryn said, "we must force her! 'Tis too dangerous to stay here!" As the smell of smoke thickened, she took the woman's other arm and helped Lora pull her from the house, then joined the others in the lane who were hurrying toward the keep.

Elga stopped resisting and their progress became easier as they were swept along in the crowd. They soon reached the keep, where throngs of Braxton's people were crowding each other to climb the steps and fill the hall.

Oswin stood just inside, and he glowered at Kathryn as she entered with Lora and Elga. "Who gave you the authority to send these people here?" he demanded.

Kathryn swallowed. "No one. It only seemed—"

"Begone with you! The lord's son is clamoring for a feeding and you are nowhere to be found! 'Twould be well for you to remember the only purpose for which you're tolerated here!"

A lump jammed in Kathryn's throat. Mortified to be so chastised before all these people, she ducked her head and hurried toward the staircase, never looking back at the crowd in the hall.

Battle was just the thing to raise Drogan's spirits, and Edric was heartened when he joined the fray. 'Twas a bloody melee, with Scots managing to slip inside the walls, attempting to cause as much damage here as they'd done to the fields and forests in past raids.

"Gildas, have your men encircle them! Cut them off!" Edric dismounted and fought hand to hand, until he spied one of his young grooms. "Caedmon, get Modig and go with him to the keep. Find the Norman woman, Kate, and have her show you where the Ferguson chief lies dead. Bring his body back here."

"Aye, my lord," the boy replied as he hurried away to do Edric's bidding. The lad was small for the task, but Edric needed every grown fighter to remain here.

He dodged a wicked blow from the ax of Robert's second-in-command, battling against the man's heavy weapon, and thrusting his sword. "Robert is dead, Douglas Ferguson!" he shouted at Robert's cousin. "Killed by one small maiden in my keep."

"You lie, Saxon, and now you will die!"

Douglas used two hands to slam his ax into Edric's side, but Edric jumped nimbly away. "Yield, Douglas!"

"Never! Braxton Fell will be ours!"

The fight continued as fires flared all 'round. Edric had no interest in sparring verbally with Douglas. He wanted an end to this fight, and he could almost taste it. Robert was dead, and 'twould likely take years before this band of filthy Ferguson raiders could muster a good fight again. Years in which

Braxton would recover and gain prosperity in spite of their Norman overlord.

"Drogan!" Edric shouted as he continued to parry with Douglas.

Drogan heard Edric's call and made his way 'round the thick of the battle. "Aye, my lord!" he shouted against the cacophony of battle.

"Take a company of men to the postern gate. Go outside the walls and circle 'round—cut off every Scotsman who would retreat!"

" 'Twill be *Saxons* retreating, not Scots, Edric!" cried Douglas.

Edric did not dignify the Scot's words with a response. He knew Drogan would follow his orders, and was certain that once the Scots saw Robert's body, they would run for the hills.

"Do you need assistance here, my lord?" Drogan asked before he left.

Edric gave a mocking laugh as Douglas swung once again. The man lost his footing and Edric took advantage, delivering the fatal thrust of his sword.

"Well done," said Drogan. "Have you a plan, then?"

"Robert is dead—killed in the hall."

Edric hardly noticed Drogan's expression of astonishment as they hastened to the wall. "I've sent for his body to be brought here. The Scots will turn tail when they see he's dead."

"And you want me to cut them off at the knees."

Edric grinned and slapped the huscarl's back. "That's the general idea."

Chapter 11

❦

"What can you see?" Bryce asked.

Kathryn looked out the window once again. "Fires. Smoke."

"Damn Oswin!" Bryce muttered.

Kathryn did not understand the young man's curse, but paced the room, paying him no heed. She'd sent Gwen away to find a guard who could be spared to come and protect Bryce and Aidan if need be. The warrior now stood outside Bryce's chamber, while Lora had taken Elga to rest in the privacy of one of the chambers above.

Kathryn returned to the window several times,

her worry for Edric nearly palpable. It burned in her throat and churned in her stomach and would not relent until she saw him again, healthy and whole.

When her feelings for the Saxon had changed, she did not know. Mayhap 'twas when he'd said she was made for his touch . . . for she knew it was true.

He'd vowed never to take another wife, but Kathryn recalled Elga's words to Lora—that she should not pine for what could never be.

Did the woman's advice apply to Kathryn, too? She would never be a wife if she went to Evesham Bridge, never bear a child. Every dream Kathryn had ever had would come to naught. Her life at the nunnery would be barren and joyless.

Yet if she remained at Braxton Fell, she had no doubt that her virtue would go the way of her dreams, for she was defenseless against Edric's allure. Her powers of reason abandoned her when he touched her, and she melted into a pool of pure sensation when he kissed her.

How could she remain at Braxton Fell when she knew what would happen between her and Edric if she stayed? 'Twas wicked even to consider such a thing . . .

She glanced at Aidan, sleeping peacefully on Bryce's bed. Her life had been immeasurably enriched by caring for the tiny bairn. Could she abandon him to some strange nursemaid?

Bryce made a small noise and Kathryn looked at him. "What is it?"

"I still cannot believe it . . . You killed Robert Ferguson."

She chewed her lip. " 'Twas Gwen who made it possible."

"She told me what happened, Kate."

Resuming her pacing, Kathryn was hardly able to keep all her thoughts straight. If Edric . . . no, *when* Edric returned to the keep, could she let herself become his leman? Every pore in her body wanted him, yet every pore knew 'twas wrong to give herself to a man who was not her husband.

Even if she loved him.

"Let me see the knife," Bryce said.

"The knife?" She felt for the strap on her leg and the knife secured there. Turning away, she reached under her skirt. Sliding it out from the strap, she handed it to Bryce without even looking at the vile thing.

"You saved Aidan from Ferguson . . . You realize you are the heroine of Braxton Fell."

"No, Lord Bryce, I simply did what was necess—"

He shook his head. "Edric will see that you are

well rewarded. 'Tis likely he will take you to Evesham Bridge himself, if that's what you want."

Trembling with indecision, Kathryn turned away and went to the window again. Nothing had changed. Smoke still obscured what view she might have of the battle. When they heard a knock at the door, Kathryn was afraid it might be Oswin, come to berate her once again for her presumption.

"My lord, 'tis Caedmon and Modig," said the guard outside.

"You can open it," Bryce said. "Caedmon is one of our grooms."

Two youths stood outside the room alongside Bryce's guard. They did not enter, but spoke to Kate. "Lord Edric sent us to collect the body of Robert Ferguson. 'Tis said you will know where it is."

"Aye. In the nursery."

The boys' eyes grew round with surprise at her words.

"Do you know which room is the nursery?"

In unison, they shook their heads, and Bryce called out to them, "Does my brother plan to display the Scot for all his men to see?"

"Aye, we think so. They'll surrender if they see their leader is dead."

"Kate, will you take them?"

She nodded. "But Aidan is asleep. I'd rather leave him here with you—under guard."

"Do not tarry, then. He may be my nephew, but I am no nursemaid."

Dismay and alarm swamped the Scots' ranks when Robert's body was dropped into their midst. They'd seen Douglas Ferguson killed and now they knew there was no choice but to retreat toward the gates, just as Edric had predicted. Drogan awaited Robert's men outside, and attacked them as they fled. Few managed to escape, and 'twas even possible Drogan let those few through to return home and tell of their defeat at Braxton Fell.

Edric hoped this would mean an end to warfare now, for Braxton needed peace in order to rebuild and replenish.

Upon the morrow, he would send Drogan to lead the fyrd to Dunfergus, where they would deal the killing blow. Empty wagons would follow him, and when Ferguson's lands were conquered, Drogan's men would fill those wagons with grain and other stores that were needed at Braxton.

The battle outside the gates lasted only an hour more. When it was done, Edric headed back to the stable to divest himself of his horse and his armor. He had only one goal in mind—to return to the keep and find Kate.

As soon as he found her, he was going to take her where she stood, and satisfy the lust that had been pounding in his veins since he first laid eyes on her.

Edric left the stable and started walking toward the keep, toward Kate, the woman who'd almost miraculously saved Braxton Fell from disaster. Killing Robert Ferguson had been a stroke of luck, something that Braxton Fell had been sorely lacking of late. If 'twas Kate of Rushton who brought such good fortune, then Edric was in no hurry to let her go.

Anticipating the pleasures they were about to share, he hurried toward the keep. Once he took the edge off his unrelenting lust, he was going to draw her into his bedchamber and remove every bit of clothing she wore, piece by piece, baring her delectable body to his hungry perusal. One hurried coupling would not be enough. Nor would two. He was going to taste every inch of her, make her cry out with pleasure, and he would sink so deeply into her that his hunger might finally be quenched.

He wanted her for the whole night.

When the keep came into sight, it looked as if every torch were burning, and Edric saw people from the eastern end of the village milling about on the main steps. They called to him for news as he approached—the chandler, the baker, a tinker. Edric did not understand what they were doing here, but he did not much care. Oswin could deal with them while he found Kate and dragged her up to his bedchamber.

He climbed the steps, but before he could enter, the door swung open and he saw a clamoring crowd inside the hall. Clenching his teeth, he realized 'twould be some time before he could go after Kate.

Chapter 12

After showing the youths to the nursery, Kathryn went down to the hall, where she walked among the villagers seeking shelter. There were so many, she ushered the poorest of them into the chapel to avoid Oswin's scorn and await word from Lord Edric or one of his men. She took particular care with the beggar family she'd seen earlier, the frightened parents and children with nowhere else to go, and no food to eat.

Just as all were settled upon benches and engaged in quiet prayer for the safety of the fyrd, Father Algar came into the chapel and began to chastise Kathryn for defiling God's house with the least welcome of all Braxton's people.

"*Mon père, s'il vous plaît.*" Angrily, she attempted to draw the priest away from those he insulted, but he pulled his arm away from her.

"Do not touch me, Norman!"

Kathryn composed herself, reluctant to rile the man any further, yet unwilling to allow him to disrupt the peace. "I beg your pardon, Father . . . Please come away. These people will do no harm and I am sure you are needed in the hall. Can you not allow the humblest of families to pray here in Lord Eric's chapel?"

He took hold of her upper arm with more strength than she would have thought him capable. 'Twas more than anger in his eyes . . . 'twas rage, not so much for what she had done here, but for who she was.

"Who are you to give orders here? You are cursed. The sooner you leave Braxton Fell, the better it will be for everyone." He waved his free arm toward the people on the benches. "Even them!"

Kathryn pulled away and hurried toward the door, stopping short when she saw the steward standing there. He'd observed her interchange with Father Algar, but said naught as she bolstered her courage and swept past him, going in search of a place that felt marginally less hostile.

Oswin would treat her with deference if he knew her true rank . . . Or mayhap not. She wondered if Cecily had been treated with respect, or if she'd met with the same disdain Kathryn had felt since her arrival at Braxton Fell. 'Twas only Lora's influence that had eased the animosity directed toward her from every Saxon here, with the exception of Drogan and Bryce.

Kathryn did not belong at Braxton Fell, any more than Cecily did, and she could hardly expect Lora to smooth the way for her at every turn.

Seeking to return to the quiet refuge of Bryce's chamber, Kathryn made her way through the crowd in the hall toward the stairs, but she did not go unnoticed. Some of the villagers called out to her.

"What news is there?" asked one of the shopkeepers she'd met near Lora's cottage.

"Naught," said Kathryn. "But 'tis early." At least, she hoped that was the only reason they hadn't heard from Lord Edric or any of the other men of the fyrd.

"I can smell smoke now," said an old woman nearby. "I couldn't before, but it's coming closer. They're burning the village!"

A ripple of panic ran through the crowd. Kathryn had to do something to help keep their terror at bay.

Uncertain and uneasy with what she was about to do, she climbed two steps and turned to speak. *"Non! Calmez-vous! Calmez-vous!* Is not Lord Edric a powerful warrior?"

Kathryn raised her voice and drew the attention of those who stood close by. "Your fyrd is the most powerful in the land. Have faith in them!"

More heads turned to look at her. "How can you think the Fergusons will prevail? Mighty Drogan stands with Lord Edric, and they fight to defend all at Braxton Fell!"

A few voices shouted in agreement and she felt encouraged to continue.

Edric pushed his way into the crowded hall and saw that most of the people were turned toward the staircase, quietly listening to the sound of a feminine voice. 'Twas Kate, and she stood on a step slightly above them, admonishing them to have confidence that Braxton's fyrd would triumph.

A feeling rushed through him, one unlike any he'd ever experienced. This maid from Normandy was calming his Saxon villagers and admonishing them in softly accented English to believe in him.

"Your warriors are the mightiest in the realm! Have you not seen them at practice? Have you never thought of the risks they take in your behalf?"

Edric caught sight of Oswin pushing through the crowd to get to her, and he thought his steward's scornful expression puzzling. She might be Norman, but her actions seemed entirely appropriate and lawful.

Edric also started moving in her direction, intending to get there before Oswin. The people made way for him, crossing themselves and calling out prayers of thanks when they realized who passed through their ranks.

Oswin reached the stairs first, and Edric saw him bend to speak to Kate. Her expression tightened and the color drained from her cheeks. Yet she stood her ground, deliberately turning away from the steward and calling out once more. "Soon your men will return to their homes and we will all be safe here, inside the walls of Braxton Fell"— she gave a quick glance toward Oswin—"just as King William intended these mighty walls to be used!"

Edric could do naught but admire her for holding her own, not only with Oswin, but through the whole night. She hadn't allowed her fears to overcome her, but had managed to keep her wits when Robert had sneaked into the nursery. She'd ensured Aidan's and Bryce's safety, and was now calming the people with her well-chosen words.

Oswin stepped away from the stairs, but when

the crowd moved aside for Edric to come forward, Kate's eyes alighted upon him. Her speech faltered and she put one hand upon her breast. Her eyes filled with moisture, and a tremulous smile warred with the single tear that rolled down her face. Edric felt a sudden, sharp pang in the center of his chest. He rubbed it away as he reached the steps and turned to the people who'd come to the hall for safety.

"The battle is done and the Fergusons gone, defeated once and for all!" Edric called out. "Return to the village now and help put out the fires!"

A cheer rose up and Edric could not resist pulling Kate into his embrace. He did no more than hug her, releasing her quickly and then going to Oswin. Beckoning the steward to his study as the crowd dispersed, Edric took a lamp and went into the private room.

"My deepest congratulations, Lord Edric," said Oswin.

"You should applaud the Norman maid, Oswin. 'Twas she who alerted us to the attack before it had even happened." He began to unbuckle the fastenings of his hauberk. "More remarkably, she was the one who killed Robert Ferguson."

Oswin made a rude noise. "That is hardly likely, my lord."

" 'Tis true. Ferguson stole into the nursery and tried to take Aidan. Kate prevented him."

Oswin placed his hands upon the desk and leaned forward, his expression intent. "Is that what she told you?"

Edric stopped moving. "Do you question the truth of it?"

Oswin straightened. "Do you think she could kill *you*, my lord? For Robert is every bit the warrior you are. Not so easily overcome."

"It matters not," Edric said, returning to the task of removing his armor. "One of the housemaids took part in the deed. Tomorrow will be soon enough to sort out the tale."

"My lord . . ."

The steward hesitated, but Edric wanted to waste no more time with the bitter old man. "Drogan will take the fyrd to Ferguson's holding tomorrow," he said. "They will finish the Scots and take what goods they leave."

Oswin nodded but said naught.

Edric took his leave, heading for the kitchen where there would be buckets of clean water. He took one outside and removed his sherte, then doused himself to wash away the stench of battle.

A moment later he was walking through the hall. He noticed the old cradle, lying near the chairs by the fireplace, and collected it before climbing the steps. Though it was not entirely proper to walk about the keep in this half-dressed manner, it seemed that he was the only one about. The servants and all those who'd come to the keep for shelter had now left.

Anyway, in a few short minutes, Edric would not be needing any clothes. He left the cradle at the door of his own bedchamber and made his way to the nursery where he found the door ajar and the room empty. Stepping inside, he held his lamp high and saw bloodstains beside Aidan's cradle. 'Twas there that Ferguson had died.

The bastard had sneaked in like a lowly mealworm and would have killed Aidan. Stomach-turning disgust filled him. The world was well rid of Robert Ferguson and his ilk. He had no doubt Drogan would be successful in routing the rest of the clan and taking what they'd stolen from Braxton Fell. He doubted it would be enough to see them through the winter, but it would certainly help.

He left the nursery and went on to his brother's chamber, hoping to find Kate there. Bryce was alone, but for the guard who was assigned to him.

"Where's Kate?" Edric asked. "Have you seen her?"

Bryce roused himself just enough to look over his brother's nearly naked form. "I'm impressed, brother," he said, "but I'm not sure the sight of so much flesh will attract an innocent maid."

"Where is she?"

Bryce pointed to the ceiling. "She might have gone to sit with Cecily's old nurse . . . mayhap she's helping Lora with Hrothgar's mother."

Edric left his drowsy brother to his sleep and took himself off to the back stairs. Reluctant to go near Berta's chamber, he went to the circular tower room first and found Lora with Elga. They looked up when they saw him.

"What is amiss here, Lora?"

"All was well until the fires started. Then Elga seemed to lose . . ." Lora shook her head in puzzlement. "She was not herself."

"Well, I've recovered, lass," said Elga. " 'Tis time we went home."

"Aye," Lora said quietly. "Edric, what news . . . What of Drogan?"

He'd seen Lora weep only once, and it had been when he'd told her of her husband's death. But a suspicious brightness filled her eyes now, and Edric realized that the huscarl's soft sentiments toward Lora were reciprocated.

"When last I saw him, Drogan was leading a

company of men to deal with the last of the Scottish stragglers. In the morn, he will set off for Ferguson lands to finish the deed."

Lora placed a hand upon Edric's wrist. "Thank you for this good news, my lord. I . . ."

He covered her hand and gave it a squeeze. "Have you seen Kate?"

"She went to Berta's room. I assume she is still there."

Edric turned to leave. When he reached the door, he looked back at Lora. "One more thing . . . When Drogan returns, put him out of his misery, will you?"

He did not wait for her reply, but quit the room and went in the direction of the bedchamber where Berta had retired. He had not given the woman much thought since Cecily's death. 'Twould probably be best to send her back home with Cecily's father when he came to see his grandson, but that would take some time. For Oswin had sent a message to Lichford only yesterday.

Turning the corner to the next corridor, he saw someone far ahead, coming out of the room. 'Twas Kate.

She hesitated when she saw him with his small lamp. "M-my lord, you startled me."

Her eyes glanced down to his naked chest and

Edric felt a punch of lust unlike anything he'd ever known.

Holding Aidan in her arms, she shut Berta's door behind her, but did not move. It occurred to him that he should tread carefully, but his lust outweighed his good judgment. Moving one step toward her, he saw her close her eyes and take a deep breath, as though girding herself against what would come. Edric closed the distance between them and drew her into his arms, holding their son between them.

No, Aidan was only *his* son, but at the moment, the distinction seemed a trivial one. With one hand, he touched her jaw, caressing her mouth with his thumb, then sliding his fingers into the hair behind her ear. He drew her close and kissed her.

He did not take her mouth gently, but claimed full possession at once, melding her lips to his in a primal fusion of her body to his. Instinct compelled him to take her there, to press her against the wall and claim her as his own. Instead, he broke the kiss, grabbed her hand and pulled her to the staircase, leading the way with the flickering light of his lamp.

He felt her tremble, but her unease did not deter him from his purpose. Partway down the stairs, he stopped and turned to her. As she stood on the step below, her mouth was level with his, but he did not trust himself to kiss it.

He slipped his free hand 'round her waist. Touching his mouth to her throat, he tasted her tender skin as he moved his hand lower, onto her gently rounded buttock.

Though he heard pure desire in the soft sound she made, her trepidation remained.

Yet he'd never wanted anyone the way he desired Kate.

"*Jesu*," he muttered, quickly resuming their descent, unwilling to give her time to draw away from him. 'Twould take but a few kisses, a few intimate caresses, to win her.

They soon arrived at Edric's bedchamber where he pushed open the door. Wasting no time, he picked up Aidan's cradle and put it inside, then set the lamp upon a small table near the bed.

The fire burned low in the grate, but neither of them noticed the chill in the air. Edric took Aidan and laid him in the cradle, covering him quickly with his blanket. He turned to Kate who stood perfectly still, shy and very much unsure.

"Do not fear me, sweeting. Touch me."

"I cannot . . . m-must not."

He took her hand and placed it upon the bare skin of his shoulder, then drew it down to the center of his chest.

Her palm was smooth and cool, and when her fingers slid across his nipple, Edric's cock throbbed in anticipation.

"Can you deny the attraction that arcs between us?"

Her throat moved tightly and he tipped his head, then kissed her softly, pulling her fully against him, causing a sweet kind of agony.

He did not think his cock could grow any more, or become any harder, but when he pressed against her, he worried that he might finish, when they'd barely just begun. Kissing her lightly on her cheeks, then on her jaw and down the tender flesh of her neck, he shifted his position, untied the laces that held her bodice closed, and slid the garment down her arms.

Edric dipped his head down and lightly licked her nipple through the thin cloth of her chemise. Her head fell back, and when he touched her other breast with his fingertips, she gave a soft cry. "*Encore,*" she murmured in French, and Edric knew the battle was won. "More."

He lifted her into his arms and carried her to the bed. Lowering her gently, he followed her down, releasing his belt and lowering his braies at the same time. She slid her fingers into the hair at the back of his head, and pulled him down for her kiss.

Hunger, raw and fierce, swept through him and he savaged her with his tongue, so aroused he had difficulty working the ties at her waist. In a haze of need, he heard the cloth tear, and broke the kiss long enough to pull her skirts from her.

Naked but for the stockings gartered on her thighs, she was the epitome of all that was feminine. Her lush breasts and narrow waist, the fleeting fragrance of lavender, her warm, wet center . . . everything about her incited him, but he forced himself to go slowly, to savor every moment.

He nipped her neck just below her ear, and allowed his hands to glide up from her waist to touch the soft undersides of her breasts. She arched in response, pushing the tips of her breasts closer to his chest.

She placed her hands upon his shoulders as he'd shown her before, but moved them down, feathering them lightly until she touched his own pebbled nipples again. He groaned, surprised at how sensitive she could make them. Never before had a woman's touch wreaked such havoc with his senses.

Her fingertips brushed him, then closed upon those sensitive points, and fire shot directly to his groin. Closing his eyes tightly, he savored the fierce burn, wondering how this untried maid could bring about such exquisite sensations.

Relishing her attentions, Edric rolled to his back and pulled her onto him, determined to prolong his endurance. He felt her moist, feminine lips open for him as she straddled his hips, and knew it would take only one fleet movement to slide his cock into her hot sheath.

He restrained himself, and drew one of her peaked nipples into his mouth. Circling that lush tip with his tongue, he felt gratified by her sharp gasp. Feeling her tremble, he reached down, seeking her most responsive part. The last time he'd spread her legs wide and touched her there, she'd come apart with pleasure.

He planned to show her heaven again, and not only once. Dipping his fingers inside her, he found her slick and hot, and ready for his entry.

Still, he held back, aware that a virgin needed the perfect seduction. As he sucked and teased her nipples he circled the center of her pleasure with his fingers, rubbing softly at first, but increasing the pressure as her hips bucked against him in a wild response to his touch.

"Aye, my beauty," he whispered. "Come for me."

"Oh!" The word was but a quiet sound upon a quick breath, and she fell onto him, her breasts against his chest, her face in the crook of his shoulder.

Her thighs tightened 'round him, but he was not yet finished with her. He turned her once again, and when she lay beneath him, he kissed a path from her neck to her belly, keeping his eyes on hers, stirred by the utter astonishment in her eyes.

He slid his hands down her thighs and felt the knife at her garter. Pulling it out, he dropped it to the floor and positioned himself between her legs.

He kissed the soft skin of her inner thigh. Nipping and licking his way up, he reached the apex of her legs and looked his fill at her womanly center.

"Edric!" She started to squirm under his perusal, attempting to close her legs.

"Hold still for my kiss," he said.

"Oh!"

He put his mouth on her, licking her slick heat, spearing her with his tongue. He felt her hands upon his shoulders, but she did not protest his actions, rather, she opened for him, exposing her very essence to him.

Her fervor drove him on, and he laved the tip of her mound, her most sensitive flesh, until her pretty bottom came off the mattress.

"Mon Dieu! Mon Dieu!"

He rose up on his forearms and positioned his cock at her entrance, ready to plunge. But he did not. The thought of her small, tight sheath both aroused and cautioned him. He did not want to cause her any pain.

Sweat broke out on his forehead as he slowly penetrated her and reached the barrier of her virginity. "Kate . . ."

Uncertainty clouded her eyes.

"Do you trust me?"

Without hesitation, she pulled him down for her kiss.

'Twas all the answer he needed. He thrust deeply into her, then held perfectly still at her cry of discomfort. " 'Twill soon be all right," he said, dearly hoping his words were true.

Her muscles tightened 'round him and she moved slightly, encouraging him to withdraw and plunge again. *"Jesu!"* he muttered. Naught had ever felt so sweet, so intensely right. "Better?"

"Oh! Aye." She quickly learned the rhythm of his movements and met every thrust of his hips, welcoming him inside. Edric's heart pounded and his breath came so fast he was nearly dizzy with pleasure. There was an odd catch to her movements, somehow increasing the erotic sensations, drawing him ever closer to his culmination.

It hit him like a thunderbolt, crashing through

his body, starting at his cock and ballocks, and shooting into his chest until it swelled and he felt as if it might burst. His muscles tightened and released in a spasm so strong 'twas almost painful, yet the sensation was exquisite. Tremors racked his body as his climax continued, and Kate's contractions prolonged it.

It seemed hours before he could move again, and he lowered himself to his side, pulling Kate with him as he stayed imbedded within her.

He was in no rush to leave her.

Chapter 13

❦

Kathryn could not find any words. Lying on her side, face-to-face with Edric, she was unsure whether to feel embarrassment or bliss. He was still inside her, and she was glad their intimate connection felt too good for him to withdraw.

He closed his eyes and brushed her lips with his mouth, and she felt his sex tug inside her. "Ah, Kate."

"Umm . . ."

She should not have submitted, should never have given herself to this man who had vowed not to take another wife. Yet she could not regret her actions. She cared for Edric, as she would never care for another.

" 'Twill be better next time."

"I do not know how that is possible," she said, smoothing his hair back from his forehead. Her hand lingered there, and Kathryn realized how much she loved to touch him. She let her fingers drift to his shoulder and down his arm, learning the swells and indentations of each muscle and sinew as she moved. She touched his chest, spearing her fingers through the dark, crisp hair that grew there.

He made a low sound and moved his hips, pulling her leg higher to rest on his hip. Kathryn closed her eyes as he growled and started nipping at her neck. He touched her intimately again, caressing the same spot that had propelled her to the height of wanton pleasure before.

It felt different now, with his fingers working their sorcery while he moved inside her. Sensations flooded her, and she heard herself whimper with delight. An instant later, she was soaring through the clouds high above Braxton Fell, her flesh and bones scattered to the wind. Somewhere far away yet impossibly close, she felt him shudder within her, felt his hot seed spill deep inside her once again.

It took several long minutes before Kathryn returned to earth and could breathe again. She knew her heart was in her eyes, but she did not care. She loved him.

"How do you do that to me?" Tenderly, she stroked the crease that had formed between his brows. "I never knew . . ."

His jaw clenched once before he spoke, and he pulled out of her. "'Tis just sex. Mating is always a pleasure."

Kathryn recoiled as if he'd clouted her. If it had been his intention to cheapen their lovemaking, he'd succeeded. She reached for the blanket and pulled it over herself, shuddering, wishing she'd guarded her heart more carefully.

Edric rolled from the bed and went to the fireplace. He laid a fire and lit it, poking at it until it caught while Kathryn tried to figure a way to get her clothes on and leave before she made an emotional fool of herself. Clearly, what she felt for him was not reciprocated and that knowledge swelled painfully in her chest. What he'd done with her was no different from what he'd shared with Cecily . . . or any other woman he'd bedded.

Perilously close to tears, she held the blanket close and slipped from the bed. She located her chemise and started to draw it over her head, but he stopped her.

"You are very beautiful naked," he said, holding her wrist in his strong hand.

'Twas not true. Oft had it been said that Isabel was the beauty of the family, and Kathryn realized Edric intended his flattery to soften his previous words. She attempted to cover herself with her hands, but he would have none of it.

"Come back to bed."

Emotion fluttered in her chest. There was nowhere she'd rather be than caught up in Edric's strong arms. She had made her decision to make love with him, and would shed no tears for what could not be.

Standing close, Edric gently pulled her hands from her body and looked his fill. He touched the engorged peaks of her breasts, then bent to lick them. "So perfect," he whispered. "And this," he added, sliding his hand down to her feminine core.

Kathryn fumbled with her chemise and held it in front of her, taking a step back. Regardless of her decision, this was too much. It was a sensuous onslaught. She needed a moment's reprieve, time to gather her thoughts and emotions, a chance to adjust to the turmoil within her.

"Aidan will wake soon and want to be fed," she said, ashamed that she had not thought of the bairn even once since Edric had taken him from her arms.

"Where is his milk?" Edric asked, pulling on a long, woolen tunic.

"In Lord Bryce's chamber." She'd left it there earlier, and had forgotten it with all that had happened since.

Edric started for the door, but came back to her, pulling her into his arms for a kiss that seared her with its potency, leaving her knees weak and her heart palpitating.

Bryce awoke when Edric entered the room, but his guard slept on, quietly snoring. The crock of milk was on the hearth, the same place where Kate kept it in the nursery. " 'Tis late," Bryce said groggily.

"Aye," Edric replied, uninterested in a midnight conversation with his brother. He had better things to do.

"Ahhh," said Bryce knowingly when Edric picked up Aidan's milk and headed for the door.

" 'Tis not your concern," Edric replied.

"Take care, brother," Bryce said. "If the Norman is a gently bred lass . . . You dabble where no one but a husband should go."

Edric barely gave his brother a glance before

quitting the room. Kate had made it clear that she would not return to her home, and he had every intention of keeping her at Braxton. He would never have believed a Norman capable of such passion in the bedchamber, but Kate had surpassed all his expectations. She was a lioness in bed who'd mistaken lust for something else. Something elusive and quite impossible.

Fortunately, he'd seen signs of a virgin's infatuation in her eyes and had set her straight about what had transpired between them. They would have many a night like this together and he did not want her mistaking their bed play for some elusive dream.

He heard Aidan's whimpers when he returned to his chamber, and when he entered, saw Kate in her thin chemise, carrying the bairn to and fro, rocking him gently in her arms. The pretty sight struck him physically, in the lowest part of his back. It weakened his legs, but heated his groin with something other than arousal. Some feeling he did not recognize.

She looked up at him then, and smiled.

Edric cleared the thickness from his throat and went inside. There was something different about her . . . mayhap a slight reddening of her nose, and he wondered if she'd been weeping. Fortunately, he saw no sign of tears over her lost virginity, so he took her hand and drew her back to bed. "Feed him here."

Divesting himself of his tunic, Edric slid in behind her and pulled her against his chest. Kate lowered the top half of her chemise, yet remained modestly covered as she fed Aidan, and Edric's cock grew against her back. She spoke soft French words to the bairn as he drank, and Edric moved her hair aside to nuzzle her neck. He wanted to hear her say those words to him.

"You could never have left Aidan," he murmured, sure that it was so. "You are more a mother to him than his own would have been."

He felt her stiffen, but when he slipped his hands 'round to her breasts, she seemed to melt. As she sighed, her body eased back into his, and he lowered her chemise to her waist, teasing the tips of her breasts, wishing 'twas her milk that fed his son.

"Edric, I lose myself when you do this," she said tremulously. "You must let me feed Aidan without distraction."

"Ah, but I cannot resist." He kissed her ear. "These globes were meant for my touch, meant for my tongue."

She shivered at his words and he knew she would have covered herself in embarrassment if her hands had not been fully occupied with Aidan.

Her self-consciousness was enchanting, but he wanted no awkwardness or shame between them.

"Is he finished?"

She gave a slight nod and took the crock from Aidan. Lifting him to her shoulder, she patted his back and he soon gave a satisfied belch.

"Will he sleep now?"

"Likely not," Kate replied. "There is more to being a nursemaid than simply feeding the bairn."

"No doubt you will show me."

He heard a smile in her voice when she spoke. "No doubt."

From Aidan's position at Kate's shoulder, he faced his father. He began to gurgle and bat at Edric with his tiny fist. "He is a fighter already."

"No he's not. He is French—*très doux*."

Edric did not contradict her. "Then it must be that I rouse his baser instincts, for he is trying to thrash me."

She laughed softly at his jest and he shifted their positions, turning her in his arms. With Aidan between them, their eyes met and Edric tipped his head down, drawing her close. He touched his lips to hers, kissing her lightly, surprising himself with the fullness of sentiment behind the gesture— gratitude for the care of his son, affection for the way she'd spoken to the crowd in the hall, respect for dealing with Robert Ferguson in spite of her fears.

She astonished him. And she pulled away first.

"My lord, he'll want to be entertained."

"As will I," Edric replied, dipping lower to nip at her breast. 'Twas so much better to keep the bed play uncomplicated, just as he'd have done with Felicia.

She pushed away and lowered Aidan to the mattress where he lay upon his back, fully awake, kicking his legs and jabbing his hands at the air. Kate raised her chemise to her shoulders and slipped her arms in, covering her breasts from his view. Still, as he leaned back against the wall, he enjoyed the delicate lines of her neck and the smooth, feminine muscles of her arms as she and Aidan amused each other. "Look what a comely lad he is, my lord," she said, touching the cleft in Aidan's chin. "He will be an exceptional man, I think."

She spoke softly to the bairn, too, gentle words he knew he would never have heard from Cecily's lips.

Kathryn awoke early, at Aidan's first whimper.

Edric slept soundly behind her, and she left the bed to bathe quickly and slip on her chemise. Gathering Aidan into her arms, she took a seat in the chair by the fire to feed him, unready to face Edric just yet.

She blushed when she thought of all they had done the night before, and winced slightly at the discomfort resulting from the unfamiliar, vigorous activities.

Clearly, he believed their activities amounted to no more than a carefree diversion. But Kathryn knew better. There would come a day when he realized there was more.

The three of them—she and Edric and Aidan—were already a family, whether he knew it or not.

But she could not face revealing to everyone in the keep what had transpired between them.

As soon as Aidan finished, Kathryn dressed and slipped out of the room with the bairn in her arms. She had no intention of returning to the nursery where she'd killed Robert Ferguson, but there were other rooms in Edric's massive fortress. There had to be one she could make her own.

'Twas still dark inside the keep, so Kathryn moved along carefully until she reached the stairs that led down to the hall. The embers in the fireplace gave her enough light to find her way to the main door. She left the keep, unsure where she would go.

In the predawn light, she saw the ravages of the night's battle. 'Twas hard to believe it had only been last night that she'd killed Robert Ferguson and Edric had gone to battle. So much had happened since her abduction from Kettwyck that she had difficulty keeping accurate track of the time. Had she been at Braxton Fell for months or was it only days? How could she have fallen so hard and so deeply for the lord of this estate and his son?

Holding Aidan close, Kathryn walked east, toward the gate that would lead to the lane where Lora's cottage was located, hoping she would find her friends at home. She crossed the bridge and saw that several of the outermost buildings had been burned. The charred shells remained standing, but the devastation was severe.

It looked as though few of the villagers had slept, for they were out and about, carrying buckets and tools to and from the burned area. When they met Kathryn on the lane going toward Lora's cottage, many of them tipped their hats to her, or gave a quick bow of acknowledgment. One woman called to her from her cottage. "'Tis said you saved the village, mistress." The woman's three children gathered about her skirts. "We thank you."

Kathryn did not know what to say, so she gave a brief nod and continued walking. But her path was soon impeded by others who stopped to thank her for her part in thwarting the Fergusons, and to ask if the rumors were true . . . that it was *she* who'd killed Robert.

She'd met many of these people before, when she'd walked this way with Lora, but she'd felt like an outsider then. This time, there was a warmth and appreciation that was wholly different, as well as unexpected. They clamored 'round her and called her praises.

"Lord Edric will reward you richly!" called one woman.

"When Drogan returns, we'll have all we need," said another.

"You raised the alarm and made us flee to safety!"

"Who would have thought 'twould be a Norman who killed the Ferguson," one of the men pondered aloud.

Someone put a shawl 'round Kathryn's shoulders against the chill of the morning. "I—I never meant to . . . He threatened Lord Edric's son so I . . ." Moved by their unexpected kindness, tears suddenly filled her eyes.

" 'Twas well done, lass," said one of the men, patting her shoulder to comfort her. 'Twas with relief that Kathryn saw Lora, carrying her own bucket toward the well. Blinking away her tears, she took her leave of the villagers and followed Lora's path, catching up to the red-haired healer as she drew her water from the well.

"Good morn to you, Kate. All is well?"

Kathryn nodded. "How is Elga?" she asked Lora.

"Better. She is terrified of fire, and last night the fires burned much too close." She narrowed her gaze. "You are out and about quite early, are you not?"

"Er, Aidan woke me, and since he did not seem inclined to go back to sleep, I decided to get some air."

Lora drew her full bucket up and out of the well. "Aye, well, the air is foul just beyond the tanner's. But thankfully, most of the village is unscathed . . . thanks to you."

Kathryn made no reply, but walked beside Lora as she returned to her cottage. They went inside where Elga was still asleep.

Mayhap Kathryn's appearance had changed since her night in Edric's bed, or 'twas her lack of conversation, but when Lora stopped and looked directly at her, the woman's brow furrowed with concern. "What is it? What is amiss?" she asked quietly, her gaze seeming more penetrating than usual. "Is Bryce—"

"No, no," Kathryn quickly reassured her. "I did

not see him this morn, so I can only assume his condition is unchanged."

What she had shared with Edric during the night was not something she could discuss with anyone. She'd wept her tears for what could never be, then made her decision to accept what affection Edric would give her. Yet she could never make her shameful position public.

She'd become his leman.

"Sit down, Kate," said Lora. "You've suddenly become so pale. Have you broken your fast?"

The healer took Aidan from her, and when Kathryn had taken a seat at the table, Lora gave her a mug of water, along with a slice of bread and a portion of cheese.

"I'm not hungry . . . I think it must just be the shock of seeing those shops burned . . ."

Lora went to the door and peered out at all the damage done by the Fergusons. "Aye. 'Twas terrible. The men worked all night to quell the flames and make the buildings safe for habitation. If not for you—"

"Where is Drogan?" Kathryn asked. Drogan was the one person who would guess that she and Edric had become lovers. He seemed to sense everything that happened to Edric and Bryce, and he would surely realize that her association with Edric had changed.

Lora returned to the table and sat down across from Kathryn. "He's gone to finish what's left of Ferguson's warriors."

Kathryn made a face and shuddered.

"No one at Braxton Fell will mourn the end of them. Not after the years of trouble between us. Besides, Drogan will bring back their harvest and all their livestock. Mayhap 'twill be all we need in order to survive the winter."

A quiet knock sounded at the cottage door. When Lora opened it, they saw Caedmon, one of the grooms, standing outside, out of breath from running. He pulled off his hood when he spoke to Lora. "Greetings, mistress. I've been sent to fetch you to the hall."

Lora gave a quick glance in Elga's direction, but did not hesitate to get her bag of potions. "She'll be all right if we leave her. Tell me what's happened."

" 'Tis Lord Bryce. He's feverish and talking nonsense."

Chapter 14

E dric's mood vacillated between jubilant and discouraged. His night of bliss had ended when he'd awakened alone. Quickly pulling on some clean clothes, he'd gone in search of Kate.

Beautiful Kate. He could barely catch his breath when he thought of her in the throes of passion. There was nothing more appealing than the sight of a woman taking her pleasure while coupling with her man. He should not have become aroused by the mere image of her in his mind, having been sated so often during the night, but his desire for her seemed endless.

He realized he should have shown some restraint with his virgin lover, and hoped she was not too tender this morn. The muscles of his chest contracted when he considered how he would make it up to her.

She was nowhere to be found in the keep. Since no one had seen her, Edric realized she must have left his bed at an early hour, indeed. It occurred to him that she must have wanted to get away from his chamber before anyone saw her.

She was embarrassed.

He frowned at the realization, but decided her unintended discretion was for the best. 'Twould not do for Father Algar to learn of their liaison, or they would have no end of sermons on the evil of fornication and the fires of hell. Nor would Oswin take it well, not after Edric's disastrous marriage with Cecily and the man's ill feelings toward every other Norman.

Edric started toward Bryce's chamber and was met by the man on guard. "My lord, I was just about to come for you."

"Aye? What is amiss, Desmond?" Edric asked, going into Bryce's room.

"Your brother became overrestless in his sleep. When he spoke, he made no sense. His speech was garbled, his skin hot, my lord."

Bryce's lips were dry. Edric reached for a mug

of water and encouraged his brother to take a sip.

"Find one of the grooms to go for Lora. She'll know what to do."

"Aye, my lord. I already took the liberty of doing so."

The guard stepped outside and Edric was left alone with his brother. He took the blanket off him and looked at the wound. The edges at one end had turned an angry red, the worst possible development after an injury such as Bryce's.

"Bryce?"

The young man moaned in response, then tried to turn over, wincing with the effort it took. Edric would have helped him move, but he thought it best not to jar him. "Here, take some more water," he said, unreasonably expecting Kate to turn up. Unreasonably *hoping* she would turn up.

'Twas an eternity before Lora arrived. Worry and concern darkened her eyes when she looked at Bryce.

"Stand aside, Edric. Let me examine him."

Lora set her canvas satchel upon the bed beside Bryce's knees and Edric stepped away. He took note of Kate then, holding Aidan as she stood under the lintel of the door. Part of the shadow that had hovered over him since awakening alone disappeared. He would have gathered her into his arms, but for her distant expression and the formal tone of her words. "Lord Edric . . . What is amiss?"

There was barely a flicker of acknowledgment of what had transpired between them and he realized she had said naught of her night to Lora.

He turned back to Bryce. "His wound has become foul."

Worry clouded her soft brown eyes, the eyes that had shuddered closed with pleasure uncounted times through the night.

Edric gave himself a mental shake. He could not relive every amorous moment while Bryce lay here so dangerously ill. "Will you come in?" he asked her.

Her delicate throat moved as she swallowed. "No, forgive me. I . . . I . . ."

He remembered her unease in the sickroom. "'Tis all right, Kate. Go and take care of my son."

She seemed torn, and he wanted to touch her, to reassure her. But she soon turned and took her leave, and Edric returned to his brother's bedside.

"Hold his arms," Lora said.

Edric did as he was told and Bryce moaned as Lora split the stitches where the wound had putrefied. She took water and a clean cloth, and washed the wound, squeezing out whatever poison had tainted it. When she was finished with the most delicate part of her task, Edric was aware of her frequent sidelong glances.

"What is it? Can you cure his fever?"

"I'll do what I can. Tell me about Kate."

"What about her?"

Lora pressed her lips tightly together as she worked on Bryce's wound and he groaned. "Keep his hands away."

"What about Kate?"

"She nearly fainted in my cottage this morn."

Edric frowned, clenching his jaw muscles. "What happened? Why—"

"I thought it was hunger," she said, stopping what she was doing to Bryce. "But she said not. Mayhap 'twas just that I'd asked about Bryce and it brought back memories of *this*."

"So hot," Bryce moaned. "Take it out. Take it out!"

"The fever has addled his brain," Lora said. "Help me raise him up."

Lora fed him a potion that was meant to cool his blood, and they gave him as many draughts of water as he would take, but the delirium continued.

"Will you stay with him?"

Lora nodded. "But will you send one of the servants to check on Elga for me? Her mind seemed right by the time we returned to the cottage last night, but I'd like to be sure."

Edric agreed, but before he could leave the chamber, Oswin arrived. He questioned Lora about Bryce's condition, then turned to Edric "If you can be spared, my lord, I would like a moment with you."

"Aye. Go," said Lora, and the two men left Bryce's chamber and went down to Edric's study.

Edric sat, but Oswin paced. "My lord, about last eve . . . 'Twas not seemly for the Norman to make herself so important here. When have we ever allowed serving maids to dictate what is done in your hall?"

"It worked out well, did it not?"

"Lord Edric, you are missing the point."

"I don't think so. At great personal risk, she raised the alarm and brought the villagers to the keep where they were safe during the course of the battle. 'Twas by her hand that Robert Ferguson met his end."

"That remains to be seen. I've spoken to Gwen—"

Edric stood abruptly. "And what does *that* maid say?"

"My lord, I would only remind you that there are other ways to look at what happened."

"I don't think so."

Oswin clasped his hands behind his back. "She is a comely maid, my lord. After your year of—"

"Of what, Oswin? Celibacy? Do you imply I am thinking only with my cock?"

The steward was visibly taken aback. "My lord, as a friend of your father . . . I beg you to think of Braxton Fell in your dealings with that giglet."

Edric took a deep breath and walked away from his desk, wondering if Oswin was right. Had his year of sexual frustration distorted his judgment? " 'Twill be a cold day in hell before any Norman holds sway over me ever again."

Oswin seemed to relax with Edric's statement. "What news of Drogan?"

Kathryn collected the milk she would need for the day and returned to Lora's cottage. She did not think Elga should be left alone, not so soon after her upset over the Scots' attack, and there was no doubt Lora would have to stay with Bryce at least until his condition improved.

So would Edric. He was as devoted to Bryce as Kathryn was to her sister, Isabel. 'Twas one of the things that endeared him to her.

Yet her feelings could never be made known, neither to Edric nor to anyone else at Braxton Fell. Their liaison was forbidden in every respect, not the least of which was her lack of honesty with him. She'd allowed him to believe she was a serving maid, but if he ever discovered she was the daughter of Baron Henri Louvet, the depth of his contempt would be bottomless.

She might have killed Robert Ferguson, but that did not alter the fact that she was a Norman. The Saxons' gratitude would soon cool and they would once again remember that she was an outsider.

Elga was out of bed and dressed when Kathryn arrived at the cottage, and she explained where Lora had gone and why. "I'd like to stay a while," she said, "and mayhap you could teach me to weave."

She sat with the older woman while she broke her fast, and after putting Aidan on the bed to sleep, the two went into the weaving room. Elga would not allow Kathryn to touch her looms, but started her with a ball of soft woolen thread and two long, wooden sticks. "Can you knit?"

Kathryn shook her head. "No, I never learned."

"What *can* you do, then?"

"Well, I'm not entirely useless. I can take care of livestock," said Kathryn proudly, but Elga did not seem impressed. "I can cipher and keep records."

The woman's eyes widened at this, and Kathryn realized her mistake. No villein on any estate would have these skills. She shrugged as though it meant naught. "I learned at the abbey . . . I—I lived there for years before coming to England."

Elga seemed placated by Kathryn's explanation, so the first lesson began.

"Go," said Lora. "Get some food in your belly. You've left this chamber only once all day and your pacing does not help."

Edric's stomach growled again and he realized she was right. He needed to eat, and he had a few other matters to attend to. Bryce was in good hands.

He took his leave and went to the nursery again, and saw that it had been tidied and the floor washed. No signs of the attack remained. Still, he did not want his son to stay in that room ever again.

The solar where he'd given Kate her first lesson in defense was close to his own bedchamber and spacious enough to accommodate a large bed—one he planned to visit frequently—as well as having room for Aidan's cradle. There was also plenty of space for the settee and two chairs to remain.

Returning to the great hall, he took note of the changes Kate had wrought and saw that it was more like the home he remembered, the place where he and Bryce had been born and raised. She'd found another of his father's banners, and had had it hung from the rafters above the dais. A quick glance at the stair reminded him of all she'd said the night before as she'd stood a step above his people—a foreigner, addressing the mob that had gathered there for protection.

Her actions were more like those of a highborn lady than a Norman peasant, and he knew there was much that she concealed from him.

Thoroughly satisfied with their situation as it was, he would not press her for information. If she did not want to return to Rushton, 'twas her own affair. But he was not going to allow her to leave for the nunnery at Evesham Bridge. 'Twould be a terrible waste.

Drogan had taken most of Braxton's fyrd with him to Dunfergus, and so there were few guards left to watch over the keep. But young Caedmon stood at the door, ready to act in defense of all within if necessary. Edric asked him to find Kate.

"My lord, she went back to the village. She stays with Elga in Lora's absence."

Edric did not acknowledge his disappointment, but returned to Bryce's room and stood by while one of the servants assisted Lora in bathing Bryce's arms and body with cool water. "The potion helped somewhat," Lora said. "But he's still too warm, still delirious."

"Is there anything else we can do?" Edric asked.

"I've expelled the poisons from the wound and

put a poultice on it. He's taken the willow bark potion for his fever, and we're bathing him to cool him. I know of nothing more to do."

"Then why don't *you* go down to the kitchen for a meal. I'll stay here with Bryce."

"Aye, I'll do that. Did you send someone to see about Elga?"

"Kate is with her," Edric said.

Lora smiled. "She knew Elga had a difficult night. 'Tis very kind of her to keep her company in my absence."

Edric frowned. He had not thought of Kate's visit to Elga as a deliberate favor to Lora, yet it must have been.

Lora left the room and Edric sat down on the mattress next to Bryce. His brother's cheeks were flushed and his eyes dull. "Edric."

Edric took his brother's hot, dry hand. "Aye. I'm here."

"Ferguson . . . He's sneaking in through the—"

"No, Bryce. Léod and Robert are both dead."

"But your son—Aidan . . ."

Edric calmed his brother with reassurances that all was well. He placed a cool, wet cloth upon Bryce's forehead and implored him to sleep.

"Guard your eyes when you look at her, Edric."

"My eyes?" Edric was unsure what new delusion clouded Bryce's mind.

"They tell what you feel for her."

"What I—?" Kate. He was speaking of Kate. "You're imagining things, Bryce. Try to rest."

He meant what he'd told Oswin. What he felt for the Norman was no more than what he would feel for any comely maid who deigned to share his bed. The only Norman who would ever hold sway over him again was King William. Now that they'd gotten rid of Ferguson, Edric might even travel south to meet with the Norman king and address the requirements of his enfeoffment. Somehow, the reputedly astute William had misapprehended the resources at Braxton Fell. 'Twas time that mistake was corrected.

"Deceive yourself if you will . . ." Bryce muttered and then drifted off to sleep.

When Kathryn left Elga's cottage, 'twas nearly dusk. For hours, she'd had to force herself to stay away from the keep and to stop wondering whether Edric would have spent the day with her had Bryce not become ill.

'Twas a foolish notion. She was not his chatelaine. She had no part in the affairs of his estate or matters of housekeeping, unless they involved Aidan. She was Edric's leman and nothing more. Soon every servant in the keep would know it, and the whole village, as well.

Kathryn tamped down her embarrassment at that thought and held Aidan against her breast. She'd wanted the affection of a husband, a chance for that small seed of sentiment to develop into something more. She'd taken a lover instead.

She hurried past the church with bowed head, aware that she should go inside and confess her sin. But fear fluttered in her chest when she thought of facing the malevolent little priest. He would surely curse her for her transgression.

And Kathryn could not blame him, for she did not repent, nor would she refuse Edric access to her bed . . . to her body, or her heart. He owned them all.

"You!"

The harsh voice startled Kathryn and she stumbled when Father Algar took hold of her and pulled her 'round to face him. She tried to tug away, but his fist felt like iron pincers on her upper arm.

"'Twill be on your conscience if Lord Bryce dies!"

Kathryn almost felt relieved that he did not confront her about sharing Edric's bed, and she trembled at the thought of what he would do when he learned of it. *"Mon père,"* she said in an attempt to placate him. "I assure you, I mean no one at Braxton any harm. 'Twas I who discovered Robert Ferguson's plan—"

Algar shook her. "And just how did you know he would sneak into the keep?"

"How did I— I did *not* know!" she cried, surprised at the priest's implication.

"'Tis just like a Norman to lie! You let him in, then you killed him to gain Lord Edric's trust!"

Kathryn managed to pull away. The man was certainly deranged if he thought she could possibly have devised such a convoluted plan. There was no point in talking to him, no point in explaining that she'd had naught to do with Ferguson beyond being abducted by him and his clan. And that she was grateful to be quit of the Scots.

He would not believe her.

She hurried away and wondered if he'd convinced anyone else of his improbable theory. Taking her skirts in hand, she rushed up the steps to the keep and let herself inside, only to run into Edric who was coming out. Caught off balance, he caught her by the shoulders.

"Kate, I was just about to come looking for you."

His words rushed through her and she smiled.

"You're trembling," he said. "What's happened?"

"Naught, my lord. Tell me of Lord Bryce. Is he . . . ?"

"The same."

"I am sorry," she said quietly as he drew her

through the hall toward the stairs. He smelled like the coarse soap they'd used at the abbey and she realized he must have bathed. She wanted to press her face to his chest and breathe deeply of him.

"Lora and I will stay with him tonight."

Kathryn nodded. She'd thought he would.

"Caedmon," he called to the young groom in the hall, "go to the barn for a fresh crock of milk. Put it in Lord Bryce's chamber."

Kathryn climbed the stairs with Edric and followed him into the solar. Closing and barring the door after them, he took the bairn and laid him in his cradle. The room had been turned into a nursery, but Kathryn had little chance to survey all the changes before Edric returned to her, taking her in his arms to kiss her.

Angling his head to deepen the kiss, he opened her mouth with his tongue and slid inside as his hands moved down to her buttocks. Kathryn did not understand how he could arouse her so quickly and easily, but she felt the hard ridge of his erection and knew he felt the same.

Aching for his touch, she pressed her feminine center against him. Without breaking the kiss, he raised her skirts and slipped his hand under them and she knew he would find her needy and hot. Passion flared with one touch of his fingers and she quaked in his arms, her pleasure culminating in an intense burst that weakened her knees and made her heart flutter.

"You are so beautiful," he said, breaking the kiss, but touching his lips to her ear, then her neck. He let her skirts down and filled his hands with her breasts, her exquisitely sensitive nipples.

Still breathless, Kathryn unfastened his belt and slipped her hands into his braies. Encircling his cock, she ran her fingers down its length and back up, then dropped to her knees. "Oh, *Jesu*," Edric said unsteadily when she licked the tip. He buried his hands in her hair and bucked his hips, sliding his erection into her mouth.

She sucked gently, then hard, pleasuring him with her mouth as he'd done to her more than once during the night.

Edric's breath came out in a halting rasp and she knew she'd pleased him. She became more daring, using one hand to fondle his ballocks as she swirled her tongue 'round his shaft. She nipped at him lightly with her teeth and reached 'round to the back of his thigh, digging her fingers in to anchor herself, and to hold him steady.

His reaction to her attentions caused a quickening in her own loins, an arousal so intense, she shuddered with it. He moaned and she felt a distinct tightening in his flesh. He jerked suddenly, spilling his seed as Kathryn met with her own fiery climax.

Kathryn sank to the floor and Edric dropped to his knees beside her. Neither of them spoke, but he put his arms 'round her and pulled her close, content in the quiet of the moment.

Chapter 15

❧

Bryce's fever continued until the evening of the third day. Finally his eyes cleared and he was more lucid than he'd been for half the week.

"You had us worried, brother," said Edric when Bryce asked for a cup of ale. He'd shaved the younger man to make it easier to bathe him and his face looked gaunt and pale. Edric went to the door and summoned a maid to bring the beer while Lora came wearily to her feet and looked at the wound again.

She wiped the poultice from Bryce's skin and sighed with relief. " 'Tis clean. Finally."

The redness was gone, and the edges had knitted together. "Will you let me up now?"

Lora smiled. "Aye. If you feel strong enough."

"What I'd like is a bath to wash the stink of this bed off me."

"Aye. You're due for some clean bedclothes," said Lora, who left to give orders to the servants.

Edric helped Bryce put on a clean sherte and got him out of the bed and into a chair. "I feel as though someone dropped a barrow full of rocks on my head. What's the news, Edric? Is Drogan back yet?"

"No, though I expect him any day."

"What of Kate? Is she still here?"

"Aye."

"No trips to Evesham Bridge, then?"

The maid arrived with Bryce's mug of ale and he took a sip. Edric did not respond to his brother's question, unwilling to discuss Kate with Bryce or anyone else, though he certainly hoped she'd put all thoughts of going to the nunnery from her head.

"And Aidan?"

"Growing." His son had started to fill out, and did not look quite as fragile as he had at first. Kate's attentions were good for the lad.

During Bryce's illness, she'd been left to her own devices and Edric had no knowledge of how she'd spent her days. He only knew that when he visited her bed during the night, she responded to him with unrestrained passion.

Thoughts of how he would make amends for his neglect brought a smile to his lips.

When the servants arrived with a tub and buckets of hot water for Bryce's bath, Edric took his leave and went down to the kitchen. He found Lora there, giving instructions to the cook for a light meal to be served to Bryce after his bath.

"You can rest easy tonight, my lord," she said to him. "Let one of the grooms stay with him. I am fairly sure the fever will not return." She yawned.

"Go and seek your own bed, Lora," Edric said. "Caedmon will see you home."

Lora nodded wearily and returned to Bryce's room, no doubt to give instructions to the grooms and to pick up her satchel and anything else she'd left there during the long days of their vigil.

Edric rubbed a hand across his beard. His whiskers were bristly and rough on Kate's skin. He thought of Bryce's freshly shaven face and remembered Kate's remark about the cleft in Aidan's chin. She had thought it would distinguish him when he grew to be a man.

He took a plate of food with him when he

267

climbed the stairs, but set it down inside his bed-chamber. Lighting a lamp, he pulled off his tunic and took the blade he'd used to shave Bryce's face. He sat upon the bed and made use of the soap and the water in the basin, and carefully shaved the beard from his face.

Kathryn couldn't sleep. She gathered her shawl 'round her shoulders and sat before the fire with her knitting. She was not needed in Bryce's chamber, and though she worried about the young man, Edric had assured her that Lora was doing everything possible.

All that was left was to pray, which Kathryn did. Fervently.

She concentrated on her work, and barely heard the door open when Edric came in. At least she thought it was Edric. His beard was gone and his hair combed back from his face.

His was a breathtaking visage and Kathryn put her hand to her breast as if she could slow her heart's rapid beating, as if she could contain all she felt for this Saxon lord.

"Bryce's fever has broken." He came to her and crouched beside her chair, taking the newly knitted cloth between his thumb and fingers.

A weight seemed to lift from Kathryn's shoulders and she gave a quiet prayer of thanks. " 'Tis the news I've prayed for."

"Aye. He will mend now."

Kathryn cupped Edric's chin with one hand. "No wonder your son is such a comely bairn." She touched the indentation in Edric's chin and ran one finger over his lower lip, wondering if he'd shaved his beard for her benefit. Then she scoffed at her own foolishness. 'Twas likely something he did every few months to keep his beard from reaching his waist.

"What are you making?" he asked.

She held up the small blue blanket. " 'Tis nothing elaborate—Elga said I should start with a simple piece."

" 'Tis well done," he said, though he hardly glanced at the work. He took a seat beside her. "Bryce will be glad to know you are practicing your sewing skills."

She looked at him aghast, but quickly realized he was jesting. He slid an arm 'round her shoulders and hugged her to him as he laughed.

"You are a fiend, sir."

"Aye. That I am. Kiss me."

She did so, dropping her knitting into her lap. 'Twas a long, gentle kiss, and when he broke it, he seemed content to sit by the fire and talk. He wrapped a short wisp of her hair 'round his fingers, and when he looked into her eyes Kathryn thought her bones would melt.

"How is it you never learned to knit? Is that not a skill most young lasses are taught early?"

She picked up her needles again, her mind racing for an answer that would not give her away. "'Twas just that I had no talent for it then. Or not the patience. Tell me, when will Drogan return?"

"Mayhap tomorrow. 'Tis a fair distance to Dunfergus and there will be work to do once he's there."

"The people of the village think he will bring back goods . . . food."

"Aye. The fyrd took wagons for the purpose of hauling back whatever they can carry."

"Then all will be well? There will be enough food to last the winter?"

He shook his head slowly. "I have my doubts. Aye, it will help, but according to Oswin's reckoning, we'll need careful portioning to make it last."

There would be more than enough at Kettwyck. Kathryn had heard the assessment of Kettwyck's harvest, and it far exceeded her father's expectations. Kettwyck lands were fertile, and they'd tried a new system of clearing swampland and bogs, making it possible to farm those areas. She wondered if her father would part with some of his harvest. She could not ask him, not without returning to their Norman society and the ridicule it was sure to mete out.

She and Edric talked a while, but eventually Aidan interrupted, demanding his feeding. Kathryn no longer felt any awkwardness when she lowered her chemise to feed him. The bairn was still uninterested in allowing anyone else to give him his milk, and Kathryn had stopped asking about possible nursemaids to replace her.

'Twas an embarrassment . . . to realize how weak her resolve had been to resist Edric. She knew it would be best to muster some kind of inner strength and leave Braxton Fell, but she could not bring herself to do it.

When Aidan finished, he fell right to sleep. Edric took Kathryn to bed and made love to her, slowly this time, drawing out their pleasure until she lay limp beside him, her body sated and exhausted beyond mere contentment.

"Now that Ferguson is no longer a threat," Edric said, "why don't we ride out among the fells tomorrow? There is more to Braxton Fell than this keep and our village."

He stroked her hip as they lay together, and Kathryn drifted toward sleep. "Aye," she mumbled, too sleepy to consider how they would ride out together without all of Braxton Fell knowing she was his leman.

'Twas dark in the chamber when Kathryn woke him. He came fully awake instantly, and reached for his sword. "What is it?"

"You must go, Edric!" she whispered urgently. "'Tis nearly dawn and the servants will soon be about."

He fell back to the mattress and turned over. "No. Go back to sleep."

"Please!" She shook him to rouse him again. "They cannot know . . ."

Sleep and the weariness of the past few days made her words incomprehensible to him. "Is it Aidan?"

"Edric, please. Listen to me. If the servants know that you and I . . . If they . . ."

He pushed up onto his elbows and looked at her, barely able to discern the shape of her face in the dimness of the chamber. "You don't want them to know we share a bed."

"Please. They cannot know that I am your . . ."

"My what, Kate?"

He heard her swallow. "I'm sure there is a Saxon word for what I am."

"Aye. You are my *mistress*, Kate."

"It is not what your servants or the villagers

would call me. Please, can you not go and leave me a scrap of self-respect?"

Edric rolled from the bed and pulled on his tunic. Without another word, he left Kate in the company of his infant son, who awoke and demanded his first feeding of the day.

Before going to his own chamber, he looked in on Bryce, who was sleeping soundly. His skin was cool to the touch, so Edric retired to his own chamber, intent upon getting another hour's sleep.

But sleep eluded him.

He dressed and left the keep, heading to the stable. No one was about yet, so he saddled his gelding and mounted up, intent upon taking the ride he'd planned to share with Kate.

The sun came up as he rode through the gates and headed west, past the mill and on toward the mountains, to the lands that were undamaged by the Scots. He'd hoped to take Kate today if the weather was fair, and show her his domain.

But he knew now that she would not accompany him willingly. Not if she was concerned with what the servants thought of her.

In the past few days he hadn't given much consideration to her demeanor toward him in public. She was distant and respectful, just as any nursemaid would be expected to behave. But wouldn't a servant take pride in capturing the interest of a powerful lord? In the years before his marriage, Felicia had certainly let everyone know she'd taken him to her bed.

He'd suspected Kate was different, and now he was certain of it. Last night he'd asked her an innocent question about learning to knit, but she'd managed to avoid giving him an answer, turning the conversation in another direction.

She did not want to divulge anything of herself.

Oswin had warned him not to trust her. But the steward spoke as one who hated Normans on principle. Kate was no threat to Aidan or to Braxton Fell. She'd killed Robert Ferguson and raised the alarm before the Scots had been able to catch him unawares.

Edric's shadow shortened as the sun rose. He'd wanted Kate with him on this ride. He'd planned to hold her in the saddle in front of him, her back to his chest, his arms 'round her waist as they wandered the fells and dales of his lands.

Clearly, she was no simple maid. He wondered if her true name was Kate, and whether she was actually from Rushton as she'd said. He should ask her directly. He should return to the keep right now and demand some answers from her. After all, she had the care of his son. He had the right to know who she was.

Instead, he rode hard through the dell until he came to the path that would lead through the wood and up to a concealed perch on one of the fells. 'Twas a place where he and Bryce, along with Siric and Sighelm, had hidden from their parents and dreamed the dreams of youth.

Edric had not been here since his young friends had been killed.

He rode as far as he could, until the terrain became too rough. Then he tied his horse to the same tree his brother and Oswin's sons had always used, and continued on foot. The path was not so easily discerned here, and that was what the lads had liked about it. They'd thought no one would ever find them if they didn't wish to be found.

They hadn't taken into account the evidence of their horses tied at the bottom of the path.

He reached the place where the four friends had sat together and discussed their fathers' errors and the things they would do differently were they in charge. Sitting on the grassy ledge to look out on his many hides of land, Edric gave a self-derisive laugh when he thought of all that had failed.

He might have other estates, but Braxton Fell was home. 'Twas where he was born, where his parents had lived in the modest keep that stood empty now; where he planned to raise his own son. Before the Normans had come, the village had prospered, even despite the occasional skirmishes with the Fergusons.

But too many men of the fyrd had been killed or maimed in their required service to King William, and those who'd been left to defend Braxton Fell two years before had failed. Edric and Bryce had been shocked on their return home to find their lands so devastated. There had been little enough they could do to repair the fields and forests, and his other estates had only what they needed to sustain themselves.

Braxton's viable fields had been harvested in recent weeks and Edric looked over the freshly mown lands. Anson Miller had not been busy enough this autumn, for there was less grain to grind than ever before. Which meant that Edric's share was significantly diminished, too.

He caught sight of a few goats rambling among the deadwood and boulders on the mountainsides, and some sheep grazing in the dale below. The few cattle at Braxton Fell were kept close by, for the Fergusons had a fondness for beef. In past years, they'd stolen many a cow from Braxton's pastures.

Edric leaned back against a rock and remembered the foolish notion he'd once had—that one day he'd bring his bride up here to see where he'd spent the lost hours of his youth, and to survey the bounty of all their lands.

Cecily was not one he'd have shared this with. Norman women did not . . .

His notion of Norman women had changed with Kate. She was not the same cold and spoiled wench Cecily was, but giving and warm. She was soft-spoken and fluent as a well-bred lass might be. She had a sense of pride that drove her to keep secret her liaison with him. And if Edric learned she was a well-born daughter of a Norman knight, honor would compel him to return her to her family.

That thought gave him pause. He was not ready to give her up, even if she was reluctant to let everyone on the estate know of their affair. She was right. It was an illicit association, and though no one would think badly of *him* for taking a mistress, *she* would be branded a whore.

'Twas not what he wanted for Kate.

Kathryn could not return to sleep, not when Edric had left her so abruptly, and without the kind of lingering kiss he'd given her with each of his prior departures. He was angry, and rightly so. Who was she to dictate how their affair was to be conducted? Edric was lord of the estate and she should not have protested his presence in her bed or asked that he keep their liaison secret. She'd given her virtue to him and had no right to care that the world knew she was his lover.

She fed Aidan, then dressed and went in search of Edric. He was not in his own bedchamber or in his brother's, but Bryce was awake and welcomed her to visit.

"I cannot stay," she said. "I am looking for your brother."

"Why? What is amiss?"

She shook her head, barely noticing that his face had also been shaved of its beard. "Naught. I just . . . I wish to speak with him."

"Find him later. Come close. Let me see my nephew." He gave a cursory glance at the bairn, but leveled most of his attention on her, his scrutiny making her feel enormously uncomfortable. "There is a different look about you, Kate of Rushton," he said. "Braxton Fell agrees with you."

Even though she was certain that he could not possibly know of her intimate association with his brother, she blushed at his words.

"I must take my leave now, Lord Bryce. Mayhap we will visit later."

She left Bryce and looked for Edric in the keep, but did not find him. Thinking he might be with his men on the practice field, she went for the door, but was stopped by Oswin, who barred her way.

"Prepare to leave Braxton Fell within the hour,"

he said. "I have a company of men who will escort you to Evesham Bridge."

His words hit her like a cold fist. "What of Aidan?" she queried. "Who will—"

"There is a woman in the village whose bairn died in the night. She will have the care of him now."

As she swallowed back her sudden tears, she reflected that Edric was not the kind of man to use an intermediary to terminate their affair. But surely Oswin had not taken it upon himself to send her away. Edric must have ordered the arrangements to be made.

Chapter 16

Edric climbed the steps to the keep and pushed open the door where he saw Kate and Oswin deep in discussion.

" 'Tis no longer your concern," Oswin was saying. "We will make do. Now go. Gather—"

The steward stopped abruptly and drew himself up to his full height when he saw Edric.

"Kate?"

"Good morn, my lord."

Her voice was different, a bit breathless, Edric thought. He looked at Oswin, who crossed his arms over his chest but said naught.

"All is well?"

"Of course."

"Then come with me." Together they walked away from Oswin and climbed the stairs. When they were out of sight, he leaned over and kissed her.

She put her hand upon his forearm, her mind reeling with regret for having sent him from her bed, and confusion over Oswin's intentions. "Edric, I am sorry. I was wrong to tell you to keep our—"

"Kate. You were not wrong. And I will respect your wishes on the matter." He'd met a number of villagers on his return to the keep, and they'd spoken so highly of Kate, he could hardly believe they referred to the same young woman they'd scorned on her arrival at Braxton Fell.

"You will?" Her eyes filled with tears.

"Of course." 'Twas bothersome how much her tears troubled him, but he would make sure that in future, she would have little reason to weep. Their bed play would keep her satisfied and happy.

"You do not wish to send me away?"

"Don't be ridiculous."

"But Oswin said I must—"

"Ignore him, Kate. 'Twill take some time before he lets go of his hatred for your people."

She rose to her toes and kissed him. "Oh, Edric,

I . . ." Whatever she was about to say, she changed her mind and thanked him instead.

They entered the nursery where Kate collected Aidan's milk and some fresh clothes for him, then wrapped her shawl about her. Edric enjoyed looking at her, observing the gentle care she gave his son and the way she sometimes fumbled self-consciously when she knew he was watching her. "Where are you going?"

"To the village. Elga's friend Diera promised to show me how to sew."

"I thought Bryce had taught you." 'Twas a jest, intended to lighten the moment when he realized how deeply she'd ingrained herself into his community. 'Twas not every maiden who could boast of killing a Ferguson warrior, much less Robert himself.

Aidan grew as the days passed, and Edric spent the greater part of every night in Kate's bed, always leaving before dawn. To his knowledge, only Bryce knew of their affair, though Lora might have suspected.

He ordered Oswin to stay away from her since there was naught to be gained by the steward's association with her. Every now and then he wondered what Kate had been about to say the morning she'd thanked him for keeping news of their affair to themselves, but told himself it had been naught.

After more than a fortnight away, Drogan finally returned. Edric and Oswin met him in the courtyard and surveyed the wagons loaded with sacks of Scottish crops. While Oswin took his ledger and wrote his assessment of their plunder, Edric questioned Drogan.

"Ferguson's women and children fled when they heard of Robert's death, and we battled the rest of his clan for the territory and the goods."

"Will they come back?"

Drogan shook his head. "I doubt it. Their lands and crops are ours. Many of our men wanted to return here to their families and their work. With your permission, we'll take others back to Dunfergus and finish harvesting Ferguson's crops from the fields."

"Aye. 'Tis a good plan."

"In the meantime, I left Cuthbert with fifty men to guard the place. If anyone challenges them, they will have an uphill battle to win."

'Twas all news Edric had wanted to hear, but when Father Algar arrived and scowled at them, his optimism faded. Oswin's news was even less welcome. "We need five times this much, my lord," he said, sweeping one arm in the direction of the wagons. "I had hoped—"

"There will be more coming, I promise you," said Drogan, but Oswin shook his head. Pressing his lips together, he walked away, studying his column of numbers as he went. "He becomes more dour with every passing day, doesn't he, my lord?"

Edric watched the tall, stoop-shouldered figure recede into the crowd of men in the courtyard. "Aye. Mayhap he tires of his occupation." Oswin's advice about the Fergusons had been wrong and his attitude toward Kate untenable. He'd known for a while it was time to seek another to serve as steward, but he'd been reluctant because of Oswin's history with his family.

Drogan shrugged and looked expectantly toward the postern gate. Many of the women had come to welcome the fyrd home, but Lora was conspicuously absent.

"How does Bryce fare, my lord? Is Lora with—"

"He is out of bed these days," Edric replied. "But Lora forbade him from coming out to greet you."

"Ah. If you don't mind, Lord Edric, I will take my leave of you." He reached up to his saddle and removed a large, delicately tooled leather satchel.

"What have you there, Drogan?"

If Edric's eyes did not deceive him, a familiar reddish hue rose from the burly huscarl's neck to his cheeks. "'Tis a gift for Lora. I bartered for it with a tinker we met on the road. Touch this. Is it not the softest leather you've ever felt?"

Edric agreed. It was very fine and he hoped Lora

would take Drogan's suit seriously. She would not find a better provider in all of Northumbria, and Drogan would never know a more good-humored wife. They were well suited to each other.

Kathryn set down her sewing when the men of the fyrd rode through the village. Excitedly, she and Diera went to the door of the cottage. "My husband will be with them!" the woman exclaimed, picking up her skirts to run after the wagons.

Kathryn knew her own excitement would be just as great had it been Edric returning after more than two weeks' absence. She wondered how Lora would react to Drogan's arrival. The healer had seemed quiet these past few days and Kathryn thought mayhap she was considering Elga's advice. She might not care for Drogan the same way she'd loved Hrothgar, but she was clearly fond of the fair-haired huscarl, and mayhap he would give her the children she'd wanted.

Just as Edric would give Kathryn a bairn. 'Twas only a matter of time before she became pregnant, and she wondered what he would do with her when she grew large with his child. They would never be a true family, not without the benefit of marriage. Mayhap he would give her a cottage in the village, or on one of his other estates, to raise their child. Their bastard child.

She quickly turned away from the door and sat down with her sewing once again. It did her no good to try to guess what the future would bring. She had to be content with the present, caring for Aidan and learning the skills the women in the village were willing to teach her. One day she would likely need those skills.

Sometime later, Kathryn returned to the keep, careful to avoid Oswin and the priest. Both men remained hostile toward her, clearly believing she was not to be trusted. She did not know what more she could do to prove her worth than to kill the leader of their enemies. She shuddered at the memory of Robert Ferguson standing so close to Aidan's cradle. She loved the bairn as if he were her own, just as she loved his sire.

But she would never tell Edric so. He had not spoken of any tender feelings for her, so she would not bare her vulnerable heart to him. Nor would she complain of Oswin's treatment of her—she was not some whining female who saw naught amiss in criticizing the man who advised both Edric and his father before him.

Fortunately, the steward kept his distance, and Father Algar's attendance in the keep had been limited to short visits with Bryce.

On her way back to the keep, Kathryn was diverted by the line of wagons in the courtyard. Each was laden with produce or goods, and men were unloading them. Edric was among them, and when their eyes met, he beckoned her toward him.

He'd been careful with his attitude toward her in public, never touching her, but giving his attention wholly to Aidan. "Drogan has returned?" she asked.

"Aye. He's gone in search of Lora."

It must have been the first thing Drogan had done on his arrival home—to look for the woman he cared for—and Kathryn felt immeasurably touched by the deed. She hoped Lora would accept him this time.

After sharing supper with Oswin to discuss their assessment of the goods from Dunfergus, Edric left the hall and walked to the old keep. A lot of his parents' belongings still remained in storage, and there was something of his mother's that he wanted to find.

He lit a lamp and carried it to the chamber his parents had shared for all the years of their marriage. The bed hangings were gone, and he realized the curtains now hung 'round Kate's bed. She'd made the nursery a warm and welcoming place, with colorful cloths and the toys of Edric's youth.

He opened an old trunk and looked inside, but

did not find what he sought. The next trunk was more of the same, but the third belonged to his mother. In this he discovered what he was looking for, two heavy shell combs she'd worn in her hair.

Wrapping the combs in a cloth, Edric returned to the keep, aware that the gift Drogan had brought for Lora was what had inspired him to collect his mother's combs for Kate. Women appreciated these tender gestures and he'd been remiss not to have thought of it before.

'Twas dark, and all was quiet in the keep when he returned, so he went up to the nursery. Kate sat beside the fire, looking into the flames. The nights were much cooler now, so she was fully dressed, with her shawl wrapped 'round her shoulders where her hair fell in loose, lush waves. As usual, Edric felt the urge to press his face to it while he listened to her softly accented words.

He took the combs from his pouch and opened the wrapping that enclosed them. "I brought these for you," he said, taking a seat nearby. But she looked at the combs as if she had never seen such things before.

"Combs. For your hair."

"You brought me a gift?" She lifted them from his hand and admired them with her gaze.

"They were my mother's."

"Oh, Edric, they are very fine."

She looked up at him with an expression that was somehow beyond gratitude, and he realized she was making more of the gift than he'd intended. "'Tis naught, Kate. You have but a length of twine to hold back your hair. These will work better."

He got up and added wood to the fire, causing it to flare, thinking mayhap he'd have been wiser to have left the combs in the old trunk.

"Thank you for this practical gift, then," she said quietly, shuttering her expression. Reaching for her hair, she raised her arms and twisted up the long tresses, then inserted the combs, which held it artfully in place. She looked elegant . . . mayhap even regal . . . and every muscle in Edric's belly clenched tight at the sight of her.

'Twas too much.

He headed for the door, reminding himself that she was little more to him than Felicia ever was— a good bed partner—as well as Aidan's nurse-maid. And it would not do for her to think it was anything more.

Edric's sudden coldness confounded Kathryn. His gift had been thoughtful and a bit sweet. Yet he'd been put off by her gratitude. If she was not mistaken, that was exactly what had sent him from her chamber.

His attitude was not reasonable. And if he thought she was going to worry about his bad temper, or make herself available to his every whim, he would have to think again. She had no intention of waiting here in the nursery for her nasty-tempered lord to return. She banked the fire, then collected Aidan and left the chamber, going up the steps to seek respite in Berta's chamber. The old woman enjoyed Kathryn's visits, and she loved seeing Cecily's child. Besides, 'twas the one place Edric would not go.

What man in his right mind wanted a mistress who did not know her place? Edric's lover was a woman who did not want it known that he shared her bed, one who would barely speak to him in public. He muttered a curse and went down to the hall.

Sending one of the servants to fetch him a mug of ale, he took a seat in one of his father's chairs, refusing to dwell upon Kate's puzzled expression as he'd left her in the nursery. There were more important things to think of. And, by God, he was going to think of them now while he enjoyed a mug of his precious ale.

Drogan had brought good news about the Fergusons' defeat. The Scots' harvest would be a welcome addition to Braxton's stores, though Oswin's assessment was likely correct—'twould not be enough.

Yet with Bryce's health improving every day, and news of the crops, there should have been celebrations at Braxton. Father Algar should say Masses of thanks and minstrels should be performing in the streets.

In years past, 'twas the lady of Braxton Fell who brought about such festivities. It had been his mother's way, but Cecily would never have seen to it. Edric knew from the depths of his soul that had she lived another fifty years, Cecily would never have adjusted to Saxon life. 'Twould have been a service to send her to Evesham Bridge.

He'd assumed Kate would be the same, but every day, he found something else different about his Norman mistress. She was no spoiled Norman maiden, not with her willingness to care for Aidan, and to mingle with the people of the village. She'd befriended Lora and Bryce, and he even had to credit her for the time she spent with Cecily's old nurse. It could not be pleasant sitting with the old woman who could do naught but weep for Cecily.

He was sure Kate would have initiated prayers and celebrations had she been the lady of Braxton Fell.

As he mumbled another low curse over his inability to vanquish that Norman from his mind, the main door of the hall opened, distracting Edric from his thoughts. He looked up to see Anson Miller and his son, Grendel, coming toward him. "My lord!"

"Aye, Miller."

The man seemed agitated, and he spoke of his problem without delay. "The millstone is cracked, dislodged from its spindle."

It took a moment for the miller's words to penetrate Edric's brain. "Cracked? How?" He'd never heard of such a thing. The same millstone had been used at Braxton Fell for as long as he could remember.

"I don't know, my lord. Grendel and I went into the village for our bread this eve. When we returned, I went up to the millhouse . . . There was clear evidence that someone had been there in our absence."

"What evidence?"

"First, my lord, the gate was open, but I was certain we'd closed it. We went inside and found an iron wedge lying on the bed stone."

"And the hopper smashed," added Grendel.

Edric stood. He clasped his hands behind his back and started to pace. "Did you see anyone?"

"No, my lord," said the miller. He scratched his head, then wrung his hands together. "'Tis a disaster."

"Aye. We must solve it and discover who the vandal is. And why he would wish to harm us this way." Edric called to Caedmon to seek out Drogan and Oswin and have them meet him at the mill. This was no simple vandalism. It smacked of the same kind of mischief as the damage done to the ale kegs. Only this time, 'twas much worse.

He wore his cloak against the cold night and walked with Anson and Grendel back to the mill. After lighting several lanterns, they went into the chamber that housed the stones and the hopper where the grain was fed inside to be ground between the two millstones.

"What of the water wheel?" Edric asked. 'Twas housed below the millstones, lying horizontally in the river, turning with the current.

"It seems in good condition, my lord. Grendel will go below and examine it when morning comes."

"How did the vandal move the stone?"

"I know not," replied the miller. "Mayhap he used one of my shovels. Or an ax pounded onto the wedge that was left here."

The thick iron wedge lay upon the lower bed stone, just as the miller had described. "Wouldn't an ax handle break with the weight of the stone?"

" 'Twould seem so." The miller looked over his tools and implements and found none out of place.

But Edric noticed two long splinters of wood, lying near the wedge.

Drogan arrived, and Oswin soon thereafter. The two men looked over the situation, but had no other ideas. "Where is the ax?" asked Drogan. "Depending upon where we find it, mayhap we'll know our culprit."

" 'Tis too obvious. No doubt the thing was well hidden," said Oswin.

Edric agreed with Oswin. "What of a Scottish saboteur? Are you sure you wiped out their fyrd, Drogan?"

"I thought so, my lord. But I'll organize a company of men to search the grounds. Mayhap we missed someone."

But marauding Scots did not explain the damage done to the kegs in the cellar of the keep. The person responsible was a Saxon, a Braxton Fell inhabitant. Edric was certain of it.

"We'll look this over in daylight, Anson," he said. "In the meanwhile, let no one in. Lock the door."

"We'll do as you ask, my lord."

Edric returned to the keep with Oswin and Drogan. Neither man spoke as they walked, but when they entered the hall and went on to Edric's study, Drogan said he thought it would be best to wait until daylight to send men to the fields and forest to look for signs of a lurking enemy.

Edric agreed as Oswin sat down, his expression grim. "Oswin, where will we find another stone?"

The steward shook his head. "I've heard of a few places . . . There is an estate to the south— Kettwyck—known for its granite. Mayhap we can trade for one."

"Trade what? Is there anything of value that we can give Kettwyck for a pair of stones?"

"I'll have to think on it, my lord."

They discussed the burgling of the mill, but Edric did not mention the connection he'd made between the damage there and the loss of his ale, waiting to see if either of his advisors thought the same.

It seemed they did not, else they'd have said so.

Oswin drummed his fingers upon the table, clearly disturbed by the vandalism. "All has gone to hell since the Normans came. Soon the whole village will rise up in rebellion."

"Well, they can hardly blame the damage to the mill on the Normans. We have none."

Oswin looked up then, and Edric realized he'd misspoken. He had Kate, but she was certainly not capable of ruining the mill. Nor had she been free to damage the kegs of ale.

"My lord, 'tis time to return to Saxon rule."

"Oswin, we've gone over this before. We *have* Saxon rule. Me. I am in charge here."

Oswin stood and walked to the window. "No you're not. 'Tis the Norman bastard who commands us."

Edric rubbed his hand across his face. "Oswin, I am weary of this argument. We are part of a Norman kingdom now, and 'tis best we remember it."

Oswin grumbled but said no more before quitting the room, leaving Edric with Drogan.

"Well, Drogan. Is there to be a wedding?"

"I did not ask her."

Edric gave a sardonic laugh. "Drogan, you are hopeless." He left the huscarl, taking the lamp and heading up the steps. He went past his own chamber, and on to the one place where he wanted to be.

He found Kate sleeping soundly, so he took off his clothes and slid in beside her. Rolling to his side, he pulled her close, savoring the soft feel of her skin against him.

Her hair tickled his nose and he pushed it aside, pressing a soft kiss, one that would not wake her, to her nape. Holding her this way, he could barely remember why he'd left her so abruptly. He should not have reacted so irritably to her gratitude. The combs meant little—they cost him naught, and gave her some small pleasure. There was no more to it than that.

He slept fitfully, dreaming of thieves who stole the combs and made Kate weep over their loss. He saw the rogues pick up the millstone and toss it into the river, and when they were finished, they took Aidan and carried him into the mountains.

By the time Edric awoke, he was glad the night was over. He felt Kate turn to him, her breast against his back, in her sleep. Her hand dropped across his chest and her fingers slid through the hair there.

He was instantly hard.

Keeping his back to her, he held his breath as her fingers slid down to his belly and lower, until she enclosed his erection in her hand. She pushed down and then pulled back up, making him surge ever larger in her hand.

"Ah, so you're awake," she whispered in his ear, and he was immeasurably glad she'd forgiven him for his surly departure the night before.

He made an inarticulate sound when she flicked her finger over the tip of his cock, mimicking the stroke she often made with her tongue, a move that made Edric's heart nearly stop every time she did it.

"So you like this, my lord?"

He sighed a shaky breath as she continued to fondle him. What an idiot he'd been to leave her last night.

"Shall I use my tongue instead?"

Before he could reply, she straddled him and leaned forward to press kisses to his uppermost nipple, licking and sucking it as she slid over to his other side. She kissed and nipped her way down his body until she reached his cock, finding it straining toward her mouth.

She gave it a feather-light lick, then pulled him fully into her mouth, sucking him deeply. He closed his eyes and imagined the sight of her swirling her tongue 'round him, an image so sensual he nearly came in her mouth.

But he quickly shifted their positions and pressed her into the mattress. Pushing her legs apart, he found her hot and wet with arousal. He drew her legs over his shoulders and kissed her intimately, eliciting her squeal of pleasure. Using his tongue on the apex of her sex, he plied her with his finger to make her arousal all-consuming, bringing her close to her peak before he entered her.

She surprised him by pulling away. Taking hold of his shoulders, she pushed him to his back and straddled him again, sliding down on his cock. She tossed her head back so her hair brushed the tops of his thighs, and Edric's heart clenched in his chest at the soft caress.

Faint light streamed into the window, so he was just able to see Kate's features, her eyes closed, her mouth drawn in passion. He cupped her breasts as she rode him, relishing their soft weight in his hands.

"Oh, Edric!" She kept her voice low, but her quiet tone did not disguise her ardor as she approached her climax.

Edric did the same, surging into her, spilling his seed with a rush of pleasure so intense 'twas belied by the brevity of their encounter.

Kate melted down to him and Edric wrapped his arms 'round her, and they lay joined together while their hearts and lungs slowed.

Edric would be content to stay there forever.

Chapter 17

No more was learned when Edric visited the mill in the morning. The upper millstone was indeed cracked and useless. A new wooden hopper could be easily made, but to what use when they had no runner stone?

"What'll we do with all the grain that's coming from Dunfergus?" asked Drogan.

Edric tapped one finger against his mouth. "Leave it there. We'll grind it in Ferguson's mill."

"And cart all our own grain up there?" the steward scoffed.

"Not necessarily, Oswin," Edric said. "We'll

bring the Scots' grain back here and use it while we wait for new stones from Kettwyck."

Oswin gave a resigned nod and skulked away. And with good reason. Enough had gone wrong at Braxton Fell in the past few months. They did not need this.

"By the time we need to grind our own grain, we'll have our new stones," Edric explained.

"Can we not bring home the millstones from Dunfergus and use them here?" asked Drogan.

They looked to the miller for their answer. "What kind of mill do the Scots have?" the man asked.

Drogan described it to Anson, who told them they would likely not work. The Braxton mill was entirely different, using a horizontal design, rather than the vertical type at Dunfergus.

"Ah, well," said Drogan. "I'll send a messenger to Dunfergus, telling them not to cart the grain away."

Obviously disgusted, Oswin left the mill. A moment later, Grendel, the miller's son, came into the millhouse to say that riders had been sighted on the western road.

Edric sent youths out to alert Braxton's warriors to prepare for intruders, then hastened with Drogan to the armorer's to put on their battle gear and make ready for their visitors. They had no reason to believe the strangers would be hostile, but with the way things had gone at Braxton these past few weeks, Edric thought 'twas better to be prepared.

They mounted their horses and rode to the head of the fyrd just as the intruders' herald called out to the guard at the gate. "Friend, we are Saxons. We come in peace under the banner of Wulfgar of Tredburgh."

Edric gave the signal to open the gate.

"Do you bring your own provisions, Wulfgar?"

A well-armed man of Oswin's age rode forth, carrying his spear in one hand. His bushy beard was the color of burnished steel and he wore his long hair tied back at the nape of his neck. A thick fur pelt was tossed casually about his burly shoulders. "We come in peace, Edric of Braxton Fell."

"That does not answer my question," Edric replied irritably. He did not need this complication. "We are known as a hospitable house, but our own stores are lean these days."

"Aye. We've brought food."

"Then enter and be welcome."

At least thirty riders followed him, including a few women and children. They seemed no better than a poor band of wayfarers, yet *this* was the man Oswin hoped would lead them to victory over the Normans?

Edric hoped that seeing the reality of Wulfgar's ilk would put an end to all of Oswin's arguments for joining the man's rebellion.

The steward came alongside him on horseback and greeted the man. "Wulfgar, 'tis an honor to finally meet you. Your exploits are legendary in Northumbria."

The Saxon grinned. "Aye. We've had a few good go-rounds with the Normans."

"I am anxious to hear of your plans," Oswin said.

Wulfgar nodded, then turned to Edric. "Your lands, my lord . . . Such devastation. What aid does the Norman king send?"

"None, Wulfgar. We deal with our own troubles at Braxton Fell."

"Aye, but—"

"'Twas the Scots who harried our fields and forests. And we've put an end to them. We needed no help from King William."

Wulfgar pursed his lips in thought. He turned and beckoned to a woman riding some distance behind. "Odelia! Come and meet our host."

A young woman spurred her horse and came abreast of Wulfgar. "My daughter, Odelia."

She was comely in the Saxon way, with pale blue eyes and yellow hair tied into plaits wound intricately 'round her head. Her clothing was plain . . . a dark red kirtle covered by a simple brown woolen cloak. "Greetings, Odelia. And welcome to Braxton Fell."

She smiled and gave a pretty nod, but Edric felt no swell of interest in her. "My lord Edric," she said. But he'd gotten so accustomed to the gentle cadence of Kate's speech that Odelia's words sounded harsh and brittle to his ear.

He looked over at Wulfgar. "Your men can spread their blankets in the barracks. The women and children . . . my steward will see what households have room for them tonight."

"'Tis more than we expected, my lord," said Wulfgar with a bow, though his obsequious manner irritated Edric unaccountably. He would give them one night at Braxton Fell, and then send them on their way. "A few days' respite from travel is all we need."

"A few days, Wulfgar? No. You will be on your way upon the morrow."

"My lord," Oswin quickly interjected, "let us not be hasty."

"Oswin, find shelter for the women and children. Drogan will deal with the barracks."

"Aye, my lord."

"Rest well today, Wulfgar," Edric said as he spurred his horse back toward the stable.

* * *

The last time Kathryn had seen Edric so angry was right after he'd rescued her from the Fergusons and Bryce had been wounded. There was fire in his eyes now as he paced before the fireplace in the nursery.

She sat quietly, feeding Aidan as he spoke.

"These ragtag Saxons are not what is needed here," he said. "They will cause naught but trouble."

"How can they? You will send them away upon the morrow."

"I have a bad presentiment about them. If King William learns that I've given shelter to a Saxon rebel . . ."

"How would King William ever learn of it?"

Edric raked his fingers through his hair and went back to pacing. He was often distracted by the damage that had been done recently in the keep and at the mill, and Kathryn wished there was something she could say to ease his mind. He was so tall and powerful, she had never seen him worry about a physical challenge—a battle against a known enemy. But the sabotage of the mill, and now the arrival of the Saxons, had him anxious and troubled.

"What is happening here?" he mused irritably. "Once King William accepted my surrender and granted these lands to me, all things should have improved. But the opposite has happened."

Kathryn touched his arm. "Surely things will start to improve now. You've dealt with the Fergusons and you have no other enemies in Northumbria."

He put his hand over hers and leaned down to kiss her. "Your optimism is good for me. You are right. I will rid myself of these rebels and we will repair the buildings damaged by the fires. The mill can be restored and we'll use Ferguson's mill until then."

Kathryn's heart swelled at the sight of his smile and the knowledge that he'd sought her out to speak of his worries.

"With careful planning, no one will starve this winter."

Kathryn thought again of the bounteous harvest at Kettwyck and her father's boast that the estate had a quarter share above what was needed. If she but swallowed her pride and went to her father for help, he would surely give assistance to the man who'd rescued his daughter.

But that would mean returning to Norman society, not only as a Scot's captive, but a Saxon's whore.

"What is it?" Edric asked.

She shook her head. "'Tis naught. I merely . . . wondered about your brother and how he fares."

"Come with me. We'll get Bryce and see if he feels well enough to sup with us in the hall."

"Edric, I should not—"

"Worry not. I will not embarrass you there. Just . . . bring my son to me while I dine."

He lifted Aidan from her arms and helped Kathryn pull her shawl 'round her shoulders. Then they went to Bryce's chamber, where Drogan was entertaining the young man with his tales of the Fergusons' defeat.

"Will you come to the hall for supper?" Edric asked.

"Only if Lora is nowhere near." He was sitting in a soft chair near the fire.

"Why?" asked Kathryn.

"Because she's become a dragon of late. She says that now that I feel better, I'm more likely to become overactive and do myself some damage."

"She is right, lad," Drogan remarked.

"You would say that if she'd told me to drink a potion of henbane."

Drogan started to bluster, but Bryce stopped him. "'Twas merely a jest, Drogan. I know Lora's advice is good."

"Do you not think Lora would allow you down to the hall?"

"'Twill be my first time."

"Then let's try it," said Edric. "Can you manage the stairs?"

"Aye."

Kathryn went ahead while Edric and Drogan assisted Bryce. She signaled the servants to begin serving, and asked Caedmon to move one of the cushioned chairs near the fireplace to the table for Bryce.

The four of them had no sooner taken their seats than Oswin entered the hall with several men and a beautiful young woman Kathryn had never seen before. The man beside Oswin reminded her of Léod Ferguson, not so much in his features, but his rough demeanor, and she pulled Aidan close as she gathered her wits.

"By damn, I did not give leave—"

Bryce interrupted Edric's muttered curse. "'Tis Wulfgar?"

Nodding, Edric stood, keeping his eyes trained on the newcomers.

"I will take my leave, my lord," Kathryn said.

"Stay," he said angrily. "Eat the meal provided you."

"Lord Edric," said Oswin when they reached the dais. "Wulfgar's company is settled, all but his daughter and his chiefs."

Edric said naught, but crossed his arms in an obstinate manner.

"Surely you offer the hospitality of your hall to these high-ranking Saxons?"

Much as he did not care to do so, Edric could not deny the generosity of his hall and his table without seeming the churl. He felt Kate drawing into herself even as he beckoned the newcomers to be seated. 'Twas not the small pleasant gathering he'd expected for Bryce's return to the hall and he was annoyed with Oswin for circumventing his wishes.

He would talk to the steward later.

Kate finished her meal quickly and, just as Aidan started to howl, took him away from the table. She retreated to the stairs, but not before Wulfgar took note of her. " 'Tis unusual to serve a slave at your table, is it not?"

"She is no slave, but my son's nursemaid," Edric replied, maddened by the question. 'Twas not Wulfgar's concern what position Kate held or where she supped. Naught at Braxton Fell was the Saxon rebel's concern and the sooner he was gone, the better.

"Ah . . . I misunderstood . . . No offense meant, my lord," said Wulfgar.

"He is a comely bairn, Lord Edric," said Odelia. Sitting beside him, she placed her hand upon his forearm as Kate had done only an hour before.

Odelia's touch did not cause the same sensations on his skin, or make his heart throb with arousal. No one's touch had the same effect upon him as Kate's.

"My lord," said Oswin. "Wulfgar has two hundred thanes under his command. They are well hidden among the northern fells and ready—"

"Two hundred?" Drogan scoffed. "What good is two hundred?"

"I assure you, I can call many thousands to my service, Drogan White. I am not without some repute on the battlefield."

"Aye, to be sure, Wulfgar," Drogan said. "But we have no need of change at Braxton Fell. These lands are under Lord Edric's command. We are content."

Edric kept his silence, allowing Drogan to do the talking while he took the measure of the Saxons Oswin had gathered here in the hall. There could be no mistaking the might of the men seated at his table. Each one had the look of a powerful warrior about him. But it did not matter how many men Wulfgar commanded. Edric had no intention of going to war again.

"My lord, 'tis said you have a Norman wife."

"Lord Edric was recently widowed," Oswin interjected.

Wulfgar nodded briefly, but offered no condolences. "At least the wench bore you a son."

Edric gritted his teeth, annoyed with the man who knew naught of his relations with Cecily, and should have at least wished him sympathy in his loss. He swallowed his last gulp of ale and turned to his brother. "Bryce, are you ready to return to your bed?"

Bryce gave a quick nod. With bare civility, Edric enjoined the Saxons at his table to stay and finish their meal without him. He helped Bryce to the stairs and supported him as they climbed. "I don't like it," said Bryce once they'd reached his bedchamber. "Why is this Saxon here?"

"He hopes to draw support for his rebellion."

"What is Oswin thinking, allowing him refuge here?"

Edric built up the fire, then stood and turned 'round, with his hands upon his hips, to look at Bryce. "He wants me to throw in with Wulfgar. I'll speak to him later."

"Edric, Oswin's advice has been faulty of late."

"Not only his advice," said Edric, "but his opinion of our situation at Braxton. He must step down."

"Aye, but who has the skills to replace him?"

Edric rubbed the back of his neck. He did not

know the answer to his brother's question. Even if he had someone in mind, he did not know how to dismiss the man whose family had served Edric's for a hundred years.

The coming winter worried Kathryn. She thought of the young boys who helped the maids in the keep, of Caedmon and Modig, and all the other young faces in the village, and considered the painful hunger they might face if she did not go to her father and petition him for help.

Yet Edric was not certain their plight was that grave. There might actually be enough, if Oswin made careful distribution of the grain and other crops from the Scots, and if they had no additional mouths to feed.

"The Saxons thought I was your slave." Kathryn did not doubt it was Oswin who'd told the Saxons she was Edric's slave. He'd purposely intended to demean her before Wulfgar and his daughter.

She had not mentioned it to Edric until after they'd made love and he held her in his arms in the quiet of their bedchamber. The Saxon's assumption was not without merit. Though she'd come to Edric's bed willingly, she was not a free woman.

He nuzzled her ear. "I told them you were not."

'Twas a small comfort, but her thoughts became muddled when his mouth was on her.

"Your steward hates me," she said. Her breath caught in her throat when he cupped her breast and slid down to take her nipple into his mouth.

"I've spoken with him."

Kathryn no longer cared. Naught mattered but what happened between them, in this room. She responded to his touch as if he hadn't made her mindless with pleasure only a few minutes before. She could not help but love him, with the attention he paid to his little son and his concern for the people of his estate. He had a fierce loyalty to all in his care, from the paupers at his door to his brother in his sickbed.

She could deny him naught.

He was gone when morning came. 'Twas a cold, dank day, a good one for staying indoors. But Kathryn had made plans to spend the day at Elga's cottage. She fed Aidan, then dressed for the day, taking the bairn down to the hall to break her fast.

Drogan was already there and greeted her fondly, as was his manner. He was a gentle man, and Kathryn was certain Lora had finally come to recognize his worth. If he asked her to marry, the healer would agree. " 'Tis a wet day, lass. You'll want to stay in."

"But I'm to spend the day with Elga. Mayhap you would walk with me to her cottage?"

"Aye. After I speak with Edric."

"Is he here?"

Drogan gave a nod toward the back passage-way. "He's talking with the miller in his study."

"What will be done about the millstone?" Kathryn asked just as Edric came out of the room. He entered the hall with the miller beside him.

"We'll just ask him, won't we?" said Drogan, standing to meet Edric as he came toward them.

The miller split away from Edric, taking his leave, and Edric came directly to Kathryn. He looked down at his son and touched his cheek. Though it would have seemed entirely natural for him to slip his arm 'round her, he kept his distance, respecting her wishes that he show her no particular familiarity outside their bedchamber.

"Oswin says the best granite millstones are to be had south of us, on an estate called Kettwyck."

Kettwyck. Kathryn's heart jumped into her throat and thudded almost painfully.

"Shall I take a company of men to barter for what we need?" Drogan asked.

"No. Send Irwin and Penrith. When Oswin returns, I'll see what he thinks we can barter for the stones."

"Irwin is already gone to Dunfergus, my lord."

"Then find another likely man to do the negoti-ating."

"Aye, my lord. I'll just escort the lass to Elga's cottage, then give Penrith his orders."

"You're going out in this storm?" Edric asked her.

Though she might have felt warmed by his concern, Kathryn hardly heard the question. Braxton men were going to Kettwyck. They would speak to her father, and there was a good chance they would mention the Norman woman they'd rescued from the Fergusons.

Her deception was nearly over.

Chapter 18

Edric had left the nursery later than usual that morn, and Rheda had seen him. He did not think the girl would keep silent about what she'd seen—him, coming away half dressed from Kate's chamber. The maid would not misunderstand the situation, and the gossip would make her the center of attention all day.

Mayhap 'twas best that Kate was spending the day away from the keep.

With the inclement weather, Wulfgar and his Saxons did not leave Braxton, although Edric was certain they must have encountered rain in their travels. At the least, they would have tents for shelter.

But 'twas not only Wulfgar's warriors who traveled with him. Edric would not turn out their women and children into the cold rain. They had brought their own provisions, so 'twas no hardship on his own people for them to stay another day.

Edric went looking for Oswin, and found him in deep discussion with Wulfgar in Edric's study.

"If you'll excuse us, Wulfgar," he said, barely controlling his anger. He took a seat at his table. "I'd like a few words with my steward."

"Aye, Lord Edric," Wulfgar said affably, as though he had no reason to placate his host. "I was just about to take my leave."

"Shut the door, Oswin," Edric said when Wulfgar had gone. At least Oswin did not insult him by pretending that naught was amiss. "Explain yourself."

"In regard to what, my lord?"

"Is there more than one issue at hand, Oswin?"

"I told Wulfgar his party could stay until the weather cleared."

"By what right? As I remember, you were ordered to show them the gates as soon as possible."

"Lord Edric, you would not—"

" 'Tis for me to say, Oswin. You have not been given leave to act in my stead."

The steward's features seemed to tighten. "Aye, my lord."

Edric's anger was not assuaged by Oswin's capitulation, but he still had need of the steward's knowledge and services. He could not dismiss him out of hand. Not yet. "I am sending two men to Kettwyck to negotiate for new millstones. What can we barter for them?"

Oswin put his hands behind his back and stepped away from the door. "A Norman captive?"

Edric stood up so abruptly his chair fell back. His blood pounded in his ears, but Oswin was undaunted.

"You must admit she is no lowly serving maid, my lord. Her return to a Norman holding would be valuable beyond compare, with no cost to us."

Edric made a conscious effort to rein in his temper. He needed Oswin now, while they were dealing with their crop shortage and the takings from Dunfergus.

"Oswin, Kate will not be part of any trade. Think of something else the Norman will take for his damned stones. And get rid of Wulfgar and his followers. When the rain clears, I want them gone."

As Oswin left, Edric channeled his thoughts toward all that Braxton Fell produced. With their resources so severely compromised, wool was their only valuable asset, yet all that they produced was mainly for their own needs. He supposed 'twould be possible to promise away the bushels of wool that would result from the spring shearing and let his people go without.

He hoped Oswin would somehow come up with a better solution.

"'Tis good to get out of the rain!" Kathryn said, hastily entering the cottage Lora and Elga shared. Drogan came in behind her, coming face-to-face with Lora. Neither one of them spoke, but Kathryn knew there was much to be said between them. "I'll just go and hang up my cloak in the back," Kathryn said. "Thank you for your escort, Drogan."

She carried Aidan to the room where Elga sat at her loom and signaled the older woman to stay quiet. She handed the bairn to Elga and removed her cloak. Hanging it on a peg on the wall, she spoke quietly. "We should not listen in."

"No," Elga whispered. Nonetheless, she and Kathryn made themselves as quiet as mice and strained to hear the low voices beyond the curtain.

Kathryn put her hand to her breast when Drogan told Lora he had cared for her for a very long time, and his feelings were not likely to change. Not even when they were both bent over with age. She heard him move, heard a rustle of clothes, and imagined him taking Lora's hand in his.

Then she heard Drogan ask Lora if she would do him the honor of becoming his wife. Lora did not reply, and Kathryn worried that the healer might refuse him. She crept toward the curtain and peered out, ready to shake some sense into her. Drogan was the worthiest of men, and would make her a fine spouse.

But when Kathryn looked into the room, 'twas clear that Lora had come to the same conclusion, for she stood in Drogan's embrace, kissing him fervently. Their kiss heated up and Drogan's big hands framed Lora's back as he pulled her close and groaned quietly into her mouth.

Kathryn stepped away, intensely touched by the deep affection shared between the two. She had no doubt that Drogan would make Lora a wonderful husband, for he was kind, as well as thoughtful. He loved her.

Elga caught her eye and wordlessly asked her question. Kathryn nodded, feeling ridiculously close to tears. Lora and Drogan would wed; their love would be blessed by the holy sacrament, and their children would not be bastard born.

She blinked away any sadness she might have felt for her own plight, and considered the joy Drogan's union with Lora would bring. "We must give them a moment alone," Kathryn whispered, "then go in and give our congratulations."

Aidan suddenly made his presence known with a sharp cry. "Your lad wants his milk," said Elga.

The bairn's breaking of the quiet in the cottage brought Lora to the curtain. Smiling, she beckoned Drogan to join her, and took his hand in hers. "We have news," she said.

"Lora has consented to be my wife," Drogan interjected, repositioning their hands so that her small one was engulfed by his much larger one, bringing them to his lips to kiss her knuckles.

The gesture caused a lump to form in Kathryn's throat, but she managed to convey her delight at their tidings. "'Tis wonderful news!" she said as Elga took Lora, then Drogan into her embrace.

"We will have Father Algar call the banns at week's end," said Drogan, "and wed three weeks hence."

Elga nodded, her expression pensive. "I am glad for you both . . ."

"What is it, Elga?" asked Lora.

" 'Tis not the time to speak of it. We will talk later."

"No, if you have—"

" 'Tis naught . . . Only that once you are wed, you should move into Drogan's quarters at the keep."

Lora frowned, but Drogan spoke. "Our thanks to you, Elga. I know 'twas a concern to Lora. You will never want for company, though."

"Aye," said the old woman with a smile. "Of that, I'm certain."

"Shall we find Edric and ask his permission to wed?" Drogan asked.

Lora laughed. "His permission?"

"Aye. Well, 'tis customary, if unnecessary."

The two took their leave, grinning happily as they hurried out into the rain. Kathryn knew that Drogan had a room in the keep near Berta's, though he did not often sleep there. Edric said he preferred the barracks. But once he and Lora were wed, they would stay there. 'Twould be difficult then to keep secret her own sleeping arrangements with Edric.

She supposed it did not matter, for soon Lora would have to learn of it . . . . once Kathryn became pregnant, she would have need of Lora's skills.

"What is it, lass?" asked Elga.

Kathryn shook off her gloomy thoughts and

laid Aidan on the bed, denying that aught was amiss, for truly, it was not. Bearing Edric's child would be pure joy. "Shall we begin our lesson?"

Edric wanted to find the tool that had been used to pry off the millstone, but he had little hope of doing so. Likely it had been broken by such misuse and then discarded. The vandal might well have thrown it into the river that powered the wheel that turned the stones. 'Twould be the perfect irony.

He wondered who hated him—hated Braxton Fell—enough to do such damage. The wasting of the ale in the cellar had not been the first incident. Thinking on it, he remembered a few other strange events that had occurred before Cecily's death, but had thought naught of them. Yet now he wondered.

Several of the shopkeepers had approached him earlier, asking what would be done about the mill and the shortages they were anticipating in the coming months. They wondered if it might be best to join with Wulfgar and cast off the unwelcome Norman yoke.

Edric used no uncertain terms to dissuade them from that line of thought. He sent them on their way, angry with Wulfgar, who had obviously been talking with them, attempting to stir them up.

He walked into the stable and searched among the tools stored there, but found no broken ax. He did the same in each of the storage sheds, the places where the wagons loaded with produce from Dunfergus were stored, and found no ax. But seeds of concern and suspicion had started in his brain.

There were few people about in the rain, but two figures came toward him, their faces obscured by their deep hoods, running through the muddy puddles in the yard.

"My lord!" called Drogan. He drew Lora up beside him into the shelter of the shed and Edric quickly realized the reason for their broad smiles.

"Aye," he said, grinning, putting his troubles to the back of his mind for the moment. "Have you finally—"

"We have. Lora has agreed to marry me. We have only to ask your blessing and announce the banns."

"You know you have my permission," he said, clasping Drogan's hand. He noticed the burly, blond warrior slipping his free arm inside Lora's cloak, encircling her waist in a gesture of possession as well as affection. "You are well suited to one another. My congratulations to you," he added, feeling distinctly on edge, in spite of their good news.

"What are you doing here in the shed, my lord?" asked Lora. " 'Tis a day for staying indoors."

Edric rubbed one hand across his face. He'd shaved again, aware that Kate had a particular liking for his naked face. "I have a feeling about the storage sheds. 'Tis a prime target for our vandal . . . if he should set fire to them . . ."

Drogan gave a harsh gasp. "By God, you're right."

"I want guards posted at each building and more men making regular rounds. We'll make it difficult for him to strike again," Edric said.

"Mayhap we'll catch him in the act," Drogan remarked.

"We can only hope . . . Not a word of my suspicions to anyone. Either of you."

"Aye, my lord. No one will hear it from me," said Lora.

"Do you remember the fire in the orchard last summer?" Edric asked.

Drogan nodded. "You think 'twas the same vandal?"

"There's more . . . The time Cecily became so ill after eating supper." Edric turned to Lora. "You thought the fish was tainted. But I remember wondering how it could be, since I'd shared the same meal."

"I thought mayhap it just disagreed with her. Do you think her portion was poisoned?"

Edric shrugged. "We can only guess now."

"But who would want to do us such damage? We have no enemies in our midst—have we?"

"Obviously, there is one who is deranged enough to want to wreak havoc on us."

"Who could it be . . . and why?" asked Drogan.

"Mayhap there is no reason," said Lora.

"I don't think so," said Edric, turning his thoughts to those early-morning discussions with Braxton's villagers. "What if someone has intentionally been trying to create mayhem . . . To foment discontent here, at the hall, and among the people."

"To what purpose?" Drogan queried.

Edric shrugged and considered his partially formed theory. He glanced outside and saw several of his men coming through the gates, riding toward the stable.

" 'Tis Gildas, Alfred, and Octa, my lord. They've come from Dunfergus."

"I'll be in the hall," said Edric. "Send them to me once they've settled in."

Through the rain, Edric went 'round to every logical place where the vandal might have hidden the broken ax, although he did not entertain much hope of finding it. Still, he went through the motions and soon returned to the keep.

Kate had not returned to the nursery, and he felt her absence keenly. The dank afternoon would lend itself to barring their door and making love by the fire until he could not tell where he ended and she began. But she was about her business in the village, learning the crafts that she'd somehow never been taught, and Edric had estate business to attend to.

Aidan had been irritable all afternoon and Kathryn sought out Lora to consult with her. She said that all was well, but that sometimes the bellies of tiny bairns became distended, or they had cramps that were difficult to soothe.

The walk home seemed to help quiet the bairn, but as soon as Kathryn stopped, he became fussy again. She entered the hall and found Edric sitting at the table with Bryce and several of his warriors. Kathryn's heart swelled with love for the Saxon lord, even though she knew the sentiment was not reciprocated. She was his chosen bed partner, and she had to make her peace with that.

She walked past the men and climbed the stairs to the nursery to put the bairn in his own crib, hoping that his familiar surroundings would quiet him. But it did not help. She attempted to feed him, but he was not interested in the milk.

Finally, as a last resort, she fashioned a woolen pouch for him by tying two ends of a blanket together, then looping it 'round her shoulder and waist. She secured Aidan inside, and tried pacing the length of the nursery, but there was not enough open floor space to pacify him with her stride.

The only solution was to return to the hall. She did not believe Edric would mind the intrusion, since he seemed always to welcome his son's presence. Kathryn thought mayhap the passageway at the back of the hall would give her sufficient space to walk, so she would not really be intruding.

"Is my son ill?" Edric asked when he saw her and heard the bairn's wails.

"No, my lord. At least, Lora does not believe so."

"Then why must you pace with him?"

"His belly is upset. Moving this way seems to be the only way to quiet him."

"I will walk a spell with him when I finish here," he said.

"Oh, my lord, 'tis not—"

"Let him perform his fatherly duties, Kate," said Bryce with a grin. " 'Twill do him good."

Aye, he was an attentive father, and Kathryn

could not help but think he would make a good husband . . . Yet marriage was something he'd vowed never to consider. Kathryn knew she was not the most comely of women and she often felt awkward and clumsy, especially beside Edric, who was fair and agile, and could have any woman he chose. Even Wulfgar's Saxon daughter.

She thought he might care for her a little, for he was a gentle, thoughtful lover. Outside of bed, they spent long intervals discussing Edric's hopes for his son, and his aspirations for his estate. Still, he'd never given her reason to believe he would take a wife again.

The men turned back to their discussion, a serious one, to judge by the expressions on their faces. She watched Edric surreptitiously, her blood heating at the sight of his comely features—the dent in his square chin, the small scar that split his dark brow, the lips that made her squirm with pleasure.

He made her feel beautiful, too, and for the first time in her life, she felt nearly as lovely—and as capable—as her sister.

Thinking of Isabel gave Kathryn a pang of guilt for deceiving her family as she'd done. No doubt they grieved for her . . . but her mother had been quite clear about the status of a woman who'd been abducted by Scots. After all that had happened, Kathryn would not be welcome in her parents' home.

Bryce's words caught Kathryn's attention as she walked with Aidan. "You say the Scots have burned their own fields?"

"Aye," replied one of the men. "But not all. Under Cuthbert's command, we routed the bastards. But we lost mayhap fifty hides of land to fire before we could vanquish them."

Kathryn watched Edric rub a hand across the lower part of his face, as he often did when he was troubled. She clenched her teeth, aware that this news could mean only one thing. Unless she went to Kettwyck and asked her father for assistance, there would be starvation this winter at Braxton Fell.

Kate's pacing distracted Edric. The sling in which Aidan rested was nearly the same blue as her gown, making her look as though she carried the bairn within her body, as if she were pregnant. With his child.

The notion was so distracting, he'd almost missed what Alfred said, and the man's words, coupled with the disturbing image of Kate, inflamed him. *"Fifty hides of grain?"* he demanded.

The three warriors nodded. "But 'tis good news,

my lord. We were able to stop them before they could do any more damage."

"Good news!" he roared. He stood and scraped his fingers through his hair. "This news could not be much worse. Do you know how limited our stores are now? We needed the produce from those fields!"

"Aye, my lord. I only meant that it was fortunate we were able to salvage most of those fields."

Alfred's statement might be true, but Edric was angry. Their luck had been absolutely abysmal ever since the Normans had come. Mayhap Oswin was right and they should throw in their lot with Wulfgar and his men.

But what would that solve? With King William's resources, Wulfgar's thousands would hardly make a dent in the Normans' shields.

In a tone rough with irritation, he called out to Caedmon, who stood near the door awaiting orders. "Seek out Oswin and tell him I have need of him in the hall. Make haste."

Anger and frustration filled him. Their defeat of the Fergusons had brought hope, yet now they were nearly as destitute as before. At every turn, something went wrong. The place was cursed, just as Father Algar had said. Edric could not even take pleasure in looking at Kate, and knowing the intimate delights that awaited him in their bed when he retired for the night. Was consorting with a Norman likely to cause him some future difficulties?

"Edric, come back to the table," said Bryce.

He clenched his teeth and did so, aware that there was no purpose to his anger against the three warriors gathered here. They only brought the news, they were not responsible for it.

The men told of the attack they'd repelled, and their frantic struggles to contain the fires that had been set. Edric's head began to pound and he only half listened, preoccupied with what they would do, how they would manage their shortfall. He wondered, too, if there was further threat to the Fergusons' fields and to the men who'd been sent to harvest the crops and mill the grain. He should probably send more men to protect them, just as he'd posted guards to watch over their own storehouses.

The door of the keep flew open and Wulfgar entered with his daughter and at least a dozen of his men, each one carrying a cloth-wrapped bundle. A troupe of musicians followed them, and with much merriment, laughter, and song, the Saxons came inside and called greetings to Edric and the others.

Edric found their jovial manner offensive, especially in light of the recent news from Dunfergus.

"My lord, we come to share our bounty. We've learned of your shortages and have much to contribute. We bring you a Saxon feast, Lord Edric! Sup with us!"

Edric was incensed. The state of affairs at Braxton Fell was no business of Wulfgar's, yet the man had the utter gall to turn up here—in Edric's hall—with his meat and his ale, as if to demonstrate Braxton's inferior circumstances. "You come uninvited and insult me in my hall? Oswin!" He called to the steward who'd come in with the Saxons. "Did I not tell you to rid us of this rebel?"

"My lord, we need Wulfgar and his—"

"You overstep your bounds, steward. Your orders were to escort these people to the gate. Their largesse is not welcome here."

Wulfgar approached. "My lord, an alliance between us will be of great value to you. Even now, the Norman bastard-king is planning to go to war with King Malcolm of Scotland. The greatest Norman knights of the realm are traveling now to join William in the conflict. All his armies, all his ships . . . They will soon meet at the mouth of the river Tees to march to Scotland. 'Tis our best chance to overthrow the usurper."

"You talk treason, Wulfgar. I have pledged my sword to King William's service. Do not presume to enter here and—"

He was interrupted by the sharp words of Father Algar, who'd entered the hall behind the crowd of Saxons, unnoticed with the confusion of Wulfgar's people and his minstrels crowding about him.

"Where is she!" the priest shouted. *"Where is the Norman whore?"*

Chapter 19

Kathryn's throat closed, making it difficult to catch her breath. Father Algar could only be speaking of *her*. Of Kathryn de St. Marie, daughter of Baron Henri Louvet, a Saxon's whore.

They'd been so careful, yet someone in the keep must have noticed that she and Edric shared a bed.

"By God, clear the hall, Oswin!" Edric said. His voice was harsh and dangerous above the pandemonium in the hall. "Octa and Gildas! Run them out!"

Kathryn held Aidan tightly against her breast.

She made her way toward the stairs, hoping to make her escape before the priest set his eyes upon her and leveled his vitriol in her direction.

"An empty hall will change naught, Lord Edric!" Father Algar pointed a skinny finger at him. "Your sin does untold damage to us all. If you do not wed the wench—"

"God's balls!" Edric roared. "I will not have some half-cocked cleric telling me—"

"Wed her!"

Edric slammed the palms of his hands on the table. *"I will not!"*

Kathryn's heart fell to her toes and tears filled her eyes. Edric's vehemence cut her deeply. Hearing him say that he would not even consider taking her to wife was an injury she could not bear, and to do so before the Saxon rebel and his kin was too much.

She handed Aidan to Gwen and ran from the hall, making her way down the back passageway toward the door that would lead to the kitchen garden.

Yet she did not want to encounter anyone outside.

Stopping short, she let herself into the first chamber she came to. She closed the door behind her and backed up against it, fully giving in to her tears. She wept for all she'd lost, and for the only thing she yearned for—Edric's love.

'Twas hopeless. His marriage to Cecily had been a disaster, one he'd vowed never to repeat. She'd known it from the start of their affair, yet somewhere in the depths of her soul, she'd hoped he would change his mind.

Despondent, she sat down at the heavy oaken table. Pushing aside a thick, bound ledger and numerous leaves of parchment, Kathryn laid her head upon her arms. Her time with Edric was over, for she could not live openly as his leman. Her shame was greater here than it would ever have been at Kettwyck had she returned to her father's estate after her abduction.

The Scots had not stolen her virtue . . . she'd given it to Edric willingly.

But now that she was confronted with her sin, she could not continue. Nor would she let anyone at Braxton Fell starve, not if her father could give some assistance.

She sat up and dried her eyes. 'Twas useless to weep over what was to come, for she'd known from the beginning that she could not stay at Braxton Fell. Once the hall was cleared, she would find Edric and tell him who she was, and how her father might help them.

Rising to her feet, she picked up the parchments she'd knocked to the floor. As she replaced them on the table, the seal at the bottom of the first one caught her eye. 'Twas the signature of King William.

Holding the document carefully, she took it to the wall sconce for better light. Surprised by its friendly tone, she wondered if she'd misconstrued all that had been said about King William's directives. She looked at the next document in her hand and saw that it was from Baron Gui de Crispin, Cecily's father. It, too, was overtly friendly, with no mention of his daughter's death, but generous offers of assistance.

The letters made no sense. Surely she had not completely misunderstood what had been said about Baron Gui and King William. Why would they lie about . . .

It suddenly struck her. They had not lied. *"Mon Dieu,"* she murmured. Even Edric did not know the contents of these missives. The steward was the only one at Braxton Fell who could read and write. He had misled Edric intentionally.

But what would he gain by doing so? 'Twas his own people who suffered from their lack of provisions, and here was an honest offer from Baron Gui, to supply some of what was lacking. It made no sense at all.

Unless he intended to foment unrest in Edric's estate. Or make Edric angry and resentful toward the Normans.

The door to the study opened and Kathryn shoved the letters behind her as Oswin entered. He closed the door tightly and approached her.

"So. You can read, Norman. What else did you neglect to tell Lord Edric?"

She held the documents out to him. "What did you hope to gain by your lies, Oswin?"

"My lies? You Normans lie. You do naught but take what is not yours."

"What of these letters? They show the generosity of King William, and of Cecily's father. I do not understand why you would want your own people to suffer, just to make Edric think that the king is an uncaring—"

"Because there was no other way to make him understand!"

"Understand what?"

"That Saxons must stand together. That your king and his ilk are naught but villains, come to steal our land and our young men!"

"You are deranged, Oswin," she said as she tossed the letters to the table. "Are you the one who did damage to the mill?"

The steward's eyes flickered with guilt.

"Edric must learn of your deceptions. 'Tis not

fair that he go on worrying so. You must tell him what you've done."

Kathryn started to walk past him, but he grabbed hold of her arm and shoved her back against the table. Before she could scramble away, he came and pinned her down. "You will not tell him!" His voice was but a harsh rasp as he held her against the hard wood, encircling her neck with one hand.

She struggled against him, trying to kick him where Edric had taught her, but he guarded himself well. She attempted to reach for her knife, but he anticipated that, too. He increased the pressure upon her neck, choking her until she could not breathe. She knew she was doomed. Her struggles soon diminished and her panic receded. At first, she saw tiny pinpoints of light behind her eyes. Then all went black.

Edric followed the Saxons out the door and all the way to the barracks. He was not going to be distracted from his purpose this time. Wulfgar and his companions must go, no matter what the weather.

With Octa, Gildas, and Alfred to back him up, he herded the Saxon troupe across the courtyard and into the barracks. Damp with the rain, Edric hardly felt the chill as he crossed his arms over his chest and watched the interlopers gather their belongings.

"You are making a mistake Edric," said Wulfgar angrily. "When we take Northumbria from the Norman bastard, you will find yourself without lands. You will be lucky to have a hovel to call your own."

"I will take my chances, Wulfgar. Now, choose someone to collect the women and children you have scattered through my village and take your leave."

Caedmon had followed along, so Edric sent him away to the stable to have the grooms saddle the Saxons' horses and hitch their wagons. He would brook no delays in their departure, for he needed to find Kate. From his position at the opposite side of the hall, Edric had seen the color drain from her face at the priest's words. She'd been hurt and upset, and rightly so.

Algar, that horse's arse, had called her a whore and demanded that Edric wed her. Edric was not about to tolerate anyone insulting her in such a manner. As his mistress, she made his cock throb with arousal at the sight of her.

Yet it was more than that . . . Kate aroused his heart and mind with her gently spoken words and her tender care of Aidan. She spoke his language, and had made it her business to befriend his people. She had hurt no one, but was kind and caring, yet she'd managed to kill his mortal enemy in spite of her near-paralyzing fear.

He knew of no other woman who stirred him as she did.

"Where is Drogan?" Edric asked Gildas, knowing he could trust his huscarl to oversee the eviction of the rebels while he went in search of Kate.

"I have not seen him, my lord."

Edric muttered a curse. If ever Kate needed his comfort, 'twas now. He would not have her off somewhere alone, lamenting the insult to her virtue. He cared too much for her.

The realization struck him all at once. He could not fall asleep unless she was in his arms. He listened to the sound of her breathing when he awoke each morn, and looked forward all day to spending the evening hours and most of the night with her. He listened for the sound of her soft voice and the trill of her sweet laughter in the hall, and knew he cared more for her welfare than his own.

He loved her.

Jesu.

He was the horse's arse. He might have vowed never to marry again, but that was before Kate. She was his woman, for now and for always.

He looked 'round for Oswin, but reminded himself the steward was not the man to trust with evicting the Saxons.

"Gildas, go and find Drogan. Octa, Alfred, we'll stay with Wulfgar's party and be sure that all of them go their way."

Once again, Father Algar seemed to appear from nowhere, his white brows furrowed, his expression screwed into a hateful façade. Edric drew his sword, a hair breadth away from killing the man. "Call the banns, priest. And ask me no questions."

"You must confess your—"

Edric raised his sword. "'Tis likely a sin to threaten a priest, but by God, I will cut you down if you say another word. I have decided to wed Kate of Rushton. The marriage will take place three weeks hence."

"She is but a—"

Edric's sword came down with a violent slash, but he stopped short of spearing the priest. The old man was suddenly prudent enough to hold his tongue.

"Never mind," said Edric, his tone as threatening as his sword, and he knew 'twould be a long time before his temper cooled. "Get you gone from Braxton Fell. Go with Wulfgar and plague *him* while I find a priest who does not offend me so."

"You will regret—"

"Not half as much as you will wish you had not insulted my betrothed."

For once, the priest was silent. With his features twisted into an ugly mask of anger and frustration, he turned on his heel and removed himself from Edric's presence, and Edric returned his attention to the grumbling Saxons. He knew he'd made an enemy of Wulfgar, but he could not afford to make him a friend. The Norman king was more powerful than Oswin or Wulfgar knew. Edric and Bryce had seen him on the battlefield. They had experience of the man's personal power as well as knowledge of his determination.

Wulfgar and his ragged followers would have no chance against William, and Edric would not bring his people into war again, even if they had the resources for it.

The Saxons climbed onto their horses in the rain and took their wagons to the gate. Edric and his men mounted their own horses and escorted them, watching as their women and children joined their party, climbing into the wagons and covering themselves with tarpaulins to stay dry. "Ride with them until they are deep into the fells," said Edric to his warriors, just as Gildas and Drogan appeared.

"My lord," Drogan said, eyeing the scene before

him. It must have seemed odd, but he did not question what he saw. "I am at your service."

"Gildas, go with them. Be certain no one remains behind, no one circles back. I want these vagrants far from Braxton Fell before they make camp."

"Aye, my lord."

"Drogan, see that Algar leaves with them and make it known that he will never be welcome here again. Order ten additional men to follow this ragged troupe and assist them in setting up their camp," Edric said, for 'twould be difficult to get settled in the rain and the dark, and he would not let the women and children suffer any more than was necessary.

Drogan did as he was bid while Edric watched the last of the Saxons leave through the gates. Then he headed back to the stable and left his horse with one of the grooms. 'Twas well past time to go after Kate.

Kathryn awoke slowly. Her sense of smell returned first, and she found herself surrounded by a sickeningly sweet aroma. She felt chilled to the bone, but when she opened her eyes, 'twas too dark even to see her hand in front of her eyes.

Her throat felt raw and bruised, and she remembered Oswin's assault. Her panic returned and she thought the steward must have buried her alive. But she could move somewhat freely. She rolled onto her hands and knees, and felt the cold, damp earth beneath her.

Where was she?

'Twas completely silent in her prison, no sounds to give her a clue to her location, but if she was still inside Edric's keep, then this must be the cellar. Taking care not to collide with the casks that would be stacked nearby upon wooden frames, she crawled forward, meeting naught but an earthen wall.

She pushed herself up to her feet, but could not rise to her full height before hitting the ceiling. It felt the same as the floor and the wall, cold, and damp, the texture of clay.

This was not the same cellar she'd visited.

She returned to her crouch and moved along the perimeter of the chamber, finding its length several feet longer than her body, yet the ceiling was a good bit shorter than her height. She kept moving and discovered a long, wooden bar lying in the center of her dungeon and thought it was a handle of sorts. A moment later, she found the cold, hard steel of an ax blade, broken off its handle.

When she found no door and no window, her breathing became rapid and shallow, and her fear advanced toward panic. She tamped it down, fully aware that it could make her situation worse. She did not know how Oswin had gotten her into this place, or even where it was . . . Mayhap she was not inside the keep. If that was so, Edric would never find her. Surely that was what Oswin intended.

Her tears started to fall when she thought of Edric and the last words she'd heard him speak: a curse, and then his vow to remain unwed. He did not feel what she felt for him, and in his anger, he would likely be happily rid of her, at least for tonight. No one would miss her until Aidan needed his milk and they could find no one able to feed him.

At least Aidan needed her.

Thoughts of her child kept the panic at bay and she made another turn 'round the small chamber, with the hope that she'd missed something. 'Twas difficult in the pitch-darkness, but if there was a way to get out, she was going to find it.

Taking the ax handle in hand, she started pounding on all the walls, hoping to find a hollow sound, or mayhap a weak spot, but she found naught. She knelt near one of the walls and bruised her hands using the ax blade to dig, even though she was afraid the effort would avail her naught.

Glad to be rid of Wulfgar and his paltry band of rebels, Edric walked through his hall and took the steps like a starving man with the promise of a meal abovestairs. He hurried to the nursery, and shoved open the door without knocking, ready to take Kate into his arms and kiss her until they were both breathless.

The chamber was empty.

No matter, she was likely sitting with Bryce, as she often did, visiting with him as she knitted the blanket for Aidan. Edric went looking for her in his brother's chamber, but found Bryce dozing lightly. He roused him and asked if he'd seen Kate.

With a negative response from Bryce, Edric went back to the hall and soon heard the sound of Aidan's demanding cry. He followed the sound, certain that wherever his son was, there he would find Kate.

Aidan was in the kitchen, but there was no sign of Kate, and Gwen was desperately trying to feed the bairn. The cook and two scullery maids hovered nearby, offering advice, but Gwen was not successful.

A feeling of dread took hold of Edric, deep in his belly. Kate might be upset—or even angry—with him, but she would not go off in a temper, leaving Aidan to the mercy of the servants.

"My lord," said the cook, "we've all tried to feed the bairn, but he—"

"Give him to me." Distracted by worry, he sat

down and took Aidan into his arms. Someone handed him the crock of milk and he put the nipple into Aidan's mouth. Immediately, the child quieted and started drinking.

Edric hardly gave a thought to the odd circumstance, but fed his son as he questioned the staff. "Has anyone seen Kate?"

All but Gwen shook their heads.

"Where did you see her last?" he asked the lass.

"Wh-when Father Algar shouted at her . . . she gave me the bairn and ran from the hall."

"In what direction?"

"Back this way. I think she ran out through the kitchen garden while you were chasing those men from the keep."

'Twas a start. Likely Kate had gone to Lora's cottage.

He left the keep and hastened through the rain toward the east postern gate, then picked up speed as he crossed the bridge and moved through the village toward Lora's cottage. He recognized he'd been a fool to ignore all that he felt for Kate. She might be Norman, but she was nothing like Cecily, and from the first time he'd seen her, so terrified and vulnerable under Léod Ferguson's bulky form, he'd wanted her. He'd wanted to kill Ferguson just for touching her.

His hands itched to touch his woman, to pull

her into his arms and tell her she'd heard him wrong . . . that he truly wanted her for his wife.

And that he loved her.

She had done what no other maiden could do, seducing him with her gentle ways and the loving attention she gave to him and his son. They'd come full circle, with Edric falling oh so deeply for the woman he'd thought he wanted only for a bedmate.

He arrived at the cottage and knocked at Lora's door. Elga answered, stepping aside for Edric to enter. "Where's Kate?" he asked.

"Not here, my lord," Elga replied as Lora came through the curtain that led to the back room.

"Is she not with Aidan?" Lora asked.

"Aidan is with the maids at the keep, but I cannot find—"

"What reason would she have to leave the bairn with your servants? She is never without him."

Chapter 20

Kathryn was going to die in that hole. She was certain of it . . . at least, as certain as she could be of anything. The air was almost gone and she felt dizzy from its lack. She'd tried digging her way out with the ax-head, but all she'd done was to deplete what little air there was, making herself light-headed and weak.

No one would ever know what had happened to her.

She lay down on her side and curled into a shivering ball, wondering if this fate was better than the one she'd have met had Léod Ferguson managed to keep her.

Aye. 'Twas.

She'd fallen in love with Edric and his tiny son. She'd have made Edric a good wife, if only he'd wanted one, for she loved him beyond reason. She'd taken him to her bed and given him all that she had, all that she was, without benefit of marriage or the promise of a future.

She wondered if there would be talk of her . . . of the Norman who'd come to care for Lord Edric's bairn and then disappeared without a word, without a trace. She'd come with naught but her ragged clothes, and left with naught.

The idea that all would believe she'd left Braxton Fell—left Edric and Aidan, and all her friends— was abhorrent to her. She was no shallow varlet who cared naught for the man who shared her bed, naught for the bairn who depended upon her.

She did care. Desperately.

And in her desperation, she raised herself onto her knees and started 'round her tiny prison once again, searching for the opening, for there *must* be one. She picked up the ax handle again and tapped every surface of every wall, but she discovered nothing more than what she'd found the last ten times she'd done it. Solid walls of clay.

Hungering for air, she sat back in frustration

and confusion, certain that her mind could not be functioning properly, else she would be able to do something about her plight. Suddenly, the darkness seemed not quite so thick. Kathryn saw faint flickers of light all 'round her, and heard the soft murmur of voices in her ears. She knew they could not be real, for she'd scoured every corner of her prison and found naught but hard, packed dirt. *No one was here, no one could help her!*

Leaning against a wall, she pressed her hands against her ears in despair, trying to block out the phantom voices, but the low sounds penetrated nonetheless. "There is a way out, *ma petite*. You must find it."

Kathryn recognized the voice of Soeur Agnes, yet the old nun could not possibly be here with her. "I know, *ma soeur*, but I've tried everything," she cried, afraid that she was losing her mind. She had to get out and get some air!

"No, you have not." This time it was Isabel's stern voice.

Kathryn could almost see her sister, the talented one, the beautiful one. *Isabel* would never have let Oswin get the better of her. She'd have fought back and won against the old man, then exposed him for the traitor he was. Edric would be proud to have such a capable woman for his wife. No doubt *Isabel* would be able to engender all the tender feelings a man should feel for a woman, feelings that would inspire him to make his marital vows to her.

"Do not be a fool, Kathryn," said Isabel. "He cares for you . . . else he would not be such a considerate lover. He would not look so fondly upon you as you care for his son. And he would have sent you to Evesham Bridge the moment you mentioned it."

"No—"

"There is a way out. You must find it and go back to those who love you!"

Isabel was wrong. There was no way to leave. No one who loved her. In a haze of regret, she raised the ax handle and brought it down hard into the ground.

"Did you hear that?" asked Soeur Agnes.

"No. There was naught," Kathryn replied. Tears welled in her eyes and streamed down her face, but they did not matter. She was essentially blind, anyway, so there was no reason to brush them away.

"But there was, Kathryn," said Isabel's voice. It swirled 'round her, taunting her with words that made no sense. "In the ceiling. When you bumped the ceiling with the ax handle, there was another sound. Wood."

"Wood? Up here?" She dropped the wood

handle and raised her hands to feel for it, for some small spark of hope.

"You are right," she whispered. The air was even thinner now and it hurt her lungs to breathe. "I feel it."

With all the effort she could muster, Kathryn ran her hands across the plank, assessing its size. If she could believe her senses, it just might be a door, large enough for her to slip through. She pushed on it, but it did not move. Rising up to her hands and knees, she used her back and shoulders to push, but again, it did not budge.

"What will I do?"

"The ax handle," Isabel whispered. "If you pound loud enough and long enough, someone will hear."

While talking with Lora, Edric's feeling of dread returned. "I said something that . . . She thinks I . . ." By God, the priest had called her a whore and Edric had not chastised the man or corrected him. "She believes I care naught for her."

"Edric, how can that be so? You— Oh, dear." Lora pressed a hand to the center of her chest, but asked no further questions.

"She's not at the keep," said Edric. "I thought I'd find her here."

"No. No one has come since Gildas left with Drogan. That's been quite some time ago."

"Has she spoken of Evesham Bridge in recent days?" Edric asked, grasping at straws.

Lora shook her head. "No, my lord. She would not leave Aidan . . . Or you. What she feels for you is evident in her eyes every time she looks at you."

Edric had seen it, too, but denied it, unwilling to accept her love.

He made a quick search of the village before returning to the keep. 'Twas full dark and he hardly noticed that he was soaked to the skin. He sent Caedmon in search of Oswin, and Modig out to the fells to summon Drogan. Then he went into the kitchen where Gwen was sitting by the stove holding Aidan, who had cried himself to sleep.

Edric wasted not a minute. "Gwen, did you see Kate leave the keep?"

"No, my lord," Gwen whispered. "She handed the bairn to me, then ran toward the back door."

"Past the chapel, past my study?"

Gwen nodded. "She must have gone through the kitchen garden and on to the barn."

"Take Aidan to the nursery and put him to bed. Stay with him there," Edric said to Gwen.

With worry clawing at his gut, Edric headed out toward the barn, retracing Kate's steps through the back passageway. Stopping when he noticed that the door to his study was ajar, he pushed inside and saw papers strewn about. The ledger in which Oswin so painstakingly recorded every barrel of ale and every bushel of wheat was on the floor under the table.

Something untoward transpired here.

Oh, *Jesu*. Kate had come this way.

"My lord?" 'Twas Caedmon's voice.

"In here," he called out to the lad.

"I cannot find Oswin," Caedmon said, his eyes going over the disorder in the room. "He is not in his quarters, nor in the stable. No one has seen him."

Edric muttered a curse. "Gather all the grooms in the hall. Kate is missing and I think Oswin might . . ." Might what? Edric wondered. Might harm her? By the appearance of his study, he'd already done some harm.

Edric's stomach clenched at the thought of it. Was Oswin's hostility great enough to cause him to hurt Kate? After the incident with Wulfgar, Edric did not know what to think, or rather he preferred not to think of what damage Oswin was capable of doing.

Still, the steward could not have left through the main gates, for Edric and his men had been there, escorting Wulfgar and his party from the estate. But mayhap the postern gate . . .

Grabbing one of the wall sconces, Edric hastened through the door with Caedmon right behind him. "Oswin might have taken her somewhere. We must search every inch of the keep, starting with the battlements and working our way down to the cellar. Tell the maids to look inside every chamber. Get someone to go down to the postern gate and ask the cottars if anyone has seen Oswin in the last few hours."

Caedmon wasted no time, but hurried down the passageway and out of sight. With only his instincts to guide him, Edric went to the cellar door and descended the wooden steps. He could not allow himself to think what Oswin might have already done to Kate, but berated himself for neglecting to see how the man's hatred had compelled him. Edric should have anticipated some rash act and dealt with him sooner. He hoped and prayed he was not too late.

Naught was disturbed in the ale room. There were no footprints in the packed-dirt floor, no sign of anyone having come through. Edric looked for a door, a passageway, any place where Oswin might have taken her, but he saw naught.

Quickly retracing his steps, he headed back to the great hall, but collided with Lora, her cloak soaked with the rain. "I heard from Caedmon. Where would Oswin have taken her?"

"He could not have gone far." Fear hovered just beneath the surface. Every muscle in Edric's body clenched tightly at the thought of where Kate was and what might already have happened.

"Edric, you must calm yourself," Lora said. "Kate needs you now, she needs your taut discipline and all your training."

He rubbed a hand across his mouth and chin. "Aye. You're right. Come with me to the battlements."

"You don't think he means to—"

"No. If he'd intended to push her off, he'd have done so already."

"Then—"

"There is nowhere else to look!" he shouted in frustration. "He would have had a great deal of difficulty going outside the walls. Where else could he . . . *Jesu!* The old keep!"

Taking Lora's elbow and spinning her 'round, he pulled her down the back passageway and left the keep. Lora could not keep up with Edric's speed, so he let go of her and ran ahead where he spied a dark figure standing at one of the tower windows of the old keep. Its shutters were open, and as the man leaned out, the driving rain soaked him.

'Twas Oswin!

Edric made it to the door and found it barred. Using all the strength he possessed, he threw himself against it repeatedly. Finally it gave way and Edric nearly fell into the old hall.

'Twas dark inside, but he remembered it well and knew where to find a torch. Quickly, he lit it and headed up the stairs toward the tower where he'd seen Oswin. He heard Lora following, but did not stop for her, his attention fully focused on keeping Oswin from pushing Kate from the tower.

"Oswin!" he called. "This is not the way to gain my favor!"

"Your favor is useless, traitor!"

"Kate!"

She did not answer, but Edric heard Oswin step outside the window and onto the tower's ledge. His heart filled his throat when he thought of the terror Kate must be feeling. 'Twas worse than dangerous. 'Twas almost certainly a fatal drop from that window to the ground.

"Oswin, hear me well! If you harm the woman I intend to wed, you will be cast out of Braxton Fell, never to return!"

"You will never find her!"

Did that mean she was not with the steward?

Edric entered the tower room and saw that all the shutters were thrown open. He thrust his torch into one of the sconces and cautiously approached the window where Oswin had climbed to the ledge outside. 'Twas a precarious stance in the wind and pelting rain, but the steward showed no fear.

"Where is she?" Edric demanded.

Oswin did not reply, but crossed his arms over his chest and laughed, as if he were not standing on an unsound perch in the worst possible circumstances. Clearly, he was deranged, and Edric felt helpless to deal with him. He was shaking with frustration when Lora entered the chamber behind him.

"Try another approach, Edric," she said quietly. "Cajole him."

He took a deep, shuddering breath. "Oswin, come inside. We can talk."

The steward made no reply, but sidled away from the window. Edric looked down at Lora. "He must have hidden her. But where?"

Lora shook her head. "Shall I keep talking to him while you search the keep?"

"Aye." Edric's heart still pounded in his throat. He could not recall the last time he'd felt such agitation, such absolute fear. Edric did not think there was a nook or a crevice in this building that he did not know. Yet where could Oswin have stashed her?

" 'Twas the Norman who ruined everything!" Oswin shouted. "All my plans! The letters . . . the discontent . . . the mill . . ."

"He is raving. Go, Edric, go and find Kate!"

Oswin began to rant. "You listen only to her, but she is accursed! I will not . . . I will not . . ."

They heard a rough clatter and rushed to the window, instinctively aware of what Oswin had done. They could do naught as they watched the steward fall to the ground far below.

Oswin lay quiet and still, his body bent and broken, clearly dead.

"God's breath!" Edric muttered, shocked by what Oswin had done. Yet he wasted no more time, grabbing the torch and heading toward the stairs.

"Take the rooms up here!" he said to Lora.

She started with the chamber where his parents had slept for all the years of their marriage. There would be no separate bedchambers for him and Kate, either. He *would* find her, and after they were wed, they would share the intimacy of one bedchamber for the rest of their lives.

He hastened down the steps and met Drogan, just coming into the hall, looking pale and shaken. "My lord, Oswin has—"

"I know. Quick. We must find Kate. I fear Oswin has done her some harm before hiding her away."

"She is here?"

"I don't know. *Damnation, I can't—*"

"Listen. Do you hear that?"

Edric could only hear the pounding of his heart.

"Down below," said Drogan. "The cellar!"

Edric heard it then, a faint, dull hammering. Together the two men rushed to the small kitchen at the back of the hall and threw open the cellar door. The pounding stopped, and Edric wondered if he'd imagined hearing it, desperate as he was.

They stood still and listened. "Where could she be?" asked Drogan.

Edric made no reply, but descended the steps. The racks that had once held barrels of ale were still in place, with a number of heavy kegs stacked upon them. They searched every corner of the cellar, but saw no sign of Kate, although Edric noticed tracks in the hard dirt floor. "Drogan, look!"

With a strength he did not know he possessed, he took hold of the rack that had made the tracks and started to pull it back. Drogan came and helped, and within moments, they'd uncovered a small wooden door. 'Twas sealed tight, and Edric looked about for a wedge to pry it open.

Holding the torch so they both could see, Drogan handed Edric his dagger. Edric shoved the blade beneath each of the metal catches that held the wood in place and bent them back. Then he pulled the wooden door off its frame. Pushing it to the side, he dropped down into the space below where he found Kate, lying insensible.

He pressed his ear to her breast and heard her heart fluttering within. Saying a prayer of thanks, he lifted her limp body into his arms and carefully passed her through the opening to Drogan who took her and gently laid her on the cellar floor.

Edric pushed himself out of the hole and knelt beside her, lifting her head into his lap. He called her name softly and watched her chest rise as she took in a full breath of air.

"God's blood," said Drogan. "Another few minutes and she would have suffocated."

Edric could not bear to think of it. "Kate," he said gently, stroking her hair, her face, her hands. "Come back to me."

She did not respond. Edric lifted her into his arms and carried her up the stairs, following behind Drogan and the torch. "Get Lora. She will know what to do."

Edric took Kate into the hall and laid her upon the long table that stood on the dais. He took her hand in his and rubbed it roughly, speaking to her, pleading with her to awaken, for he did not want to face a cold and empty life without her. Surely he had not found her below the cellar of his father's keep, only to lose her now. "You are my life and my love, sweet Kate. Come back to me and be my wife."

Now she was hearing Edric's voice, but she knew it could be no more real than those of Isabel and Soeur Agnes.

"*Non, je ne suis pas Kate*," she said to him, though she was not sure whether she spoke aloud, or only heard the words in her mind. Her muscles ached from trembling, but she could not seem to stop. "*Je suis . . .*" She moistened her lips. "I am Kathryn de St. Marie."

She heard a gruff sound very close to her ear, then Edric's voice. "Aye," he said. "Kathryn. My Kathryn."

She felt his warm breath on her skin and she shivered with the chill of her damp clothes.

"Awaken, my beloved. I will not let you slip away from me. I love you, Kate—Kathryn. I need you."

Other voices came to Kathryn then, both male and female, but she could not make out their words. She suddenly felt something cold and wet on her face and opened her eyes with a gasp.

'Twas Edric's face she saw first. Then Lora and Drogan behind him. Were they real? "Edric?"

He said naught, but pressed his forehead to her breast.

365

"I thought you were . . . You found me!" she cried, suddenly remembering the dark hole Oswin had put her in.

"Aye. I'd have searched heaven and earth for you. *Jesu,* I was afraid I'd lost you."

She gave a weak nod. "I was afraid, too." Was still afraid her mind was playing tricks on her. He could not possibly have said he loved and needed her.

Could he?

"You are cold. Here," said Lora, taking her cloak and draping it over her.

"I'll get a fire started," said Drogan.

There was a bit of noise and activity away from Kathryn's view, but Edric did not leave her side. He pressed gentle kisses on her hands, then her forehead. "What of Oswin? Did he tell you where I was?"

"No, Kathryn. Sweeting, he's . . . He fell from the tower. He's dead."

She felt a lump form in her throat. "I ruined all his plans. He is your saboteur. He did all he could to make you resentful of King William, and of Cecily's father. Those letters . . . He told you lies, Edric. The letters offer help and encouragement."

"What?"

"He told falsehoods with the hope that you

366

would become frustrated with King William's rule and join Wulfgar's revolt."

Edric frowned. Oswin's actions would make a perverse kind of sense to a demented mind. The steward had never gotten over his grief for his two sons, and it had made him bitter and irrational.

"He wanted you and everyone at Braxton Fell to feel angry with your lot. He did what he could to foster discontent."

Edric lifted her from the table, and carried her to the fire where Drogan had moved a large, dusty chair. She was still trembling with cold, so he sat down with her, keeping her nestled in his lap as Lora and Drogan disappeared.

"You read the letters?" he asked, holding her close.

She nodded and pressed her face against his chest, her body finally starting to warm. 'Twas time to tell him the truth, even though she knew what the consequences would be. She'd lived this moment a number of times in her mind, and feared she knew how Edric would react. "Oswin was not the only one to tell falsehoods. I misled you, too."

Edric rubbed one hand along her side and leaned down to kiss her. "I care not, Kathryn."

"Edric, my father is one of King William's most powerful barons. He—"

He stopped her words with his kiss, a long, sensuous seduction of her mouth, her body, and her soul. "Say no more. We will wed before I know who you are and feel compelled to ask your sire for your hand. As Kate of Rushton, you can easily be mine."

Kathryn closed her eyes. "No. It cannot be."

Edric knew she cared for him. She could not be refusing to marry him. Yet she broke away from his kiss and cupped his jaw. "This is too important, Edric."

"Aye. We're agreed on that. We will marry as soon as—"

"No, I mean we must go to my father," she said. "I won't risk your losing his favor by marrying me without his consent."

"Kate—"

"My father is Baron Henri of Kettwyck. His harvest was better than expected and he will have grain to spare . . . And millstones to replace the ones Oswin ruined."

"Kettwyck? Your father is lord of Kettwyck?"

She nodded, but Edric realized that he did not care. He wanted her as his wife as soon as the law allowed. As Kate of Rushton, she could wed him.

"I love you, Edric, and there is nothing I want

more than to be your wife. But we must go to Kettwyck. My father will be a powerful ally."

"Only if he gives his consent. Marry me now, Kate. Be my wife and we will face your father together."

She looked up at him with tears in her eyes, her expression clouded by indecision.

Epilogue

Edric settled his wife on the saddle in front of him, and rode through the dell and up to the base of the fell where he'd spent so many boyhood hours in useless dallying. They reached the place where he and his brother and their friends had always tethered their horses, but Edric did not dismount, stopping instead to turn and capture Kate's lips in a searing kiss.

"I love you," he said. He'd never meant any words the way he meant these. Kate was his heart and soul. She was the world to him.

He dropped down from the saddle and reached

up for her, taking her hand as they climbed to the top of the fell, to the ledge where he would show her all his lands, the hundreds of hides that were hers to command.

In the past few weeks, she'd reviewed Oswin's ledgers, and found them just as inaccurate and misleading as the letters he'd translated to his own purposes. Braxton Fell would survive the winter without help from anyone, and when they adopted the techniques being used at Kettwyck for draining bogs, there would be more arable land for planting in spring.

He drew Kate up to the hidden ledge, tossed a blanket to the ground, and sat down on the soft mossy grass with his back against the rock wall. Pulling Kate down to him, Edric situated her on the ground between his legs, her back resting against his chest.

" 'Tis beautiful here," she said.

"Aye, but only half as beautiful as my wife."

"Edric, we should have waited to wed."

"No, love." He slipped his hands 'round her waist and let his thumbs drift to the undersides of her breasts. "Our nuptials were long overdue. Besides, your sire will not object, not when he reads the letter you sent him, describing your valiant rescue from the Fergusons."

She tipped her head back, giving him access to

her slender neck. He kissed the pulse that beat there, and slid his hands up to cup her breasts. They were much fuller these days, and the tips had darkened slightly. He'd noted a slight rounding of her belly, and knew that she often slept in the afternoons when Aidan napped.

She carried his child.

"Are you warm enough?"

She nodded slightly. "But I see you've brought a blanket."

"Aye. 'Tis for lying on."

"Ah," she said, turning in his arms. "I thought you brought me here to see all of your realm, my dear lord, not to seduce me."

"And so I have, sweeting," he said, laughing. "But a bit of seduction was also part of my plan."

She put her arms 'round his neck and nipped at his lips. "Aye," she whispered. "But not until I tell you my news."

Next month, don't miss these exciting new love stories only from Avon Books

How to Seduce a Duke by Kathryn Caskie
An Avon Romantic Treasure

Mary Royle may—or may not—be the "secret" daughter of a prince, but what she lacks in pedigree she makes up for in determination. When Mary sets her cap for Viscount Wetherly, she is foiled by her "intended's" older brother, the Duke of Blackstone, who will do anything to stop the marriage—even wed the chit himself!

Secrets of the Highwayman by Sara Mackenzie
An Avon Contemporary Romance

Nathaniel Raven was a notorious highwayman until his betrayal and murder. Now, awake in present-day England and determined to avenge his death, Nathaniel turns to Melanie Jones, a beautiful solicitor from London, for aid. But can they overcome the odds and find the peace that true love can bring?

Deliciously Wicked by Robyn DeHart
An Avon Romance

When Meg Piddington stumbles into the Viscount Mandeville's arms, neither expects it to become the perfect alibi. Wrongfully accused of a crime, Gareth tries to focus on clearing his name, but Meg is more of a distraction than he anticipated, tempting him to claim something he has no right to want.

Taken By Storm by Donna Fletcher
An Avon Romance

Imprisoned while trying to track down his brother, Burke Longton is stunned to meet his rescuer, the beautiful and courageous Storm. But there is something mysterious behind those deep blue eyes of hers, and Burke is determined to uncover the truth about the woman he has come to love.

Avon Romantic Treasures

Unforgettable, enthralling love stories, sparkling with passion and adventure from Romance's bestselling authors

DISCOVER CONTEMPORARY ROMANCES *at their*
SIZZLING HOT BEST FROM AVON BOOKS